Cindy Anstey

LOVE,
LIES *and*
SPIES

Swoon Reads   New York

A Swoon Reads Book

An Imprint of Feiwel and Friends

Library of Congress Cataloging-in-Publication Data

Names: Anstey, Cindy, author.

Title: Love, lies and spies / Cindy Anstey.

Description: First edition. | New York : Swoon Reads, 2016. | Summary: In the early 1800s, when her father sends her to London for a season, eighteen-year-old Juliana Telford, who prefers researching ladybugs to marriage, meets handsome Spencer Northam, a spy posing as a young gentleman of leisure.

Identifiers: LCCN 2015026917| ISBN 9781250084033 (paperback) | ISBN 9781250084064 (ebook)

Subjects: | CYAC: Love—Fiction. | Spies—Fiction. | London (England)—History— 19th century—Fiction. | Great Britain—History—1789–1820—Fiction. | BISAC: JUVENILE FICTION / Love & Romance. | JUVENILE FICTION / Historical / Europe.

Classification: LCC PZ7.1.A59 Lo 2016 | DDC [Fic]—dc23

LC record available at http://lccn.loc.gov/2015026917

Book design by Anna Booth

Our books may be purchased in bulk for promotional, educational, or business use. Please contact your local bookseller or the Macmillan Corporate and Premium Sales Department at (800) 221-7945, ext. 5442 or by e-mail at MacmillanSpecialMarkets@macmillan.com.

First Edition—2016

3 5 7 9 10 8 6 4 2

swoonreads.com

For my family, especially Mike, Deb, and Chris

CHAPTER

1

*In which a young lady clinging to a cliff
will eventually accept anyone's help*

"OH MY, this is embarrassing," Miss Juliana Telford said
aloud. There was no reason to keep her thoughts to herself, as she was alone, completely alone. In fact, that was half of
the problem. The other half was, of course, that she was hanging off the side of a cliff with the inability to climb either up
or down and in dire need of rescue.

"Another scrape. This will definitely give Aunt apoplexy."

Juliana hugged the cliff ever closer and tipped her head
slightly so that she could glance over her shoulder. Her high-
waisted ivory dress was deeply soiled across her right hip, where
she had slid across the earth as she dropped over the edge.

Juliana shifted slowly and glanced over her other shoulder.
Fortunately, the left side showed no signs of distress, and her

lilac sarcenet spencer could be brushed off easily. She would do it now were it not for the fact that her hands were engaged, holding tightly to the tangle of roots that kept her from falling off the tiny ledge.

Juliana continued to scrutinize the damage to her wardrobe with regret, not for herself so much as for her aunt, who seemed to deem such matters of great importance. Unfortunately, her eyes wandered down to her shoes. Just beyond them yawned an abyss. It was all too apparent how far above the crashing waves of the English Channel she was—and how very small the ledge.

Despite squishing her toes into the rock face as tightly as possible, Juliana's heels were only just barely accommodated by the jutting amalgamate. The occasional skitter and plop of eroding rocks diving into the depths of the brackish water did nothing to calm her racing heart.

Juliana swallowed convulsively. "Most embarrassing." She shivered despite a warm April breeze. "I shall be considered completely beyond the pale if I am dashed upon the rocks. Aunt will be so uncomfortable. Most inconsiderate of me."

A small shower of sandy pebbles rained down on Juliana's flowery bonnet. She shook the dust from her eyes and listened. She thought she had heard a voice.

Please, she prayed, let it be a farmer or a tradesman, someone not of the gentry. No one who would feel obligated to report back to Grays Hill Park. No gentlemen, please.

"Hello?" she called out. Juliana craned her neck upward,

trying to see beyond the roots and accumulated thatch at the cliff's edge.

A head appeared. A rather handsome head. He had dark, almost black, hair and clear blue eyes and, if one were to notice such things at a time like this, a friendly, lopsided smile.

"Need some assistance?" the head asked with a hint of sarcasm and the tone of a . . .

"Are you a gentleman?" Juliana inquired politely.

The head looked startled, frowned slightly, and then raised an eyebrow before answering. "Yes, indeed, I am—"

"Please, I do not wish to be rescued by a gentleman. Could you find a farmer or a shopkeep—anyone not of the gentry—and then do me the great favor of forgetting you saw me?"

"I beg your pardon?"

"I do not want to be rude, but this is a most embarrassing predicament—"

"I would probably use the word *dangerous* instead."

"Yes, well, you would, being a man. But I, on the other hand, being a young woman doing her best not to call attention to herself and bring shame upon her family, would call it otherwise."

"Embarrassing?"

"Oh, most definitely. First, I should not have gone out in the carriage alone. Carrie was supposed to come with me, but we quarreled, you see, and I got into a snit, and—" Juliana stopped herself. She was beginning to prattle; it must be the effects of the sun. "Second, if I had not been watching the swallows instead of the road, I would have seen the hole before my wheel decided to explore its depths—very scatterbrained of me. And third, if I return home, soiled and in the company of a gentleman with no acquaintance to the family, I will be returned to Hartwell forthwith in shame. All possibility of a Season and trip to London will be gone completely."

"Well, that is quite an embarrassing list. I do see the problem."

"Is there someone down there?" another voice asked.

The head with the blue eyes disappeared, but Juliana could hear a muffled conversation.

"Yes, but she does not want to be rescued by us. She says she needs a farmer."

"What?"

Juliana leaned back slightly to see if she could catch a glimpse of the other gentleman, but that dislodged a cloud of dirt.

"Achoo."

"Bless you," one of the voices called from above before continuing the conversation. "Yes, it seems that we are not the sort—"

Juliana's nose began to itch again. She scrunched it up and then wiggled it, trying to stop another burst. To no avail. *"Achoo."* This time her left hand jerked with the force of the exhaled air and broke several of the roots to which she was clinging. Slowly, they began to unravel, lengthening and shifting Juliana away from the cliff's side, out into the air.

"Oh no." She let go of that handful and reached back toward the rocks for another, hopefully stronger, group of roots. But she was not so lucky. Twice more she grabbed, praying that the tangle in her right hand would not get the same idea.

Just as she had decided the situation was now possibly more dangerous than embarrassing, a hand grabbed her flailing wrist. Relief flooded through her, and her racing heart slowed just a touch.

"Give me your other arm."

"I beg your pardon? You cannot expect me to let go."

"Well, if I am to pull you up, you are going to have to."

"Oh dear, oh dear. I really do not want to."

"I understand completely. But I am afraid we have no length of rope, no farmer is in sight, and your predicament seems to be proceeding into the realm of peril. Not to worry, though. I have this arm firmly in my grasp, my feet are being held—sat upon, to be exact, so I will not topple over—and all that is left for you to do is to let go. I will grab your other arm, you will close your eyes, and up you will come. Back onto terra firma."

"This is terra firma." Juliana pointed with her nose to the rugged cliff wall.

"Yes, but I doubt very much that you want to stay there."

"I like the idea of dangling in the air so much less."

The head nodded sympathetically. "Life is full of these trials, I am afraid."

"They seem to follow me around. I am a magnet for trouble."

"That is sad news. However, perhaps it would be best to

discuss your penchant for interesting situations when we are on the same ground level—say, up here. It would make the discussion much easier to conduct."

"In other words, I should stop dillydallying."

"Exactly so."

"I really do not want to do this."

"I understand."

Juliana took a deep breath. "I am only eighteen, you know."

"I did not."

"That is much too young to die, do you not think?"

"I quite agree, which is why we are going to do everything we can to help you make it to nineteen."

"All right, I will do it."

"Brave girl."

Juliana felt anything but brave. Her knees were starting to wobble and her hands had decided to shake. She took several deep breaths, counted to three in her head, and then let go. She stretched her arm up quickly and for a flash of a second wondered if he could reach her. Then a firm viselike grip locked onto her wrist, and she did as the man had suggested: Juliana closed her eyes.

At first, his touch brought relief, but it didn't last long . . . for she didn't seem to be moving. She was just dangling. It was better than falling or hitting the rocks, but she really would rather be going up, definitely up.

Juliana opened her eyes a slit. She could see that the man with the friendly smile was not smiling anymore. His expression was more of a grimace. Lifting her was clearly an effort, and Juliana shut her eyes again. She squeezed them so tightly that colors danced inside her head. Or was that because she wasn't breathing? It could be either one.

Juliana felt the sharp punch of an interfering cluster of rocks upon her upper leg and couldn't help but regret the thin nature of her muslin gown. Next time she flew off a cliff, she would try to remember to wear her worsted skirts. Perhaps then, *ouch*, she would not have to suffer additional bruising.

"It is all right now. You can open your eyes."

Juliana was startled. The voice was intimately close. Her eyes flew open and met those of the blue-eyed stranger. She lay on her side not two feet from her rescuer. The lopsided smile contrasted deeply with his beet-red face and his labored breath. Glistening perspiration dotted his forehead and dripped down his temples.

Juliana smiled broadly and was about to thank him when two other hands grasped her waist and lifted her to her feet as if she weighed no more than a feather. Her rescuer rose as well, and all three set about dusting themselves off. It took quite some time, as they were all thoroughly dirty.

Juliana was the last one finished. In fact, she wasn't done so much as she finally gave up. The streak on her hip was too in-grained to succumb to a brushing. She would have to sneak into the manor the back way and bribe Nancy to clean it without a word to anyone. If her aunt were to find out . . .

Juliana suddenly realized that she had to swear these

gentlemen to secrecy. At the very least, she had to convince them that the least said the sooner mended, or something like that. Juliana straightened up.

Two young men, who looked little more than her age, stared back with frank interest. Her rescuers were tall, handsome, and well built, but while one had dark wavy hair and blue eyes, the other had sandy locks and brown eyes. The sandy-haired man had a round face with a cleft in his smooth chin, and he moved with pent-up energy. The blue-eyed man with the friendly smile was rather loose-limbed, with a square jaw and an air of athletic grace.

Juliana was momentarily at a loss for words, a strange condition for her. It didn't last long.

"Sirs, I cannot thank you enough." She ventured a quick glance toward the cliff's edge, once again noting the huge drop. "My initial reluctance to accept your kind offer of assistance was not in any way due to a lack of appreciation. My disinclination was due solely to the fact that my shortcomings were about to cause my family grief. I do apologize for asking you to go away—"

"Oh, do not even consider it." The sandy-haired gentleman dismissed her hesitance with a wave of his hand.

"Still, I was wondering if you might not mention it to anyone."

"I beg your pardon?" His hand stopped midair.

"As gentlemen, I am sure you realize that my . . . adventure . . . was a little . . . unladylike. Or at least that is how—"

"How your relatives will see it?"

Juliana turned toward the blue-eyed gentleman; his friendly smile was back.

"How very perceptive, sir. I know that your efforts showed a great deal of bravery, but I was wondering if . . ."

"Say no more. Your secret is safe with us."

"Once again, I must thank you for your exquisite generosity." Juliana was almost limp with relief.

"If—"

She was suddenly stiff and alert again. "If?"

"If you would do us the same courtesy."

Juliana brought her brows together and tilted her head.

"We will not mention having to pry you free from certain death, if you do not mention having seen us on this side of town . . . to anyone. An easy arrangement, don't you think?"

The sandy-haired stranger nodded. "Good thinking. Wouldn't want tales to reach the ears of my dearest mama."

Juliana smiled. "Well, yes, sir, that is easily done—since I do not know to whom I owe my gratitude."

"Wonderful, then it is established. You have never seen us before; we have never seen you. And should we at some time meet in any official capacity, it will be for the first time. Agreed?"

Juliana, smiling larger than she had in some time, dropped into a deep curtsy. "I am most pleased to forget you, sir." She turned and did the same to the sandy-haired man, who was watching her closely with a grin tugging at his lips.

Having settled the arrangement amicably, Juliana turned

with renewed energy to her pony cart, and her stomach plummeted to her toes. The cart was on its side—one wheel still encased in mud from the deep rut that had been the cause of her ordeal—and the pony was gone.

"Oh dear, oh dear."

"Not shed of us yet, I am afraid," the blue-eyed young man said at her elbow.

Juliana almost jumped in surprise but held her reaction in check. Or at least she thought she had until she caught his look of amusement and his bold wink. She straightened her shoulders and lifted her chin.

"Not to worry, the cart is not heavy. We will have it over in a trice," he said easily, as if unaware of his improper proximity.

"That is all well and good, but without the pony, it may as well stay where it is." Juliana sighed. She raised a hand to her bonnet to shield her eyes and began scanning the horizon.

It was fortunate that the day's early-morning fog had rolled out to sea; it had left the rugged coast sparkling in warm sunlight. The vista was expansive, rich in textures and colors, and the visibility couldn't have been better.

The rooflines and chimney pots of Ryton Manor rose out of the forest canopy in the distance. Below the ancient manor, in an asymmetrical pattern of hilly fields and thick shrubbery, the bright yellow-green foliage of reawakening vegetation contrasted deeply with the blue-gray hues of the ocean. The pony's dappled black-and-white coat stood out most profoundly.

It had not gone far.

"There," Juliana said with great satisfaction. She pointed to a clearing just up the winding road.

"Ah, you are right, I see him. Bob—" The young man started to call to his sandy-haired companion. He glanced quickly toward her and then continued. "Could you get the pony while I right the cart, old boy?"

"Right-oh. Will do."

While the sandy-haired man walked away, Juliana half-heartedly tugged on the rail of her cart, testing the leverage. It didn't budge. This was not going to be as easy as the gents had surmised.

"I think we are going to have to wait for your friend to get back before we attempt to set the cart upright."

"Nonsense, just move your comely little self out of harm's way, and I will take care of it."

Juliana blinked at the none-to-subtle condescension. Perhaps she deserved it. This stranger could not help but have a skewed idea of her capabilities. She must look like a silly girl, a babbling, inattentive silly girl. Juliana gave him an elaborate bow and made sure that he saw her intentionally vacuous smile and fluttering eyelashes. "Of course, kind sir. My poor, helpless self will be waiting just over there." She pointed to the shade of a majestic oak on the other side of the road. It did look like a nice place to while away the time. And, likely, that is where she would be until the sandy-haired man returned to help, just as she had suggested in the first place.

Juliana backed up a few paces and then, after watching the

man poke and prod various parts of the cart, she stepped forward and offered to hold his coat.

"That might not be a bad idea," he conceded as he handed it to her.

He still thought he could do it alone, foolish fellow.

Standing by the raised side of the cart, he began rocking it back and forth, using the momentum of the cart's own springs to bring it up farther with each dip. Then, in a great effort, he pulled the cart toward him. The vehicle tipped up into the air on one wheel.

Juliana was very impressed until she noticed that the cart was no longer moving. It was just hovering, hanging in the air, neither up nor down. "Sir?"

"Yes," came the strained reply.

"I think it might be easier to drive were both wheels on the ground."

"Likely."

Juliana tilted her head to see around the cart's railing. The man's face was red again with effort. "Would you care for some assistance?"

"Well, now that you mention it."

"Are you certain?" Juliana inquired politely, enjoying the feeling of vindication. "After all, I am standing away, as you directed."

"A slight nudge might do the trick."

"By me?"

"Ah, yes, that was the idea."

The cart started to shake slightly with his continued strain. With all due haste, Juliana crossed the road and levered her back against the railing. It took much more than a nudge; it was more like a shove, and a hard one at that.

At last the cart tipped toward the stranger, who smartly stepped out of the way, and came to rest on the crest of the road—on both wheels.

Without a word, he circled the cart and held his elegant but soiled hand out for his coat. His face held a languid, almost bored look, a very different expression from that of just a moment ago.

"Oh, I do apologize." Juliana rushed back to the tree, picked up his coat, dusted it off, and sheepishly handed back to him. "I, ah . . ."

"Dropped it?"

"Yes, most careless of me. I was not thinking."

"A habit?"

"Well, actually no. I am seldom accused of not thinking. It is more on the order of being overly opinionated or easily distracted, but only by my aunt. Father would never say so."

"Very kind of him."

"Well, no, not really. I only seem to do imprudent things when it is expected of me. Strange, do you not think? Father has great respect for my intellect, so I am invariably witty and wise in his presence. Difficult to imagine, is it not?"

"Very difficult."

Fortunately, the fellow's friendly smile had returned, or

Juliana might have been piqued. He was teasing in such a subtle manner that he was almost being familiar.

They continued to assess each other in companionable silence. It was a rather pleasant sensation, and somewhat surprising. Juliana had not expected to experience any headiness this Season—not in London, and certainly not in the backcountry of Dorset. Apparently, one should never underestimate the allure of a mysterious stranger.

"Here we are, friends and neighbors," a voice interrupted her musings.

Both started guiltily and turned toward the sandy-haired man. He was leading the dappled pony at a brisk pace down the road. The pony looked calm and unfazed by the adventure.

"There is the cart, all ready for you," he told the pony. "Good job, old boy," he said over his shoulder. He led the pony to the front of the cart and started reattaching the leathers. He continued to soothe the pony with his monologue. "Now, did I not tell you that you were going home? Would I lie to you? I am sure, Miss, ah . . . I am sure your mistress will make sure you have plenty of sweet hay." The sandy-haired stranger looked up at Juliana for confirmation.

"Absolutely, the sweetest. Bonnie always gets the best . . . after all the other horses, of course." Juliana was amused by his attitude toward the poor pony. She was a sorry example of horseflesh, made all the more obvious by the gentlemen's fine specimens tethered to a nearby shrub, but he used a tone that was gentle and full of kindness. Admirable.

The sandy-haired stranger nodded. "Right-oh. As I said, Bonnie will get you the best hay."

Juliana laughed. "No, no, I will do it for Bonnie. The pony is called Bonnie; it is not my given name."

He looked up at her and smiled. "I think Bonnie is most apt for a damsel in distress."

"Oh no, not at all. A damsel would be called Amelia or Octavia, even Brunhild. Bonnie is such a simple, unassuming name; it would not do at all."

His brown eyes twinkled. "Ah, but it might, for such a bonny young maid."

Juliana felt sudden warmth on her cheeks and turned her eyes to the ground briefly. She glanced up in time to see his companion roll his eyes.

The stranger completed his task without further comment or flirtation, patted the pony on the flank, and slowly walked toward Juliana. The wind gently lifted his sandy hair, splaying it across his forehead in a wild fashion. "Your carriage awaits, my lady." The gallant held his arm out to lead her to the cart.

Juliana recoiled slightly. She sidestepped, almost bumping into the blue-eyed young man in her haste. "Thank you again," she said to cover her acute discomfort.

She was so gauche, so unpolished. She had made a cake of herself. The art of conversation was a talent that she had long since mastered, well able to hold her own on the topic of natural sciences—particularly the lady beetle—but this art of flirtation was another thing. She had always known her country manners to be a little coarse; it had never bothered her before. However, the contrast between the gentlemen's smooth manner and her awkward response . . . well, she would have to try harder if she were to blend into London society.

Juliana climbed into the cart, settled herself on the hard, wooden bench, and took up the reins. Doing her best to recover some dignity, she nodded with a benign smile and flicked the leathers. Unfortunately, she noticed the amusement in the young men's eyes, and Juliana ruined the nonchalant effect she was trying to impart by chuckling and grinning broadly. Oh well, perhaps next time.

Juliana directed Bonnie around the offending rut and back onto the crest of the road toward Grays Hill Park. She flicked the reins across the pony's back to encourage a little more haste and prayed that Paul, Aunt's wizened head groom, would see her coming. She knew that he would be more than willing to institute a little subterfuge to protect her from Aunt Phyllis's sharp tongue. It was easy to spot a confederate.

Juliana kept her gaze firmly on the road ahead. No swallows could distract her now; the invigorating smell of the salt air could not entice even the slightest diversion or glance to the water. No, no more accidents or incidents, at least not today. She would be the staid, mindful lady that she needed to be. But just as the road twisted inland, Juliana couldn't help herself. She turned to look behind.

Disappointingly, both strangers were no longer looking in her direction. She had already been dismissed from their minds.

Juliana took a deep breath and let it out slowly. It was not that she was truly attracted to either one—how could she be?—but it would have been ever so flattering if they, or even just one of them, had found her intriguing. No, it would seem that the vast, empty ocean had captured their attention instead. They both stared at the waves. Not flattering at all.

It was only then that Juliana realized that while she had been forthcoming, far more than was necessary, about her reason for this harmless conspiracy of silence, the gentlemen had not. Actually, they had divulged hardly anything at all, while she had . . . Juliana shuddered in recollection of her babbling tongue. She really needed to take hold of that organ and cultivate the silence that exudes a more knowledgeable air.

Juliana sighed. Perhaps the delay to London was a godsend. It gave her more time to school herself in the ladylike arts of elegance and witty discourse; she had spent too much time wielding a net and not enough time fluttering a fan.

CHAPTER
2

*In which a locket of great sentimental value is lost
and a locket of a suspicious nature is found*

"ONE WOULD THINK THAT A MODISTE WOULD BE able to design a gown that a lady could shed by herself. But it would appear not," Juliana complained as she waited impatiently for Nancy to finish undoing the back buttons of her mucky walking dress.

"Yes, Miss."

There had been no disapproval or alarm in Nancy's expression when Juliana had arrived in complete disarray, hair falling about her ears, out of breath, and in a severely soiled gown. The short, freckled maid simply dropped her armload of linens on the closest flat surface and rushed after her. She hadn't even inquired as to what had occurred. In less than a month, Nancy had become quite accustomed to Juliana's uncommon behavior.

"The cart hit a rut," Juliana explained needlessly, avoiding any reference to being out alone or falling off the cliff.

"Yes, Miss." The maid's tone was excessively neutral.

All twenty tiny pearl buttons were at last undone, and the dress dropped to the floor. Nancy laid the muslin ruin upon the bed in such a way that the ingrained dirt was concealed. She knew to be cautious. Aunt Phyllis often entered a room unbidden. "It was such a handsome dress, Miss. The latest fashion."

"Just the latest fashion for Lambhurst, Nancy. I imagine it would . . . will look rather rustic next to my cousin's London styles."

Juliana realized that she sounded petulant. It was unintentional, for the dress had been her idea. She had asked her aunt to help her find a local dressmaker for her London Season wardrobe. Lambhurst fashion was a vast improvement over anything she could have had made in her hometown hamlet of Compton Green. Aunt Phyllis had protested that all the best styles came from London, but, as Juliana was covering her own costs for the Season, there was little that her aunt could say. Besides, seeing her niece in country fine while Carrie paraded in London elegance suited Aunt Phyllis perfectly.

The fact that Juliana could afford gowns to rival the most moneyed in society but chose not to, well, that was a source of great amusement for her aunt—one that she pretended to hide. Perhaps Aunt Phyllis did not resent having to present her niece to the *beau monde* at the same time as her daughter, but her barely veiled hostility hinted at such a possibility.

The woman need not have worried. Carrie had her youth, as she was one year younger than Juliana, and her social ease, due to countless elocution, dancing, and etiquette tutors; and soon she would be a fashionable beauty enjoying the Season. Carrie would eclipse Juliana utterly—which played into Juliana's plans exactly.

Juliana intended to put her time in London to better use than shopping and attending frivolous fittings. She would be seeing to the publication of the Telford research—a fascinating project about the *Coccinellidae*. It was an important study on the lady beetle, which had begun simply as a common interest between Father and his motherless daughter, but it had grown to the point where it now formed the basis of their lives. It was something that Aunt Phyllis would never understand and certainly never approve of.

And so Madame Greville, the renowned modiste of the town of Lambhurst, had been called in and put to immediate use. Aunt Phyllis had helped pick the beautiful fabrics in the dullest of colors—and suggested an abundance of lace and flounces, which Juliana had immediately censored. The resulting wardrobe was a mixed set of gowns—some suiting Juliana's tastes and others suiting her aunt's—all well made, if somewhat classic in style.

"I would very much appreciate anything you could do to make the dress serviceable again, Nancy. I really did like it."

"Yes, Miss, you looked rather corky in it."

Juliana smiled and dropped a coin on the girl's palm.

"Miss?"

"That is in case you need to replace any part of the skirt. Keep any left over."

"Thank you, Miss. I will have it back 'ere in the mornin'." The vow of silence was implicit between them. Aunt Phyllis would not be informed.

The coin quickly disappeared behind the maid's frilled white muslin apron. "'Ow about yer Pomona green gown, Miss." Nancy opened the doors to the large wardrobe sitting in the corner of the ivy guest room. It was deliciously full.

Juliana felt a rush of pleasure at the sight of all those rich materials. As she was not usually prone to such frivolous feelings, the emotion surprised her. She snorted and shook her head. She had a touch of vanity in her after all.

Nancy brought over a gown that had long, full sleeves tied in three places with ribbons. As the maid pulled the gown up over her shoulders, she made a startled sound and Juliana turned.

"Is something wrong?"

"Oh, no, Miss. Just surprised is all."

"By what?"

"Yer locket, Miss. I never seen you without it afore."

Juliana's hand went to her throat. Her neck tensed, and the pounding of her heart filled her ears. She pulled away from Nancy's ministrations and rushed over to the mirror. Nancy was right. Her fingers were right. The locket was gone.

"Oh dear, oh dear," Juliana lamented. "I had it on this morning. The clasp must have broken. It could be anywhere."

"I'm that sorry, Miss. It were special, weren't it?" Nancy

met her eyes in the mirror with a twinkle. "From a particular gentleman?"

Juliana smiled at the ludicrous suggestion. "Nothing so romantic, I am afraid, Nancy, but just as sentimental. It was my mother's." She laid her hand across her empty neckline. "Father gave it to me last August, on my birthday." She swallowed against the sudden lump in her throat. "I thought very highly of it."

Nancy resumed fastening Juliana's buttons in silence. It gave Juliana the opportunity to fret in earnest. The locket had been a special tribute, a gift from her dead mother upon reaching her majority. A lovely necklace, not too large or ornate, it accented most of her dresses and could be hidden under those that were not set off by the etched silver. Best of all, it held a tress of her mother's straight dark hair, so unlike her own wavy reddish brown. Juliana touched the widow's peak on her forehead. That was a gift from her mother, too. Or so she had been told.

"Primping again, I see," Carrie Reeves teased from the doorway. She ambled across the floor, wafting lavender as she did so. Stopping at the full-length mirror, she swept her hand up under her carefully piled coiffure. It was a new look for her. It added the height she needed but was too severe for her youthful face.

Juliana stepped behind her cousin and pulled a few honey-brown tendrils from around the nape of Carrie's neck. Juliana worked absentmindedly, her thoughts focused on the loss of her locket. Nancy completed the last of her buttons, curtsied and started toward the door.

"Where have you been, Juliana? Mama was looking for you

earlier. We have news." Carrie watched Juliana from the mirror. The tendrils had done the trick; Carrie looked like a fragile porcelain doll, no longer her mother in miniature.

"I told ya, Miss Carrie," Nancy quickly interrupted, "Miss Juliana were out walking in the gardens." She glanced toward Juliana, who nodded her appreciation and dismissed her at the same time.

"No one could find you," Carrie persisted after Nancy closed the door.

"I went farther than I had intended—into the park." It was almost the truth.

"You really ought not to do that, Juliana." Carrie's concern sounded genuine. "There are a lot more rules here than you are used to—and a lot more eyes to make sure you abide by them." She sighed deeply. "Ladies are expected to act with an abundance of decorum in Lambhurst. It will be worse in London."

Carrie shook her head and turned. First staring at the floor and then the bed curtain, she avoided Juliana's watchful gaze in a studied fashion. Walking over to the window, she pulled back the green draperies and gazed out at the gardens, as if she were more interested in her surroundings than the conversation.

"I hadn't planned an excursion . . . but I was piqued, remember," Juliana prodded.

Carrie sniffed, lifted her chin, and then paused—drawing a ragged breath. She dropped the curtain, and the pretense, finally turning to meet Juliana's eyes. "Yes, and I do apologize. I didn't mean to be so vile—you can talk about bugs anytime you wish."

"Insects."

"Yes, yes . . . those horrid little creatures that you find so fascinating. I did not mean to imply that you are a bluestocking."

"I don't mind the name, goose. I was quite pleased with the label; it was the way you said it. With such disgust, as if to be knowledgeable were a terrible affliction. One that you share, I'd like to point out."

"Yes, I don't know what came over me. Frustration perhaps? It's this infernal sitting around waiting. I almost wish there were someone else who could present us—but no, that would preclude Vivian, and I wouldn't want to do that."

"I am sorry, too, for I knew you not to be in earnest—it was quite unlike you." It was more like her Aunt Phyllis, but Juliana kept that thought safely tucked away.

Carrie smiled and grabbed Juliana's hand, pulling her out into the hall. "Enough of that. I must tell you my news." She brought them to a halt on the top step of the grand staircase. But her words were to remain unspoken, her excitement stifled.

Clicking on the marble below announced the arrival of Aunt Phyllis.

⚬⧓⚬

"You cannot control yourself, can you, Bobbington?"

"Whatever do you mean?"

Spencer Northam watched Lord Randolph Bobbington line

up his ball, blowing his sandy hair out of his eyes. He stared with such tiresome and painstaking concentration that Spencer knew his friend had not heard a word of his advice.

The two young men were sequestered in the large, heavily paneled billiard room of Shelsley Hall, Bobbington's cavernous ancestral home. They had not lingered long on the cliffs of St. Ives Head. It had not seemed prudent. To stay longer would have invited discovery, by someone other than a young lady intent on keeping her own small secret.

Spencer curled up the right side of his mouth into a lop-sided smile, recalling the odd miss who had diverted him from his purpose a few hours ago. Very different from the sophisticated, calculating young ladies he usually encountered. No, this one was rather fetching, country fresh and quite a talker . . . a green but intelligent girl, certainly with a mind of her own. Confident, until Bobbington had flustered her with his cocky flirtation.

Spencer frowned. Lambhurst society was small. It was probable that they already knew her aunt. Spencer hoped that the miss was true to her word and found no reason to mention their appearance on the Head. He had no desire for his name to be bandied about the country as a young man too ripe and ready by half. He had woven the air of passivity into the tapestry of his persona for too long for it to become unraveled at this late date.

"Whatever do you mean?" Bobbington eventually repeated. "I can, indeed, control myself." He was leaning on the table with his cue resting beside him. The ball he had so laboriously studied lay stagnant and untouchable on the far side of the table. "In what way?"

Spencer realized that he could be accused of woolgathering just as much as his friend. He straightened his back and his thoughts. "For the better part of a fortnight you have extolled the virtues of one Miss Vivian Pyebald. A litany of her marvelous qualities has followed me around every corner of Shelsley, as well as assurances that your devotion is so complete, so constant, that she will live in your heart until you gasp out your dying breath. And then along comes this pert miss and you forget your unalterable fixation. In a blink, you cast your net around a new candidate. We wouldn't have been on the blasted cliff had you not insisted on staring wistfully at her manor . . . against the express wishes of your dear mama."

"How can you say that? To flatter an obviously comely young lady is merely courtesy. I could never turn my thoughts from dearest Miss Pyebald. She lives in my heart—"

"You will have to pardon my lack of enthusiasm, Bobbington. We have been friends since Eton, and in that time, I believe your complete and exclusive devotion has been passed from—let me see, there was darling Miss Wilson last autumn, virtuous Lady Harriet in July, stellar Miss Barnard just before Easter, beloved Miss—"

"But this is different."

"Really? How so?"

Bobbington flushed and shifted his weight from one side to the other. "Because my feelings are returned."

"The beautiful Miss Pyebald, daughter of Lord Reginald Pyebald, has informed you of her devotion though you have had but three encounters and she is not yet out? That is miraculous. Have you spoken to her father?"

"Oh, Northam, leave off, will you? You know I have done no such thing. She has been gone since March. I am simply awaiting her return."

"Then why, oh why, do you believe that Miss Pyebald returns your regard?"

"We had a moment just before she left."

"Would you care to elucidate?"

"That would not be gentlemanly."

Spencer sighed. He rubbed at his temple. "Well, then, my friend, you might want to leave off flirting with strangers on a lonely cliff-side, or you might find yourself in a compromising situation, thereby losing all hope of winning your fair Miss Pyebald."

Bobbington shook his head in sharp jerks. "That is not likely to happen."

"Despite your lack of funds, your title holds great allure. You would not be the first to fall victim to a scheming mama and her daughter."

"Our miss has an aunt."

"Do not be so literal, Bobbington."

"You cannot believe the girl threw herself off a cliff in order to gain my attention."

"Perhaps not. That would be going a bit too far."

"Indeed. I believe the true nature of your disapproval is not that I brought her to blush, but that I did it before you had the chance."

"Rot."

Bobbington gave him a victorious smirk.

Spencer bent over the table and hit his ball with a little more force than he had intended. As he watched Bobbington play out his turn, he fingered the delicate ornament in his pocket. He wondered about the lock of dark hair and the *fleur-de-lis* etching. It had been lying in the thatch beside the oak. Was it a love token dropped by the traitorous French spy? Did it indicate a cliff-top vigil or simply a passing vehicle? Was there any significance in its location? Was it a signal? It was not a busy thoroughfare; the locket could have been there for some time—perhaps it meant nothing.

As he speculated, Spencer lamented his inexperience—the ability to know and understand exactly what an object represented might be years away. He looked forward to when his espionage skills were honed enough to match those of Bibury and Lord Winfrith. It is likely that they would have been able to see the locket for what it was.

However, Spencer did not yet have their mastery, and he reasoned that St. Ives Head would need another look as a result;

it would also afford him another opportunity to observe Ryton Manor.

⌧

"GIRLS, come down here at once." The tenor of Aunt Phyllis's voice was unreadable. But the variables were small: She was either annoyed or very annoyed.

Juliana didn't wait to find out. With as much haste and grace as she could—lest she bring on a tongue-lashing for unladylike behavior—Juliana scrambled down the wide staircase. Carrie followed closely behind. Aunt abhorred dawdlers.

"Juliana, it has come to my attention that . . ." Aunt Phyllis began the minute Juliana's feet touched the ground floor. Then she stopped.

Chester, the footman, entered the main hall carrying a large candelabra destined for the dining room. Maisie was busy in the back corner, dusting the family portrait, and Mrs. Belcher, the housekeeper, passed into the little hall with her keys clunking and jingling as she moved.

Aunt Phyllis swooped her hand impatiently to the morning room, indicating that their private discussion would continue in there.

Juliana entered the pastel blue room with a surge of resentment taking up residence in her spleen. She simply would not allow the woman to rail at her again for nothing. Aunt might deserve respect for the mere fact that she was older, well positioned in society, and Father's sister, but that did not give her the right to—

"Juliana, do not slouch."

"Yes, Aunt." Juliana acquiesced as sweetly as possible. Position and familial connections did not give Aunt Phyllis the right to belittle her moral character, insult her education, or—

"Juliana, straighten your gown."

"Yes, Aunt." Juliana ran her hands down the perfectly placed bodice. She simply could not . . . would not allow her aunt to intimidate her. Juliana raised her chin and turned to face the enemy.

Aunt Phyllis was a beautiful woman. She was small in stature, but her fine bone structure was in proportion to her height. She had thick honey-colored hair, with a few touches of gray that were allowed to see the light of day only occasionally, very occasionally. Her voice was always calm but held a sting, a malicious message that seemed indiscernible to gentlemen but was infinitely clear to other women.

Juliana slowly descended onto the closest brocade settee with exaggerated grace. Aunt did not like that most people towered over her, even when it was by mere inches, as was the case with Juliana.

"There must be some mysterious voice emanating from the shadows that only you can hear, Juliana, for I am quite certain that it was not I who suggested that you sit before I do—the height of disrespect."

"I beg to differ, Aunt. The voice I heard was, indeed, yours—just yesterday you mentioned the strain of having to look up." Juliana smiled sweetly. "I wouldn't want to be a pain in the neck." After appreciating the ceiling for a calming moment, Juliana returned her gaze to the martinet, doing her best to look attentive—while clenching her jaw.

If this had not been the only way that she could get to London with her true purpose undetected, she would have gracefully marched back up the stairs, neatly thrown her possessions into her trunks, and calmly run from the house. As it was, she had to put up with the derisive treatment and snide remarks, or return home unpublished. It was now or never—for she had heard that another natural scientist was putting his theories forward—studies that borrowed heavily from the Telford research.

"Juliana, it has come to my attention that you were out alone. Again. This, after I so delicately stated that such wanton behavior is vulgar and common. You must refrain from voyaging abroad immediately, even in our own park as you were today. What if you had been seen? Walking, without an escort. It is likely that you only barely avoided an incident today. I will not brook another one."

"Yes, Aunt." Thank the heavens she had requested the silence of her cliff-side rescuers. "However, you must recall that I am unused to such restrictions and find them chafing."

Aunt Phyllis's small but strong hand drummed dramatically on her upper bodice, in the general area of her poor, taxed heart.

"That is irrelevant. You are no longer in the primitive environs of Compton Green. The Ton has standards, and I will not be associated . . ." Aunt Phyllis artfully collapsed into the small chair next to her escritoire. Her hands fluttered like a small bird and then came to rest, with a twitch, in her lap. The exquisite lavender gown flowed and puddled around her.

"I will not be associated," she began again for emphasis, "with anyone about whom there might be a hint of poor breeding. We must do our utmost to hide your mother's French taint."

This proved too much for Juliana's sense of justice. "Aunt Phyllis, how can you deride Mama's heritage? She was the daughter of a comte. Hardly an example of poor breeding."

Aunt Phyllis arched her left brow in a practiced expression of superiority, then she turned toward the fireplace, staring at the painting above the mantel. It was a depiction of a tree— the Telford family tree to be precise.

"I shudder to think what my great-grandfather, the Earl, would say about your bloodlines, Juliana. France is our enemy. We are at war." She continued to stare with her lips curled into what could be mistaken for a smile; she was entranced by the long list of names.

Juliana refrained from pointing out that Phyllis Reeves had never actually met "the Earl" and that her name was on one of the lowest branches of this revered family tree. With great forbearance, Juliana placed her tongue between her teeth and held it there on the off chance that it would escape and say all manner of vulgarities, with great force.

"Now I must tell you the glad tidings." Aunt turned back to the girls, looked critically at Carrie, and then frowned. Her eyes focused on the soft tendrils curling prettily about her daughter's neck. She pursed her lips momentarily but continued with no reference to the altered coiffure. "Our vigil is over; Lady Pyebald and Vivian have returned. An elegant, articulate letter arrived just a few hours ago. Apparently, the holiday in the Lake District was most successful, although the journey home has been overlong and taxing on the delicate constitution of our dearest Vivian. A brief respite is required, but we will be able to leave for London within five or six days . . . perhaps a seven-night. Certainly not more—now what say you to that!"

Despite herself, Juliana smiled. "That is good news, indeed, Aunt." Juliana glanced at her cousin. Their eyes met in mutual excitement. At last they were going to London.

When Juliana had arrived at Grays Hill Park, it had been with the expectation of leaving for London within a fortnight. She had planned to use those fourteen days to procure the necessaries for the Season, catch up with her cousin, whom she hadn't seen since the previous summer, and be apprised of the who's who of London society by Aunt Phyllis. It would have been a tight schedule, but one that Juliana had thought was best suited to her needs—predominantly, her need not to spend any more time with Aunt Phyllis than was absolutely necessary.

However, no sooner had Juliana arrived than she had been informed of a delay. The ladies of great Ryton Manor, with whom Carrie and Juliana were to share the Season, had not yet returned from their visit with relatives in the Lake District. Some sort of ailment had laid Vivian low, and they had been required to postpone their departure by a full week.

As the Pyebalds were to enjoy the hospitality of the Reeves family while in London—their own opulent residence being in need of unspecified repairs—there was nothing to do but wait upon the return of these grand dames if the entrance into good society was to be assured. Now at last came news of their return.

"We have been invited to the Great-House tomorrow. You, in particular, Juliana. Although it was not stated, I do believe Lady Pyebald wishes to assess your suitability to our little party. You would do well to keep your mouth firmly closed, your eyes cast upon the floor, and your opinions to yourself. Do you take my meaning, girl?"

"Yes, Aunt. You would prefer me to be someone I am not."

"Good, then we understand each other. You will not attract the attention of anyone, least of all the good lady. Wear the yellow gown I directed you to buy."

"Yes, Aunt." It was the least attractive of her new gowns, fashioned in a pallid yellow that made her look sallow. However, Juliana would match it with her apple-green pelisse, and the effect would be charming.

Having imparted the required warnings, Aunt Phyllis rose and glided to the door. No doubt she had Cook to harass or Mrs. Belcher to criticize. The moment the door closed behind her, Carrie was on her feet.

"Oh, this is too splendid by half, Juliana. I thought this day would never come." Carrie reached over and gave Juliana's hand an affectionate squeeze.

"Do you refer to the social call or the Season?"

"Goose, the Season, of course." Carrie laughed, then sighed deeply and stared dreamily into the air. "The balls, the gowns, the music. Handsome gentlemen and starry romance. It is too delicious."

"Lechers with sweaty palms and crowded smelly rooms."

"Juliana. One would almost think you had no interest in catching a man's eye."

"Well, I do not."

"Then why, pray tell, are you about to place yourself upon the most notorious marriage stage?"

"To dance the night away, laugh at deplorable comments, and be frivolous and lighthearted. Go to the theater, visit the museum, and ride down Rotten Row. Need there be more than that?"

"Yes. A handsome man who picks you as his one and only and asks you to marry him. I could go on."

"No need." Juliana laughed. "I don't think the gentleman exists who would support my research—something I would not be willing to give up."

"Is it that important, Juliana? I mean, would you forgo a home of your own for your bugs?"

"Insects, Carrie, lady beetles."

"Yes, but—"

"I already have a home of my own in Compton Green with Father and have had the running of it for many years now." Juliana understated her aversion to the institution of marriage—not wanting to scare her cousin off. Carrie, after all, would face a lifetime of Aunt Phyllis should she be unsuccessful in the marriage mart.

"Yes, but—"

"Fine, Carrie dear. I shall keep the possibility open in my mind . . . but without any expectation."

Juliana's hopes were not pinned on any gentleman but on a small red insect with black spots . . . and years of research. Yes, and a fascinating compilation of facts:

COCCINELLIDAE: A THOROUGH STUDY OF THE HABITS AND HABITAT OF THE LADY BEETLE AS OBSERVED IN THE VILLAGE OF COMPTON GREEN—BOOK ONE.

"Glad to hear it."

Juliana started and then realized that while her mind had gone off in a different direction, Carrie's had remained focused on her romantic dreams.

With a sigh, Juliana shrugged. They stood together, locked arms, and proceeded to the hall. While Carrie sustained the conversation with a seemingly endless list of diversions, Juliana turned her thoughts to another subject altogether. She tried to conceive of where she could have dropped her locket.

CHAPTER
3

*In which there is a lengthy discourse on the advantages
and disadvantages of marriage*

T HERE WAS A MUTED BUSTLE AND SCURRYING about the nether regions of Grays Hill Park as Juliana crept down the back stairs. The family rooms held no occupants and were, therefore, devoid of sound. This welcome tranquillity would not be shattered for quite some time. The sun had only just come up over the horizon, bringing with it an unusually fine day. The warm yellow glow of the dawn was invigorating.

Or was it just the thought of defying her aunt yet again?

It was a mark of his thorough training that Chester did not start or remark when he came upon Juliana in the main hall unlocking the front door. He merely grasped the handle, pulled the door open, and bowed a graceful sweep that would have satisfied even Aunt Phyllis.

"I am not going out, Chester," Juliana said as she stepped across the threshold. "I am sleeping in due to a slight sick headache."

Without any obvious glimmer of interest or amusement, the tall, lanky footman nodded. "I am sure Nancy will be pleased to look in on you from time to time, Miss Juliana. Perhaps a cup of tea would be in order."

"Yes, indeed. That might do the trick."

"Shall I instruct Nancy to bring it to you, say, just as the family begins to make an appearance?"

"Thank you, Chester. I am sure that will help. I will likely be feeling better shortly after that."

"Perhaps you will be taking air in the garden, to rid yourself of the remnants of your ache before breaking your fast? I am sure Nancy will find you there. I understand the red roses are beginning to green."

Juliana smiled broadly. "Why, what a coincidence, I had thought to look in on them this morning. I am not sure how long I will be out there and, in fact, might not need too much air."

"I am sure Nancy will see you the moment you are feeling better."

"Thank you, Chester." Had Juliana looked away, she might have missed the wink that flashed across the bland, expressionless face.

"Any time, Miss."

Juliana was dressed in her old riding costume. She did

not want to repeat yesterday's fiasco—no more ruined outfits before she saw the chimney pots of London. The deep blue material was not as much out of mode as the rest of her original wardrobe, and it was comfortable and flexible. At this time of day, the likelihood of encountering anyone but a dairymaid or tenant farmer was rather small, and they would care not a whit about the unfashionable style of her jaunty but weathered top hat.

As she had expected, Juliana found Paul amenable to her early-morning escapade. He had a horse saddled and ready in quick time. He even offered to accompany her, with a nominal nod to propriety, but Juliana's stubborn independence cut too wide a swath, and her fear of Aunt's discovery too strong for her to risk the notice of a missing groom.

Juliana led her horse behind the stables to a little-used path that meandered through the back hills of the park and then out to the coast road. It was a picturesque passageway, well worth the extended time to travel west by going east. It was also the best way to avoid being seen from the house.

It was another handsome day, which made two in succession. The trees and hedges were alive with multitudes of skittering squirrels and trilling birds. Their songs, the sweet smell of dew-covered earth, and the lack of pursuit instilled in Juliana a sense of calm that had evaded her since the discovery of her missing locket.

When the rugged spit of St. Ives Head came into sight, Juliana directed her horse to the protective oak of yesterday and swung the reins lightly across a gnarled branch. She turned, giving the ground a cursory glance, but, as usual, providence was not on her side. There was no glittering hint of the locket. The probability of recovery was minute.

Not surprisingly, Juliana had an aversion to the cliff-side. She was reluctant, in the extreme, to approach the eroding precipice unless such an action proved absolutely necessary. She decided to begin with the road instead; the rut and the general vicinity of the overturned cart were as likely as any other to conceal her locket.

However, when that site proved to be unproductive, Juliana returned to the majestic oak from beneath which she had watched the blue-eyed stranger struggle with her cart. She smiled at the recollection of their lively banter, sighed deeply with an unformed regret, and then returned to her search.

The only object hidden among the grasses was a neatly folded playbill for *Hamlet* at the Theatre Royal Drury Lane in London. The program was covered in circles and squares, and the curt scribbled order, *do not fail*. Juliana sighed. It must have fallen from the gentleman's coat. She refolded it and consigned it to her pocket. She had no idea if she would encounter the gentleman again, but if she did, she would return his souvenir.

Juliana drew a very deep breath and exhaled slowly between her pursed lips. She had no choice; she would have to approach and examine the cliff-side after all. She could hear the crashing of the waves so very, very far below her.

Juliana slowly inched toward the eroding brink that had

held her life in balance less than a day ago. The nearer she came to the edge, the faster her heart beat. She looked, in a studied, nonchalant manner, all around. No one was in sight. She dropped to her knees, thanked the heavens for her foresight in wearing old, stained gloves, and crawled slowly to the edge. It was most undignified, and had Aunt seen this demeaning posture, she would have fainted dead away or become apoplectic. Both were good reasons for Juliana to be on her own.

The ledge was alarmingly small when viewed from this height. The miraculous discovery of it while sliding down the cliff had been nothing short of, well, a miracle. As she had told the gentlemen yesterday, her aunt would never have forgiven her had she plummeted to her death. More important, neither would her father.

While Juliana pondered the incredible event that would be etched permanently in her memory, she swung her head back and forth, scanning the rocks. At last she was rewarded for her diligence and tremendous bravery.

A glint. A metallic shine. Could it be her locket?

Unfortunately, Juliana could not reach it. She needed a little more length. She lowered her trunk and slowly pulled herself half over the cliff's edge.

She could almost reach it. It was just at her fingertips. Juliana dug her toes into the ground and with a great lunge grabbed it.

"Miss!" a voice barked.

The surprise and consequent start pitched the silver coin

from her hand. Juliana watched it bounce, roll, and clatter against the rocks until it dropped soundlessly into the waves below. She was rather glad that it had turned out not to be her locket.

Suddenly, Juliana was seized by her booted ankles in a completely improper manner. Before she could protest, she was unceremoniously dragged across the thatch and jerked onto her feet.

"Did you not have enough excitement yesterday?"

It was the handsome, blue-eyed stranger, with no hint of his friendly smile.

"Sir, while I appreciate your interest in the well-being of my person, I was not in any peril whatsoever." Juliana was both embarrassed and piqued. This man shouldn't be gadding about the country hauling young women off cliffs without so much as a by-your-leave. She was neither a sack of potatoes nor addlepated, with no sense of propriety. "I knew what I was doing. I was not in any danger."

"I believe your aunt may be correct in accusing you of heedless behavior."

Juliana did not appreciate that in the least. To hide her discomfort and shaking hands, she brushed off her skirts, pulling bits and flecks of straw from the material with great concentration.

"What were you about? Trying to finish the job that you had begun yesterday?"

"I beg your pardon?"

"Trying to do yourself an injury?"

"Of course not. I thought I saw something."

"What, pray tell?"

"It was only a coin, and I lost it when you startled me."

"I see. You were seeking your fortune."

"Hardly." Juliana laughed without mirth. "It was merely one coin."

"Then not worth the effort."

Juliana felt foolish, naive, and unworldly. It was amazing that this stranger could do all this with so few words. He was quite adept at it, for she was sure that had been his intent.

"I lost something yesterday and I thought I saw it on the cliff."

A frown flashed across his face so quickly that Juliana was not really sure she had seen correctly. He turned a troubled expression to the Channel but almost immediately turned back to her with a calm mask.

"I did not mean to be judgmental. It was most ungentlemanly." His tone was conciliatory, and a smile began to tug at the corner of his mouth. "I believe it was the possibility of your pitching over the side that caused my tongue to acquire such an unreasonable edge."

Juliana faced him, her furrowed brows smoothing. She was not one to hold grudges. "I do not believe I would have gone for a tumble. I was trying to be cautious. I will, however, thank you for your concern." She smiled at him in an effort to encompass all those sentiments in her countenance. She had the pleasure of seeing him grin. It should have done much to calm her racing pulse, but somehow it didn't. Instead, she discovered a strange connection between his expression and the fluttering in her stomach.

To hide her momentary discomfort, Juliana seized upon the only other subject clanging about her misty brain. "Now that we have settled our differences, pray tell me, is your friend about? Is he not in your company?"

The grin fell slightly. "No, I believe him to be still abed. It is rather early. In fact, I was surprised to see you about at such an hour."

"Even without any knowledge of yesterday's . . . incident, Aunt Phyllis forbade me from tramping about the countryside unescorted. I was not likely to get away any other time."

"You should listen to her. Your reputation is at risk."

"That is of little consequence."

"My dear Miss, there is many a gentleman who will be scared off by a whisper of scandal, and it takes very little for it to become a roar."

"I care not, truly, sir. I am not in the market for a husband."

"That is a most peculiar statement coming from a young lady on her way to London for the Season. What other motive can she entertain but the desire to have a bevy of suitors flatter her?"

Juliana laughed. "Yes, well, that would be most entertaining. I would quite enjoy the novelty, but, while I am going to see the opera, dance at balls, and eat odd delicacies, I am not husband hunting." The need to visit Dagmar & Sloan Publishing was on the tip of her tongue. But that was, perhaps, more information than one should share with a stranger, no matter how open his expression.

The fellow was still not convinced. "Whyever not?"

This was the second time in as many days that Juliana had been asked to explain her lack of interest in matrimony, and yet it gave her pause. Carrie had not been listening—not really. Yet this stranger gave every indication that he was truly interested. And still, it was hard to articulate—perhaps because there was no one definitive reason.

When her father had first encouraged her to waste a summer in the frivolity of a Season, she had reluctantly lifted her head from her studies to evaluate the purpose of this enterprise . . . and consider the results. She had observed the marriages around her and determined that few couples were well suited. A lifetime of disappointment was more the order of the day. Certainly not enticing, no matter how many pretty dresses came with the occasion. No, to enjoy all that the Season encompassed while doing something productive—finding a publisher—was all the excuse she needed for the journey. A trip to the altar need not be included to make the enterprise worthwhile.

Besides, dearest Father, as much as he urged her to put aside their research—temporarily—he could not proceed much further without her assistance, even if it was simply to wield the net.

A puzzled expression stole onto the stranger's face, and Juliana realized that her silence had been overlong. "My father is a widower and has need of me." Her bald statement had the advantage of being true and being an explanation that didn't expose her innermost thoughts.

"Still, most fathers would want to see their child happily settled."

"Yes, indeed. He would be one of the first to wish me well . . . but . . ."

"But?"

"Change is not his ally. Father doesn't realize it, of course, but he falls into a decline whenever there is the slightest deviation of his routine. He leans on it most heavily and would tumble if the prop disappeared. Even my summer away will be detrimental to his well-being."

"Indeed?"

"Yes, indeed, most heartily. I have reports that he has not been eating as he should. Needs my cajoling, I suspect."

"Still, your papa would not want to see you sacrifice your happiness for his."

"No more than I would want to sacrifice his happiness for mine."

"Dear me, that is quite the quandary."

"Yes, quite."

"He might be more adaptable than you think."

Juliana held up her hand to stop his continuing protest. "Do not believe it is in any way a hardship on my part. I have other interests that keep me well occupied." She could safely allude to her research without actually tipping her hand.

"Such as watercolor and arranging flowers."

"Not to mention walking around with a tome on my head."

"Yes, I can see how that would keep you busy." He paused and glanced at her bonnet, as if the imaginary book were sitting on it. "Would you read said tome?"

"Of course, especially if were something truly fascinating like Latin verbs."

"Or how to grow grass."

"Exactly." Juliana laughed, quite enjoying herself.

"There are some that have no choice." The stranger's expression had turned serious.

"You refer to the security of a well-heeled purse."

"I hesitate to be indelicate, but yes."

There was no missing the glance that traveled up and down her old riding costume.

Juliana shook her head and tried, unsuccessfully, not to grin. "I have no concerns in that regard."

He was silent for some moments. His gaze swept out to the gray waters and then back to her. "Well, are we not a pair?"

"I do not take your meaning."

"I, as well, have no intention of entering the stormy seas of matrimony."

"No need to feather your nest?"

"None at all."

"No lineage issues?"

"My cousin has already produced three boys and two girls as well as chosen a new color for the morning room of my manor."

"My, he is well prepared to take over your estate. Your mother does not harass you? Beseech you for grandchildren?"

"Certainly not."

"Then it would seem that we are, indeed, kindred spirits."

"If I knew who you were, I would promise to visit you in your dotage."

"Most kind of you."

"No trouble at all."

They stared at each other in a relaxed, friendly way. Juliana had been more open with this stranger than she had ever been with anyone. Being incognito certainly had its rewards.

"I must say that I am glad to learn that your leanings are not in the direction of my friend."

"Really? How so?" Juliana's brow puckered.

"I am afraid his interest is engaged at the moment." He glanced toward the large, ancient manor in the distance, home of the Pyebalds, particularly the delightful Miss Vivian Pyebald.

"That is marvelous."

"I am not sure that it is, as I cannot be sure that his affection is returned. And believe you me, I have nursed him through enough broken hearts to know that it might not be pretty."

"Another reason for my rejection of the condition."

"Quite right."

"I will be making a call there later today." Juliana turned

her head slightly but obviously toward Ryton Manor. "I might be able to observe if there is an impediment."

"Would you, indeed?"

"I cannot say rightly, but I have found observation to be an excellent tool."

The stranger smiled. A warm wind flushed Juliana's cheeks and sucked the air from her lungs. She should have worn a lighter coat.

"Are you planning an early ride again tomorrow?"

"One can never tell."

"It would give you the opportunity to give evidence of your observation skills."

"Indeed, it would. If it is not raining."

Juliana loosed her horse and brought him forward. The stranger cupped his hands to support her foot, and she lifted herself into the sidesaddle.

"So perhaps we will meet again, sir." Juliana inclined her head and urged her horse forward.

"Until then," he called after her.

Juliana turned as she entered the tree line just as she had done the day before. This time, however, she was rewarded. She raised her hand in reply to his wave and then straightened, watching the road ahead once more.

The path was much shorter on the way back to Grays Hill. She had barely enough time to contemplate the exquisite elegance of the gentleman's cutaway coat, his embroidered saffron waistcoat, the sophistication of his knotted neckcloth, or the breadth of his shoulders. It was only as the stable came into sight that she began to puzzle as to why her blue-eyed stranger had been at St. Ives Head at dawn.

SPENCER NORTHAM WONDERED WHY THE PRETTY MISS had been at St. Ives Head at dawn. She had mentioned looking for something. Was it the locket? The French locket? Her moves had been furtive, from her close scrutiny of the land to her dangerous observations off the cliff. Her motive could be suspect; she was behaving in a most irregular fashion.

If Spencer's better nature had not overcome his need to lie low, he might have discovered her true purpose. He could look to no one but himself for that folly. He should not have rushed to the rescue. Thank heaven there was none here to judge. No one need know of his error, least of all the War Office.

Raking his hands through his hair, Spencer returned to the fallen tree that had provided him a seat for the past two hours. It was concealed behind the evergreen leaves of a common boxwood, back far enough from the cliff that he could see in either direction but forward enough to include the water in his vigil.

The young lady was an unusual package. She exuded innocence, but with such independence of spirit that he almost doubted his own ears and eyes. Was she in earnest in regard to marriage? That seemed almost impossible to believe.

And then, what had she to do with the traitorous activities

that had brought him to this particular spit of land? Why had she offered to observe the situation in Ryton Manor? Was that part of her scheme? Was she involved?

Spencer considered the evolution of his mission, how he had been assigned to infiltrate the lair of the enemy only to discover that French spies were using smugglers to pass messages. It was a great discovery, for they could now beat the French at their own game—feed Napoleon . . . Boney . . . false information. Yes, Spencer just had to be patient—wait for the ship to land, for the communiqué to reach London, the traitor exposed, the lies passed . . . patience for a long process.

Spencer shifted in an attempt to get comfortable. He would stay only an hour more. By then the sun would be far enough into the sky that he could be certain that no ship would approach for fear of discovery.

The hour passed quickly and easily—much faster, in fact, than the previous two. Spencer kept his mind busy. To ensure that his faculties were honed sharp in observation, Spencer tested his memory on the enigmatic personage of the pretty cliff-side miss. He recalled her eyes: sparkling green; her hair: rich brown with reddish highlights; her figure: enticingly round in the right places and firm in . . .

Spencer stood up. It was time to return to Shelsley Hall. Bobbington would soon be stirring. Spencer would not want his friend to suspect that his stay was anything other than the escape from a randy widow that he had claimed it to be. It was an exaggeration, of course. Lady Rayne had no more than fluttered her eyelashes in his general direction, but her reputation was such that Spencer's evasion required no further explanation.

Years of familiarity had taught him that Bobbington was a tried and true friend: supportive, loyal, and obliging. But Bobbington was also completely inept at keeping his thoughts and feelings from his face. A friend like that was not an asset in Spencer's line of work, when all could be exposed with a careless comment. As it was, Spencer had had to be inventive with his excuses; Bobbington was always asking questions. Inquisitive fellow—his curiosity could place Spencer in a bind.

As Spencer placed his toe in the stirrup and pulled himself astride his black stallion, a recollection of white petticoats and lace flashed through his mind. It had come unbidden, and it rested uneasily in his mind. He began to wonder if Bobbington would have a better idea of who their miss could be, now that the aunt had acquired a first name. She had said Aunt Phyllis; surely there could not be too many ladies with that name in the exclusive society of Lambhurst.

Perhaps he would approach their miss on the morrow with a more thorough knowledge of her true character. He might be able to catch her in a lie. It might give him an edge, an opening. And a seemingly guileless means to inquire after the object that she had slipped into her pocket.

CHAPTER
4

*In which Miss Telford encounters a bevy of Pyebalds
and is in need of rescue yet again*

THE EXCITEMENT IN THE REEVES FAMILY'S COACH
was palpable. Aunt Phyllis had dressed to the extreme.
Her new sapphire-blue carriage dress of corded muslin accented
her fine figure and matched to perfection the ribbons in her
high-crowned bonnet—decorated with an excessive profusion
of peacock feathers. Carrie was an intentional foil; the simplic-
ity of her gown accented her mother's elegance while at once
declaring her own refined innocence. Her bonnet was small and
demure, sitting on her neatly upswept coiffure. Not a tendril
was in sight.

Juliana sat staring out her window at the passing scenery,
perfectly content in her sedate outfit of yellow and green. She
had no desire, or need, to impress the good Lady Pyebald with

her looks. Juliana had divined that her inclusion in this adventure would be better secured if she proved to be of no competition.

The visit to Ryton Manor had played into Juliana's hand most handsomely. Both her aunt and cousin had been much too occupied before luncheon to show any interest in Juliana's early-morning whereabouts. The excuses that Juliana had prepared were not needed.

Juliana was relieved. She might employ the same ruse at some other time. She was sure that both Chester and Nancy would fall easily into her plans, say, on the morrow if the desire for another dawn ride struck her. Who could tell how she would feel?

As the coach labored across the road roughened by winter's assault, Juliana had her first glance of Ryton Manor in close proximity. It was a huge formal house in the Palladian style, where symmetry reigned supreme. Windows abounded on all three levels, with tall chimney pots springing from the roof. The gardens were extensive but dull, due to the earliness of the season.

Ryton Manor was majestic in age and proportion. The family's noble lineage reached so far back into history that its superiority went unchallenged by all in the area—with the exception of a family some miles north of Lambhurst. Shelsley Hall, or so Juliana had been told, was in much the same predicament as Ryton. The line was deep, but the pockets were shallow. Mismanagement of lands and tenants coupled with extravagance had put a strain on many a peer's coffers.

There were few signs of this unfortunate happenstance as the coach pulled up before Ryton's great doors and two footmen in elegant, navy-braided livery rushed to their aid. However, once inside the large hall, the less-than-sound footing of the Lord's financial status became obvious with the subtle odor of decay. The carpets were worn and turned, the walls shadowed by missing paintings, and the air laden with must.

The drawing room doors were thrown open as the ladies approached, and Aunt Phyllis glided into the stiflingly hot room with an exclamation of delight. "Oh Lady Pyebald, how good it is to see you," she gushed.

Lady Pyebald was not as Juliana had expected. She was a corpulent woman with gray hair hanging in insipid ringlets about her face, in a young, rather girlish style. Her eyes had not the calculating edge that was present in Aunt Phyllis's, but a calm, almost vacuous reflection. Her gown was of the latest style, and yet it hung oddly and was far from flattering. She was not at all the sort of woman that Juliana believed her aunt would emulate and call a member of her close society.

"Mrs. Reeves, what a grand surprise."

Aunt Phyllis was not taken aback; in fact, she laughed and took her bow before replying. "Lady Pyebald, you haven't changed a whit, still funning. For you did write and expressly request our company today. And here we are."

"I did?"

"Yes—"

"Yes, Mama, you did." A winsome young girl swathed in throws answered with an exasperated tone. She lay upon a settee close to the blazing fire surrounded by cushions. Her face was flushed with the heat, but in all other respects she was recognizable as the delicate beauty of the house. Her hair was golden—dressed in an intricate style that must have taken her maid some time to complete. Her eyes were bright blue, but hard to read, and her face was a perfect oval. Juliana could quite understand the sandy-haired stranger's interest; Vivian Pyebald was quite lovely.

The beauty knew herself to be the object of scrutiny and met Juliana's stare as one accustomed to the admiring adulation of inferiors. She cast her gaze languidly upon Juliana with a glimmer of interest until, after having swept the length of Juliana's serviceable gown, even that light disappeared. She dismissed Juliana with a cursory nod and turned to the youngest member of the party.

"Carrie, lamb, you have come to see me."

"Oh yes, Vivian. How could I not? Are you well? I have been concerned."

"Oh dearest friend, I was forced to subsist on milk bread one whole day. I shan't trouble you with such tedium. I refuse to bore you with my trials, though they have been wearisome."

She patted the seat of a delicate chair conveniently placed beside the settee. "Come sit beside me. You must tell me all about Lambhurst. I am so rusticated. I have heard nothing of good society for a whole month."

Juliana looked at Vivian Pyebald with admiration. She was playing the room well. There was no doubt that all eyes of the company were upon her.

"Dearest friend, I did warn you," Carrie chided. "You should never have attempted such a journey—you were testing providence. And see how it responded. I hope it was a lesson learned, and you will never again endeavor to tax your fragile self. In fact, we should not hazard a step toward London until we are assured of your ability to handle the rigors."

Lady Pyebald laughed, a snide sort of snuffle. "Not to worry, dear child, Vivian is well able to get about. She is merely weary of being bored. She would not hear of any further delay."

Turning her head, Lady Pyebald stared at Juliana, who was still standing in the middle of the drawing room. "Is this person with you, Mrs. Reeves? For she has not gone away."

Juliana swallowed her laugh and turned it into a tactful cough. Not only had the good lady forgotten the invitation and the interview, she had apparently forgotten Juliana's existence.

Neither Aunt Phyllis nor the two young ladies blinked at Lady Pyebald's lack of memory or manners. Juliana found it remarkable that those esteemed as paragons of polite society were often the most discourteous dragons. But then, her knowledge was limited. Perhaps London would teach her otherwise; Lambhurst certainly hadn't.

Juliana curtsied to Her Ladyship as the introduction was

made, and then, as much to please her aunt as to provide herself with a modicum of relaxing obscurity, she perched with ladylike stiffness upon a chair as far from the others and the fire as decorum would allow. She could see past the red draperies and admire the dull brownness of the gardens while listening to the tales of woe that Vivian divulged—with more detail than was needed—as well as overhear Lady Pyebald and Aunt Phyllis discuss the upcoming particulars of the London journey.

The call would last longer than the requisite quarter hour as the matriarchs had so much to resolve of major importance. They had just dealt with the delicate matter of the coach seating arrangements when the drawing room doors were thrown open and a tall, slender man in his early twenties entered with a flourish. His presence filled the room with an energy and awareness that had hitherto been missing, and Juliana noted the look of interest in Aunt Phyllis's eyes.

"Oh yes, Maxwell, do come in and greet the ladies." Lady Pyebald recalled to his memory her great friend and neighbor and her charming daughter—who would no doubt break many a heart in the near future—and to theirs her son and delightful rascal Maxwell Pyebald, who seldom graced this part of the county with his presence. Vivian's nod toward the window had to be repeated three times before Lady Pyebald remembered Juliana's existence.

"Oh yes, and this is Miss Tetley."

"Telford."

"Just so, Miss Tetley."

No sooner had the imperfect introductions been conducted than Juliana was summarily excluded with a flick of Lady Pyebald's thick wrist. Juliana returned to her obscurity by the window. However, her attention was no longer directed out of doors.

While she had easily taken the measure of the ladies of the house, she found she could not do so with the heir. In looks, there could be no doubt of his association; Mr. Pyebald had his family's golden locks, blue eyes, and oval face. But there was an undefinable quality in his conversation, as though saying one thing while he meant something entirely different, or perhaps deeper. It was almost as if he was toying with his obsequious listeners.

Juliana caught an occasional glance in her direction from various members of the group, but she was not included in any of their conversations. She felt secure in her insignificance. It was only after having flattered Carrie into blushes and whispers, and steering the older ladies' discussion back to the practicalities of their London excursion, that Mr. Pyebald approached Juliana with a nonchalant air. He exuded the aura of a gentleman offering the wallflower a token, something to sigh about in the darkest part of the night. It would have been a kindness had Juliana been affected by such sentiments. But she was not.

"So, Miss Telford, are you agog with anticipation at your upcoming Season? Planning to set the town afire?"

Juliana appreciated the accurate use of her name, so she allowed him the haughty lift of his chin without demerit. "Yes,

Mr. Pyebald, I am looking forward to London, with all its sights and grandeur. But agog might not be the term best suited to my emotional state."

Mr. Pyebald took the seat across from Juliana, sweeping his tails out from under him—their knees almost touched. Juliana noticed the glance cast in her direction by his sister. The questioning look was more than enough to inspire Juliana to sparkle before her company. It was petty, perhaps, but there was something about Vivian that rankled.

"Oh come now, your excitement does not put you to shame. See my sister over there." He turned his head slightly and winked when he saw Vivian's eyes upon him. "My sister makes no pains to cover her excitement, or her intention to ensnare any and every gentleman who might stray into her path. You cannot possibly be as nonchalant about your prospects as you suggest. That is, unless you already have an admirer and require no other."

Juliana smiled. She saw the tightening of Vivian's lips and almost opened her mouth to imply that she had, but then rethought the matter. The small victory would not be enough to offset the discovery that there was no smitten gentleman waiting in the background—not to mention the impropriety of it all. Juliana decided to prevaricate.

"I do not possess the same youthful advantages of your sister or of my cousin. Therefore, my expectations are tempered." After all, seventeen was so much better suited to a Season than eighteen.

There was a slight pause in their discourse as Mr. Pyebald looked—no, stared—into her eyes. It was as if he were trying to take her measure, and, for some reason, Juliana found herself wishing that she had worn her cerulean-blue gown. She opened her eyes wider, lest he see the discomfort he had initiated, and smiled. Best change the subject.

"Are you to join us on our journey, Mr. Pyebald? Take in the sights, or balls and assemblies yourself?"

"I am, indeed, although that had not been my intent originally."

"How so?"

"I was prevailed upon by Lord Pyebald, who feels two months of conversation pertaining solely to matching gloves and ribbons might be too difficult for his constitution. While escorting my sister is to be my primary function, I am, as well, obligated to talk in great quantities of hounds and horses."

Juliana laughed. "I can well understand his discomfort, for I believe my uncle would claim the same. However, I believe Mr. Reeves is to accompany us, thereby providing said conversation."

"I believe you to be right. It was likely the gender imbalance of our small party that my lady mother found intolerable."

"Do you not tremble in fear, Mr. Pyebald? For, if I am not mistaken, there is still an almost two-to-one ratio."

"Petrified, Miss Telford. Absolutely petrified."

Juliana smiled, feeling much more comfortable with her circumstances than she had for some time. It did not even nettle when Vivian gestured her brother to the fire on a pretext of needing his opinion.

When all was said and done, the visit had served its purpose. The travel plans were set for Thursday next, Carrie was pleased to see her friend hale and hearty, and Juliana had gone unnoticed by Lady Pyebald.

Juliana had discerned no impediment that might quash the sandy-haired stranger's hopes to secure Vivian's affections, aside from the fact that she was a perfect ninny. But it was none of Juliana's concern.

The young ladies had included many a gentleman's name in their discourse, but none more than once. Alas, that also meant that if her cliff-side rescuer had been mentioned, he, too, did not rate more than a passing comment. But Juliana was not about to point that out. Although it was likely that it would have been noticed . . . if he had been in the room. He did not seem to be overly obtuse.

It was a strange thing that, as Juliana thought of the sandy-haired stranger intermingled with thoughts of Mr. Pyebald, it was a lopsided smile that came to mind. She wondered if that particular fellow ever visited London.

❧

THREE UNEVENTFUL DAYS LATER, Juliana stared through the window of the glove-maker's shop onto the bustling main thoroughfare of Lambhurst, lost in thought. She barely attended the discussion behind her between her aunt and cousin. Her attention was not required; the sale had been made. All that remained of their business was for the proprietor to congratulate Aunt Phyllis on her exquisite taste while gathering the merchandise together.

Juliana was startled out of her ennui when she watched two familiar strangers stop across the street—one of whom had meandered in and out of her thoughts far too often of late. An animated discussion ensued, after which the sandy-haired gentleman waved and disappeared from sight. The blue-eyed stranger stood in place, rocking on his heels, waiting. For what, Juliana could not know . . . though he did keep glancing in the direction that his friend had taken.

Puzzled and a tiny bit enthralled, Juliana continued to observe her specimen. The blue-eyed stranger rocked several minutes, until some inner thought brought him to an abrupt halt, and then he, too, marched up Balcombe Street.

Juliana felt an immediate need of fresh air. She glanced behind her and called to the young man still boxing up their parcels.

"I will show you the carriage," she said quickly. Juliana ignored his startled look, as well as those of Aunt Phyllis and Carrie. She quickly grabbed the polished brass door handle, pulled the door open, and stepped out onto the sidewalk. She slammed the door and stomped down the steps, making as much noise as possible.

Despite her boisterous efforts, the blue-eyed stranger disappeared into the crowd without a glance back; he was oblivious to her presence. Juliana shook her head. She wished she could call after him—but that would scandalize her aunt even more than exiting a store with undue haste.

Juliana chewed at the side of her lip and turned back toward the shop. She looked up, and seeing the shadowed figures of her nearest and dearest hovering on the other side of the glass, she decided to remain out of doors. She ambled over to the carriage, a mere three paces from the store, and nodded to Mr. White, the coachman. He was a chubby-cheeked man with a large red nose and a silent, sour expression. There was something about his squinty, judging eyes that put Juliana in mind of her aunt. Yes, Aunt Phyllis would be out all too soon with a similar expression and more than a few words. Unpleasant words.

Juliana glanced heavenward at the overcast sky. If only it had been this fine yesterday or the day before. But, no, the early mornings had been filled with rain and fog, followed by drizzly days in which even Paul would not allow her to venture beyond the gardens.

For some reason, the groom believed that she would be lost in the fogs. Had she been at home, Juliana would have overridden his objections. But at Grays Hill? She wasn't at all confident, especially in her sense of direction. She had very firm memories of the cliff-side—her bruised upper leg showed just how firm. As her destination would have been a mere thirty paces from that offending abyss, she allowed Paul his obstinacy.

Still, Juliana couldn't help but wonder if her blue-eyed

rescuer had gone to St. Ives Head despite the weather. She wondered if he had anticipated a meeting as much as—

The sage-green door of the shop was pulled open from the inside. The soft tinkle of a bell echoing in the interior announced Aunt Phyllis's departure. She marched down the steps, layered in ruffles and indignation. "Whatever possessed you, Niece?"

Carrie trailed behind her mother in a simple ivory gown; her bland expression was an approximation of a demure countenance. The parcel boy followed her onto the landing and then waited for direction.

Aunt Phyllis did not pause long enough for Juliana's excuse—which was just as well since she was still working on it.

"Can you never comport yourself properly? I swear you are becoming a veritable hoyden, what with your sudden fits of temper, unruly behavior, and sullen moods!"

"Sullen moods?"

"Mama, that is me," Carrie owned.

"Be that as it may, if you cannot behave in a decorous fashion, I will set you off to Compton Green on the next mail coach."

It was an idle threat made at least five times a day. While Juliana knew there would be repercussions for a scrape, it would have to be something that Aunt Phyllis could cite as being completely beyond the pale. This was not dire enough, not by any means.

Juliana laughed—enjoying her aunt's startled look. "A premature exit from a stuffy shop does not qualify as indecorous behavior, Aunt Phyllis. I merely needed a breath of air, and by leaving when I felt an oncoming fit of the coughs, I actually prevented you from being subjected to the commotion it would have caused."

Aunt Phyllis harrumphed and wordlessly pointed the boy with the packages to the back of the carriage. Mr. White stowed them away.

"Fine. Enjoy your air, but stay by the carriage. We have more shopping to do." Aunt Phyllis pulled at the corner of her glove as though the item should not have dared slip down her wrist.

She harrumphed again, with as much dignity as one can while breathing that deeply, turned, and stormed down the street. She almost bumped into an adorable, grubby-faced urchin, but, fortunately, he saw her coming and quickly jumped out of the way.

Carrie looked apologetically at Juliana and rushed after her dear mama. Aunt Phyllis marched down the block toward the milliner's. She gained the store rather rapidly.

Juliana sighed. She was not disappointed about missing the milliner. She didn't need to purchase another bonnet—she already had more than she could ever use. But the stationer was just across the street from the milliner, and Juliana wished to purchase a notebook. She had found a collection of lady beetles under the leafing roses that needed to be sketched and their scurrying habits recorded.

Perhaps she could slip across the street while Aunt was in the milliner's. She glanced up at driver's bench of their carriage.

Mr. White stared back at her. His initial disapproving expression dissolved into that of a composed mask. Still, it was obvious. Mr. White would not turn a blind eye. He was too firmly entrenched in Aunt Phyllis's camp. Juliana would have to remain by the carriage—if not actually in it—and return to Grays Hill empty-handed.

Mr. White sniffed. He clearly disapproved of her ways. He hadn't even offered to hand her in before he had climbed to his own perch.

Juliana decided to take advantage of his breach by waging a slight rebellion. She would obtain her latest book from the back in among the packages. She would not sit upon her aunt's pleasure but while away the time lost in *A Treatise on Some Insects Injurious to Vegetation* by Thaddeus William Harris. It promised to be an exciting read.

The pile of parcels secured to the back of the carriage was much larger than she had anticipated; they had bought far more than she realized. The book she was seeking had inadvertently made its way to the bottom of the pile. The boxes were rather heavy and quite cumbersome, but at last Juliana had the tome in her grasp. She had no intention of allowing it to slip back into its hiding place, and she tugged with strength.

More than the book broke free of the constraints. Several boxes flew across the sidewalk, and one landed in the middle of Balcombe Street. Juliana glanced around the folded hood of the landau. Mr. White was staring straight ahead in an I-see-nothing manner. He would not be put upon to retrieve the package.

Juliana lifted her chin, stalked to the middle of the road, and bent to retrieve her cousin's half dozen or so pairs of gloves. Suddenly, an arm whipped around her waist and lifted her off her feet. Without even so much as a how-do-you-do, she was yanked back to the sidewalk with her heels dragging.

"My dear Miss, what the deuce do you think you are doing?"

Juliana was much relieved to hear the familiar voice of the blue-eyed stranger complaining in her ear. She had no more time than to recognize the needless concern in his tone when a wagon, which she had not seen, barreled past them. It was a large, heavy wagon pulled by six very large, very heavy dray horses—with equally large, heavy hooves; twenty-four of them.

Juliana swallowed with some difficulty as the wagon disappeared down the street. Perhaps she had been too hasty. There might actually have been a valid reason for his concern. It would not have been a pretty sight had she still been in the middle of the road.

"I did it again, didn't I?" Her question caught in her throat.

"You did, indeed. How it is that you have survived to eighteen is beyond me."

His breath puffed out the small escaped hairs at the nape of her neck and sent tingles down her spine. She could feel his hard chest and pounding heart along the length of her back, and she almost leaned into him. She swallowed and placed her hand on the arm that was still wrapped around her waist. He released her instantly, and Juliana almost fell. The stranger quickly held out his arm for support, and two or three gulps of air later she was steady enough to stand on her own.

Juliana looked around the street, expecting a multitude of eyes to be upon them, but there were none. All was as it should be. All were about their own business, and none interested in an event that never happened. There had been no accident, and the gentleman's arm had been around her for no longer than a moment. It had only seemed longer.

And now the gentleman held an armload of rough packages; they were scuffed and dented as if they had seen hard times. When he stretched out his arms toward her, Juliana recognized them as her aunt's boxes. He had picked up the troublesome flying parcels.

"Oh yes, thank you so much." Juliana quickly divested the fellow of his burden.

"Are you alone? I am surprised that your aunt would allow you to travel about without a chaperone."

Juliana laughed lightly. "For someone who knows me not, you understand my aunt quite well. She is but a block farther, seeking yet another bonnet to match my fair cousin's complexion."

"The milliner afforded you no interest?"

"I needed a breath of air." She held up the book still in her hand. "I was hoping to read while I waited."

"Well, I should leave you to your reading then. You would not want to be caught talking to a stranger and cause any injury to your aunt. I presume that she is prone to apoplexy."

Juliana smiled and nodded. "Regularly."

"I shall continue then. Shopping can be tedious—though there is no helping it."

Juliana frowned slightly, noting that the gentleman was quite free of parcels. He must have sent his purchases on. She also discerned the direction toward which he was heading.

"Excuse me. I do beg your pardon . . . I am quite loath to ask, but . . . well, are you going to the stationer?"

"Stationer? Yes, of course. I need to get some . . . ink. Yes, ink. Is there something I can help you with?"

"I need a notebook for . . . well, notes. I was going to pick up one myself, but . . ."

"Say no more. I shall return with it presently."

Juliana smiled her thanks and watched the gentleman cross the street. However, no sooner had he left her side than the voice of her aunt floated around the carriage, erasing the lingering pleasure of her encounter with the young gentleman.

"It would not do, Carrie. There is nothing left to discuss."

"But, Mama, it was lovely."

"No, Carrie, it was overlarge. Much too flamboyant for an innocent. It smacked of vulgarity, as do you when you take such a pet over it."

"But, Mama."

"Do not *Mama* me. I—Juliana? Juliana? Where is Juliana, Mr. White?"

"Here, Aunt," Juliana answered, and stepped out from behind the carriage. "I am afraid I rumpled the parcels while trying to retrieve my book."

"Never mind, never mind. Just get in. You, too, Carrie. We are going back to Grays Hill. I am feeling rather peevish."

Mr. White jumped down from his bench and handed Aunt Phyllis carefully into the carriage. He also offered Carrie and then Juliana assistance, as if he would never do otherwise.

Mr. White had just ordered the horses to walk on when Juliana saw her rescuer exit the stationer. He stared at her as the carriage rolled past. He lifted up a small notebook clasped in his hand, and Juliana glanced to her aunt. The older woman was glaring out the other side of the carriage, hand pressed against her temple.

Juliana looked back; the stranger stared at her with a perplexed expression. She raised her shoulders slightly, hoping he would notice and understand the gesture.

He did.

Mimicking her shrug, the gentleman dropped his arm to his side. He continued to stare at her as the distance between them increased. He shifted his head slightly when another carriage passed between them and then resumed his stare. Eventually, they lost sight of each other behind the crowds of the milling populace of Lambhurst.

CHAPTER
5

In which Miss Telford is officially introduced to
Mr. Northam and they can conspire at will

SPENCER WAS IN A PUCKER, and he didn't know why. Well, at least he told himself that it was an unexplained mood, but the fact that his brooding increased every time he thought of the cliff-side miss made it evident that the cause was not as elusive as he wanted to pretend.

How could he concentrate on the complexities of his mission when his mind was constantly deviating to that lovely, heedless idiot? She was a danger to herself. Not that she wasn't capable of handling herself—he knew that she was—but she just didn't allow for the chaos of the world around her. She was too sheltered. Or was that an act?

No, she had truly been in danger, again; that dray would not have stopped in time. She would have been crushed.

The thought of her fragile, soft body assaulted by hooves and wheels caused his stomach to plummet. She needed someone to watch over her. It was outside of enough that she had professed an aversion to marriage. How else would she get to her aged years? She needed a robust, clear-thinking gallant to keep constant vigil over her.

The possibility of volunteering flashed through his mind but was summarily dismissed. His words on the cliff had been heartfelt. He was not going to ever willingly step before an altar. No, it was not the life for him. An agent, such as he, needed to be unfettered, able to pick up and move on at a moment's notice—a wife would frown heavily upon such comings and goings.

Besides, there was the miss's puzzling connection with the rendezvous point. She was an enigma as much as a concern. Was there any association between her and his quarry?

"I am rather disheartened," Bobbington muttered.

Spencer echoed the sentiments, although not for the same reasons.

"She has but arrived and now is rushing off to London."

"Yes, that is most disheartening," Spencer sighed silently. He could have muttered the same sentiment referring to a different she.

The return ride to Shelsley Hall from Lambhurst was more a plodding tramp along winding lanes than an invigorating chase through fields, which had been the manner of their arrival. The lacey yellow-green of burgeoning trees from which birds sang appeared to do nothing to capture Bobbington's attention. Neither did the sweet smell of overturned earth, nor the nods and smiles of passing tenants. Bobbington seemed to be lost in thought. A lion dressed in a lavender bonnet would likely not have drawn his attention.

Bobbington's thoughts were not difficult to fathom. He had learned, somewhat inadvertently, that his darling Miss Pyebald was to soon quit the area and ply her charms in the sparkling assemblies and balls in London. She was to have her Season; the search for a suitable match was on. Bobbington was not pleased.

"You must have realized that she would be presented. She is of an age, you know, or you would not have noticed her."

"Yes, but she has been ill. What can her family be thinking? Taking her to the city, where she might encounter any manner of deadly diseases."

"I am sure her family and relations would not put her in any danger. They will take care."

Bobbington harrumphed and fell into silence. It suited Spencer. It allowed him time to calm his wild thoughts, school his reaction to a soft, supple figure pressed against him, and refocus on the task at hand.

"Bobbington?" Spencer's thoughts had formed a safe enough question.

His friend merely harrumphed again.

"The pretty miss was in town. Did you see her?"

"Just in passing."

"Did you recognize her carriage?"

Bobbington pulled his brows tightly together for some moments. When he released them, he straightened his shoulders and nodded. "Well, I have been mulling that over." He patted his bay gelding absentmindedly. "That might have been the Rumblys' carriage . . . but no, the lead horse was too black, perhaps the Stamfords'. Oh no, I believe they have already gone to Town." Bobbington swayed slightly as the gelding ambled down a knoll. "I have it. The Reeves family's, yes, indeed. It was them; when I think upon it, I did recognize Miss Reeves. Childhood friend of Miss Pyebald."

Back to Miss Pyebald.

"Are you certain? It is not just an association of your mind, being that you can think of none else?"

"No, indeed." Bobbington sniffed. "I shouldn't wonder at our miss going to London, as it is said that the Pyebalds are to reside with the Reeves family in Town."

"Are they, indeed?"

"That is the chatter."

"Anything else?"

"Just that Mrs. Reeves's niece is visiting from Compton Green. Yes, there, you see, that must be our pretty miss. No . . . no, I must be wrong, for the rumor mill implied that the niece was rather peculiar, counting on her connections rather than her charms to secure a match. That could not be our miss, for she is quite enchanting."

Bobbington was entirely too susceptible to the female form for his own good. He would need a wife one day, although

Spencer doubted it would be Bobbington's darling Miss Pyebald. The mamas would object, strenuously. Both families needed an infusion of funds.

"There it is," Bobbington said with the intonation of an announcement.

"There what is?"

Bobbington's thoughts had apparently gone off in a direction quite separate from Spencer's.

"I must pay Miss Pyebald a call. I must show her that she has imposed on me and that we suit. And I must do it before she leaves."

"Miss Pyebald is likely filled with excited anticipation of the pleasures of Town. She might not favor any suggestion that would prevent her from enjoying those delights."

"I cannot let anything keep us apart," Bobbington said dramatically.

"Bobbington, tell me of your moment. This shared intimacy that you believe has demonstrated a budding attraction." Spencer watched his friend's complexion deepen to that of a beet. "If it is of no true consequence, then you will make a great cake of yourself."

"I . . . I would rather not say, as I might have embellished a trifle. That is, I might have seen something more than was there. But I truly believe the possibility is strong that we would get on."

"Get on?" Spencer rubbed his hand roughly across his face.

"Bobbington, you are not going to declare yourself. Wait until she returns—"

"No, Northam. She is a beauty with a title. She shines everyone else down. She will be riveted long before she returns. I could not bear it. If I was there, in London, I could bide my time. But to while away my days in Lambhurst, imagining any number of swells of the first stare toying with her . . . well, it is too much to be borne. I must . . . I must to London. Yes, that is the way of it. You and I, we will partake of the Season as well."

Unless darling Miss Pyebald was off to London with brother in tow, it would not suit Spencer's purpose at all. "It is not everything that it is cracked up to be."

"That is of little consequence. My darling would be there. I would be there, with a whispered word in the garden, a hand clasped in a dance."

The poor fellow's romantic sensibilities were getting quite carried away.

"We could get lost in the crowds," Bobbington said dreamily.

"Not with her mama around, you could not."

But it no longer mattered what Spencer said. Bobbington had seized upon the possibility and was running away with it.

"It would make Mama prodigiously pleased . . . putting my oar in the matrimonial waters, as she would see it. She has been making very loud noises in that direction."

"Have you any blunt?"

"Of course not. My pockets are to let. I will stay at your place, and I know you will spot me."

Bobbington knew him too well.

Spencer was torn. His options were fewer the longer the conversation continued. He had to either convince Bobbington that they should remain in Lambhurst or tell him the true purpose of his visit. Both risked a heated reproach. Neither appealed.

However, there was a third possibility. If his quarry were journeying to London as well, then Spencer could continue his vigil without showing his hand. Perhaps a visit to Ryton Manor was in order, after all.

Now, if only he could prevent Bobbington from making an offer to his darling Miss Pyebald in front of the company. It would be a monumental task, far more difficult than following the secret communiqué of a French spy.

⚬⚭⚬

JULIANA TRIED TO CRY OFF, citing a terrible headache. But it was not to be. The moment Aunt Phyllis discerned Juliana's distaste for the visit, the lady became deaf to her excuses.

"No, Juliana, the megrims is not improved with a calm, tranquil setting. Light company and gaiety, such as you will find in the drawing room of Ryton, will do the trick. We will visit as planned, and you will accompany us."

Juliana could say nothing after that. She was destined to endure the condescension of Lady Pyebald, who might or might not remember her, the mindless chatter of the girls, and the sly flirting of the heir. All the while holding the pain in her temple at bay. Juliana wondered if this London endeavor carried too large a price.

At Ryton, the trio of Grays Hill ladies was, once again, led to the paneled drawing room, where the lady of the manor, her daughter, and her son awaited. This time, however, Lady Pyebald recalled Juliana's association, if not her name, and did not glower at her entrance. It was a step in the right direction.

"Miss Telford," Aunt Phyllis repeated again, with a light careless air.

When Juliana lifted her eyes from the worn geometric designs of the Bokhara carpet, she found herself being introduced yet again. The Pyebalds, it would seem, were not alone. When the gentlemen stepped forward to bow, Juliana altered her gasp into a gentle clearing of her throat.

Two impeccably dressed, familiar strangers smiled back at her with reciprocal interest. It was with great pleasure that Juliana could now identify her blue-eyed rescuer as Mr. Spencer Northam and the sandy-haired gentleman as Lord Randolph Bobbington. Better still, they were now included in her social circle, and she could interact with them at will—under the steely eyes of watchful barracudas, of course.

Suddenly, Juliana greatly regretted the pain in her head, which gave her an ashen pallor, and decried the overly frilled cut of her gown—another suggestion from Aunt Phyllis—and the offhanded manner of the other members of the party. It illustrated only too well her lack of consequence.

When the other ladies had settled and resettled on various seats, Juliana crossed the floor to the small grouping of chairs by the window. She perched on a red brocade seat that faced into the room, allowing her a full view of its occupants. It was as far away from the exuberant conversation of the girls, the stifling fire, and the repetitive discourse of the matrons as she could politely devise. She was close enough to answer any unlikely question or comment that might be cast in her direction, but not too close to create the discomfort of an uninvited guest.

The gentlemen meandered about the room, joining the discussion of the ladies from various positions. Juliana was pleased to see that while Lord Bobbington did show an interest in Vivian, he was neither too besotted nor without enough sensibility to exclude Carrie. For their part, the young ladies demonstrated, by way of their posture and conversation, no distaste for the young gentleman. Juliana found herself feeling more kindly disposed toward Vivian.

So entranced by the subtle dances of the dissimilar personalities of the room, Juliana was unaware that Mr. Pyebald had approached.

"Let us hope for fine weather on the morrow. It is such a messy business to travel in the rain."

Mr. Pyebald's address was of a benign nature, and yet he stood between her and the rest of the company—as if to cut her off from them. His predatory stance made her uncomfortable. When she realized that this discomfort was derived from a concern that Mr. Northam would misinterpret the relationship, she shifted slightly to see if his eyes were upon her.

They were. She lifted her eyebrows slightly and curled the corners of her lips. It was meant to be an invitation to join them. His casual stare did not reply.

Juliana turned back to Mr. Pyebald. She motioned to the seat across from her with her eyes, and she was pleased to see that Mr. Pyebald was not as obtuse as he was arrogant.

"Yes, indeed, it is difficult to make time on muddy roads," she finally replied.

"However, the turnpikes do improve the closer one gets to London, but then the traffic increases as well; vicious circle."

Juliana sighed silently. This conversation was as interesting as boiled potatoes. She was trying to devise another method of luring Mr. Northam to the window when she heard a muffled step headed in their direction.

"Are you to Town often?" Mr. Northam addressed Mr. Pyebald. He stood slightly to the side, as any well-bred gentleman should, not sequestering the lady but allowing her the company.

"No, not really, not above four or five times in a calendar. My interests keep me in Bath for the better part of the year."

"Charming city, Bath. The upper crust there is quite up to snuff. Do you take the waters regularly?"

"Whenever I can, but it is not frequent." Mr. Pyebald flicked a speck from the knee of his cream breeches.

"Your interests must be demanding. Whatever could keep

you from the restorative qualities of the water and the charming society that surrounds them?"

Juliana couldn't help but wonder at the hard edge of Mr. Northam's casual inquiries. She tipped her head in his direction to catch his eye, but he seemed not to notice.

"This and that, nothing of consequence." Mr. Pyebald waved his hand in the air. "Though the time is coming when I must keep to Lambhurst. There is much to running an estate of this size, all of which I must learn."

"Surely that is the purpose of your steward. A man such as yourself would prefer the company of the Ton to the birds and trees."

Mr. Pyebald laughed without mirth. "Perhaps you are right. And yourself? Do you frequently vacate your estate to your steward and enjoy the pleasures of Bath and London?"

"Bath, not as often. But London is another matter. In fact, we are for Town shortly as, I have learned, are you."

"What a happy chance," Juliana replied as was expected, and she found that it was, indeed, a welcome disclosure. The prospect of never seeing Mr. Northam again had caused a feeling of inexplicable discontent. It was agreeable to cast off that emotion before it had to be examined too closely. "Will you be there for the Season?"

"That is our intent. But one never knows."

"A willow in the winds, are you, Mr. Northam? No desire to make plans?"

Juliana wasn't sure if she heard derision or envy in Mr. Pyebald's tone.

Mr. Northam smiled and then bowed. "As little as possible." He turned without another glance in her direction and rejoined the group by the fire.

"Not one such as we, eh, Miss Telford. We have plans aplenty."

"I beg your pardon?" Juliana had not been attending Mr. Pyebald's scintillating words.

"I have it on good authority—my sister as opposed to my mother—that there is already a possibility of procuring vouchers for Almack's. Think on that, Miss Telford, the exclusive temple of the *beau monde*: the most hallowed of social clubs. Could there be anything more fulfilling to a young lady such as yourself?"

Juliana could think of several things, but she was not about to enlighten the man. He was trying to entertain her in his own banal fashion.

All too soon, Juliana heard Mr. Northam urging Lord Bobbington to make his good-byes. Their call had come to an end, and Juliana wished she could say the same. As the departing gentlemen stepped around the furniture, Juliana rose and moved farther into the room, ostensibly to fill their vacuum. With a nod, Mr. Northam crossed behind her, and she felt his fingers brush hers as he passed.

With amazing deftness, she found a small object pressed

into her palm. Juliana recognized the shape and slight crumple: a notebook. She held her hand slightly behind her skirt, hiding the notebook in its folds.

It wasn't until Juliana was once again in the echoing corridors of Grays Hill Park that she realized that along with the notebook, she had been handed a message.

SPENCER PACED BENEATH THE OAK AT ST. IVES HEAD. A light mist hung off the coast, filling the air with the smell of salty dampness. The sun had just come up over the horizon and was tinting the sky in pastel shades of yellow and pink. Whether it was to be a fine day had yet to be determined, but for now, at least, rain was not anticipated.

Spencer took a deep breath and exhaled slowly. He had still not resolved Miss Telford's role in this game of subterfuge. Her acquaintance with the Ryton family appeared tenuous, but was that just artifice? Maxwell Pyebald had adroitly prevented any quiet conversation between them yesterday and exuded an intimacy with her that could disclose an association of longer duration than that implied by Lady Pyebald. But then Miss Telford was a comely young woman; perhaps Mr. Pyebald had merely been demonstrating an interest.

Miss Telford could be the innocent blunderer that she appeared to be. However, her willful disobedience of the dictums of her aunt might be not a sign of frustrated rebellion but a personality that saw rules as inapplicable to her person. If she were a blunderer and nothing else, she might make a fascinating accomplice. If, however, she were an adept manipulator, she might be his quarry's decoy. He sincerely preferred the former explanation to the latter one.

As the sun rose higher in the sky, Spencer's doubts rose with it. The likelihood of Miss Telford riding up the road lessened with each passing moment. He would have to devise another method to encounter her in London.

Just as he had decided that his wait had been futile, Spencer heard the sound of movement in the bushes. He stepped behind the oak and into the obscurity of the shrubbery. He was relieved and surprised to see Miss Telford step out from the brush onto the road up ahead. Her russet coat was damp with falling dew, her limp bonnet askew.

Spencer regained his casual position by the oak. "Miss Telford, what are you about?"

She started slightly at his words and then frowned. She closed the distance between them as her brows became more deeply entrenched in their pucker. "Why do you ask, Mr. Northam? I was under the impression that you requested this interview."

Spencer smiled and nodded. "Yes, indeed. However, I did not expect you to walk. It is a fair distance from Grays Hill."

Juliana's expression lightened, and her brows spread back across her face. "Ah, but the household is all sixes and sevens, what with our departure at midday. Pressing Paul to either saddle a horse or prepare a cart would have been most selfish and unjust of me. I could do little else but walk."

"You might also not have come."

"Yes, I might not have. But I believe London is going to be very regimented. This might be my last taste of freedom for some time."

"Are you not looking forward to these elegant affairs, Miss Telford? For to hear you talk, one would suppose not."

"Well, I am approaching it, as I do most things, as an adventure. My vexation at the moment is derived from my expectation of no independence."

"You have had a peculiar upbringing, I believe, Miss Telford."

"Yes, thank heaven. You are quite right. My father has left me unfettered."

"Rather eccentric, is he?"

"Oh no, well, yes. But not in the manner you mean. He is merely focused—we both are. My mother's passing left him bereft, and as a result, he threw himself into research; it became his passion. The condition was quite contagious, of course. Now, we eat, sleep, and think *Coccinellidae*—"

"I beg your pardon. You think what?"

Miss Telford laughed. "*Coccinellidae*, lady beetles. We are studying their habits, their varieties, food sources, life cycles—any number of things. We have been doing so for a fair number of years and will likely be doing so for a fair number more. And while doing so, I have also been responsible for Hartwell. With that responsibility came independence."

Spencer stared at her for some moments before comment-ing. "You are not really eighteen, are you, Miss Telford?"

"No, you might be right, Mr. Northam," she said quietly, meeting his eyes directly. "I feel a good deal older."

Spencer considered her for some moments more until she shifted in discomfort. He swallowed, shook himself mentally, and asked her directly what he had intended to approach with subtlety. He no longer felt the need to hedge.

"You found something in the grass last time you were here. Put it in your—"

"Oh yes, I am so glad you brought it up. I made sure to bring it with me. It must have fallen out of your pocket when I carried your jacket over."

Miss Telford passed him the crumpled piece of paper with such an open expression that Spencer was flooded with relief. He hadn't realized how desperately he had wanted her to be no more than what she appeared. To associate with a traitor did not mean that she shared in the betrayal. After all, turncoats hid their deeds from even their nearest and dearest.

Spencer took the paper from her, purposefully touching her hand as he did so. He glanced up to see a slight flush spread across her cheeks. The shy look that accompanied it caught at his chest. The reaction startled him. He slowly and deliberately smoothed out the paper on his knee, concentrating on calming his suddenly accelerating heartbeat.

"Did you enjoy the show?" she asked.

Spencer looked down at the paper. It was a playbill. He took note of the squares, circles, and scribbled order before answering. "I am afraid, Miss Telford, that I have not yet had the pleasure of seeing the Drury Lane *Hamlet*." He saw a quizzical look form on her face. "This is not mine."

"Oh dear, I am sorry. I found it by the oak tree. I just assumed. That is, I thought. Well, then it is of no consequence."

Spencer turned to the tree, running his hand across the rough gray bark. He ducked under its lower branches for a closer look at the trunk. The tree was gnarled, bent, and old, and, yes, it possessed a burrow of a size in which someone might hide a message. He would have to replace the playbill after Miss Telford was gone.

It was clear by the markings across the face of the theater program that it was being used to arrange a meeting—a convoluted procedure to protect their identities . . . or perhaps enabling two people to meet who would not normally. The playbill had to be seen in order for both traitorous parties to arrive at the same time and place . . . where the smuggled communiqué would continue its journey deeper into the heart of Britain. Yes, the playbill would have to be replaced.

Spencer straightened and stuffed the paper into his pocket as if it truly were of no consequence. "You must be wondering why it is that I asked to meet you?"

"No, indeed. I know perfectly well."

Spencer was taken aback. "You do?"

"Yes. Did you not wish to know if I observed an impediment for Lord Bobbington in regard to his affection for Miss Pyebald?"

Spencer frowned slightly and then nodded. "Yes, that is it exactly."

"Well, as best as I can tell, Miss Pyebald is without any fixed affections. Unfortunately, Mr. Northam, that would include Lord Bobbington." As she spoke, Miss Telford leaned forward in a conspiratorial manner.

Spencer enjoyed the proximity; he could smell the sweet scent of roses drifting around her and feel the radiant warmth of her skin. "Not to worry, Miss Telford. As long as there are no prior attachments, Bobbington might have a passing chance at winning her."

"Is that why you are to London? For I was rather surprised to learn that you are about to participate in the Season."

"As you surmised, it was a last-minute decision."

"Lord Bobbington?"

"Exactly."

Miss Telford laughed, a delightful tinkling sound.

"We must do all that we can to bring him and Miss Pyebald together," she said.

"My very thought. Could I be so bold as to . . . ? No, that is pure presumption on my part."

"I cannot say yea or nay until you ask, Mr. Northam. Believe me, I do very little that does not suit me."

"Yes, I have seen the proof of that." Spencer looked out

across the road to the gray rolling water. The mist was pulling back farther, allowing the warm morning sun to reflect in the crests of the waves. "If it appeared that I had developed an attraction . . . that is, if I appeared smitten and visited . . . that is, as I know you are not setting your cap . . . what I mean is—"

"Mr. Northam, worry not." Miss Telford smiled kindly, deceived by his feigned discomfort. "I see what you are about. I will be the excuse needed to account for your and Lord Bobbington's frequent presence in our midst. It will not show Lord Bobbington's hand immediately, that is, not overtly. Oh, this is marvelous."

Clearly, Miss Telford was warming to the idea.

"I can inform you," she continued, "of which assemblies, routs, and balls we are to attend. I will keep an ear to the ground for any comments Miss Pyebald should make in his regard, and I will expect nothing from you other than a companion to whom I shall not have to be false." Miss Telford smiled brightly and nodded with finality. "I cannot but wonder if they are a good match, but that is not for me to say. Love can make one single-minded."

"You are a matchmaker, Miss Telford."

"And you, sir, are a romantic and a devoted friend. How many gentlemen would do half as much for their comrade?"

Spencer felt a flush of guilt wash over him and quickly suggested that Miss Telford hurry back before being missed. Her artless smile and wave tugged at his conscience, but only for a moment. The practicality of his suggestion was too obvious. He now had a confederate in the household, the delightful Miss Telford. He would not even consider the possibility that his proposition had sprung from a desire to spend more time in her company.

CHAPTER
6

*In which a sleepless night fills Miss Telford with doubts
while Mr. Northam discusses the culpability
of those in her party*

JULIANA STARED OUT THE COACH WINDOW. With the other ladies in the following carriage, her fellow travelers required neither attention nor conversation. Opposite her, Lord Pyebald napped and Uncle Leonard read—despite the swaying jerks produced by the less-than-smooth London Road. The scenery before her eyes was a picturesque but monotonous blend of fields and vales. It took little concentration to take her thoughts inward.

Juliana found her mind dwelling on a handsome young man with an appealing smile. She recalled the conversation with Mr. Northam in which she had, rather emphatically, dispelled the notion that she was going to London to secure a match. It had been a wise dialogue seen in retrospect. Had she not truthfully informed him of her intention to retain her heart, he would likely never have thought to include her in this harmless plan to assist his friend. He was too much of a gentleman to infer an attachment where none had developed. Mr. Northam was resolved to remain unfettered as well; they were of a like mind.

At first, Juliana would not even consider the possibility that falling in with Mr. Northam's proposition sprang from a yearning to spend more time in his company. Still, there was no denying her lighter heart at the prospect. There could also be no doubt of her awareness of him as a gentleman, with his strength of character and appealing physique, but when she turned her thoughts on him, it was as a friend or comrade. She told herself so, over and over. Who would not admire the cut of Mr. Northam's coat or the talent of his neckcloth? Or the way his hair curled at the nape of his neck or his ability to convey a deep interest with few words?

By the time the small parade of two carriages and lone rider had left Ryton Manor four hours behind schedule, Juliana had changed her mind about the wisdom of the plan and Mr. Northam's proximity . . . several times. Until at last she admitted to herself that Mr. Northam had, in fact, already imposed upon her. And yet knowing this did not worry her overly.

It was a situation in which she knew the outcome. She had but two choices: to deny herself the delight she felt in his company and struggle to cast him from her heart before she was lost any further, or to enjoy what little time they had together, knowing that they would part as friends. The latter would leave her with memories enough to keep her warm for a time. It might also allow her to understand the strange predilection of those around her to enter a state that she recently believed held little enticement.

Mr. Northam's assurances that he would never consider any match between them would allow Juliana the freedom to enjoy the sensations of attraction. She could marvel at him and never fear that there would be any upset to her original plans. Yes, there would be disappointment in their final parting, but it would be for her and her alone. Juliana could think on it as an experiment such as she and her father might devise.

By the time Mr. Pyebald rode up to the coach window just north of Eastleigh, Juliana had found the peace that her countenance implied. Although she had seen nothing of the charming villages and farms that had slowly passed by her window, her smile suggested she had found tranquillity in the scenery. It was soon apparent that Lady Pyebald had not.

"My Lord," Mr. Pyebald addressed his father. He had to call several times through the glass to awaken the man.

Juliana contemplated tapping his Lordship resoundingly on the shoulder; however, she could only reach his knee. That was too personal for her, and she dithered for a moment with indecision.

Fortunately, Lord Pyebald snorted and snuffled and then sat

bolt upright. He heard the call again and unhooked the rope holding the window in place. It dropped with a thump.

"The ladies, my lady mother in particular, request that we find an inn for the evening. They say they can go no farther."

"We are to stop at The Unicorn and Bugle in just outside of an hour. Surely they can wait until then."

Mr. Pyebald nodded in deference, but his expression held excessive doubt.

"Very well, very well. Know you of any post inn of quality nearby?" Lord Pyebald rumbled.

"Yes, my lord, not a mile farther. I have had occasion to stay there in the past, and while it does not boast as large a stable as The Unicorn and Bugle, The Double Rose has a passable kitchen and clean rooms."

"Fine."

Lord Pyebald flicked his hand at his son, his fingers wagging limply. "Tell them; it will be so." He tugged the rope and ended their short discourse.

"Lawks, never travel with women."

While it appeared that Lord Pyebald had forgotten there was a young lady sitting across from him in the coach, Uncle Leonard had not. "You must excuse him, my dear," he addressed Juliana. "The discomfort and cramped conditions never put any of us at our best."

"What are you going on about?" Lord Pyebald tried to look affronted, but the strain of maintaining a glare was too much for his constitution. His eyes closed before the question was finished.

Juliana shook her head in disgust at the lethargic figure. The man was well into his cups; the flask of refreshment that he had brought along to alleviate the journey's tedium lay empty on the floor.

Lord Pyebald suited his wife as best as Juliana could tell from such a short acquaintance. His form was as substantial as hers, particularly about the middle, his conduct did not approach intelligence, and while he was reputed to patronize the best clothiers in the country, he resembled a vagabond.

Uncle Leonard glanced up from the snuffling, snorting figure beside him. Juliana gave her uncle a worry-not smile that smoothed his folded brow.

Uncle Leonard was a kind, quiet gentleman. His features were somewhat disjointed: He had a large bulbous nose on a narrow, lean face; and his gray hair was sparse, but his side whiskers were thick curly red. He was a tall man who stooped, likely from the years of discomfort towering above the heads of others. In personality, he couldn't have been more dissimilar from Aunt Phyllis; he was sensitive and understanding. It was from him that Carrie had inherited the tendency to self-deprecation—either that or it was from living with Aunt Phyllis through the years. One had to take culpability to maintain peace. Yes, poor Uncle Leonard, he was overrun by his wife.

As promised, The Double Rose was an easy distance from

where the request to stop was granted, and not much of a detour from the London Road. No sooner had the coach pulled within the confinement of the stable yard than the vehicle's door was flung open and Mr. Pyebald offered to help Juliana step down. It was a deference that both surprised and pleased Juliana: surprised, because one would have thought that he would have attended the second carriage containing the majority of the ladies before turning to her, and pleased due to her stiff limbs, which necessitated a hand down.

Once on the firm ground, Juliana felt a rush of blood to her extremities. She rolled her shoulders, placed her hands on her hips, and stretched her back. It was wonderful to move.

Before he stepped away, Mr. Pyebald gently took her right hand and bowed over it, holding her eyes in his gaze as he did so. His bold stare made Juliana uncomfortable. She frowned and tilted her head in puzzlement. Fortunately, the noises from the other coach drew his attention, and Mr. Pyebald excused himself. However, as the gentleman passed behind her, Juliana felt something slide across the top of her skirt, along the crest of her bottom.

Juliana jerked. Had Mr. Pyebald just touched her? On her bottom? It had certainly felt like an intimate touch. But, no, it was ridiculous. What a preposterous idea. Why would he want to, need to? The stable yard was spacious and almost deserted. No reason to pass so closely. It must have been . . . Juliana glanced around.

There were two saddled horses tied to a post in the corner, a mule drinking from a trough by the stable door, and a plethora of pigs, chickens, and dogs lazily milling about. The rain barrels were about the right height, but they were near the entrance. There was nothing nearby that she could have brushed against that would have given her the sensation of being touched.

That could only mean . . . no. Juliana shook the idea from her head. She pinched the bridge of her nose.

Foolish, overtired, and too imaginative.

Juliana lifted her head and glanced around. Everyone was occupied, including Mr. Pyebald. No one looked her way. Juliana slowed her breathing and swallowed.

Mr. Pyebald was a gentleman, and she was in the company of her relatives. A man would not take liberties under these circumstances. Philanderers needed dark, shadowed rooms and deserted innocents . . . or so she understood.

"Are you coming in?" Carrie interrupted Juliana's muddled thoughts. Her cousin's face was pert but still showed signs of strain. The wrinkles on her soft brown cloak mirrored the multitude on Juliana's dove-gray coat. "Or would you rather get some air?" Carrie's question held a tone of appeal.

Juliana looked over to see her family and their friends, including Mr. Pyebald, headed toward the door of the inn.

"I would rather stay outside, even just briefly . . . to stretch and move about."

Carrie nodded her thanks and then called over her shoulder. "Mama, Juliana and I will be there presently. We need some air."

Aunt Phyllis turned. "I should say not. You will both come in at once."

"I would be pleased to escort the young ladies, Mrs. Reeves, if you wish to be settled inside. We will walk to the main road but no farther."

Aunt Phyllis glanced from Mr. Pyebald to her daughter and back again. "Thank you, Mr. Pyebald; that is very good of you to indulge my poor puss."

Juliana rubbed at her temple. This wasn't quite what she had in mind, but . . . she arched her back again, stretched her arms before her, and turned toward the road. Carrie skipped to her side, and they locked elbows.

"Oh Juliana, was it horrible?" her cousin asked quietly and quickly before Mr. Pyebald reached them. "All talk of shooting and horses? I think it highly unfair of Mama to insist that the carriage cannot seat more than four on a long journey. I am certain Vivian would not care a whit if we were crushed more than we already are."

"Thank you for your concern, Carrie. But I am comfortable where I am. There is little conversation; I have time aplenty for contemplation."

A dislodged stone, kicked forward with force, indicated the close proximity of Mr. Pyebald. But like a perfect gentleman, he remained a respectful distance from them, and Juliana began to relax. It had been her fatigue, nothing more. Her imagination had led her astray.

∞∞

THE BRIGHTNESS OF THE FULL MOON SHONE THROUGH the multipaned window, casting deep shadows and filling the room with a ghostly blue tint. The inn was at last quiet. The rollicking voices from the common room below finally hushed, and the movement in the yard stilled.

While all the foreign noises beyond the door had kept Juliana awake for the first part of the night, it was the unholy sounds emanating from beside her that threatened to prevent Juliana from ever closing her eyes for the second part.

Both Carrie and Vivian snored. While Carrie wheezed and sometimes muttered, Vivian would have put an aged laborer to shame. The racket she made was long, loud, and never-ceasing. The small room echoed the cacophony. Juliana had no idea how Carrie could sleep.

Finally giving up, Juliana shifted to the side of the bed, a mere inch or two. She slowly drew back the counterpane and slipped her bare feet onto the cold floor. There was no point in staring at the ceiling anymore. Watching the shadows claw across the beams was fine for a few hours, but it had definitely entered the realm of tedium by midnight.

Juliana reached for her coat, hung on a peg behind the door, and threw it about her shoulders. She tossed aside the clothes lying on the roughly hewn chair and lifted it just above the floor. As quietly as possible, she walked to the window and placed the chair by the glass. She sat, wiggled to get comfortable, drew her legs up, and wrapped the coat around her knees.

It little mattered if sleep remained elusive. There was nothing to do while bumping and rocking on the tiresome road to London. She was not required to make scintillating conversation, not any conversation, for that matter. No arrangements needed her consideration, and no observations had to be made. It was almost as if Juliana were in limbo, simply waiting. Sleep became redundant.

Perhaps that was the problem, Juliana postulated. She had not done enough to tire herself out. She should have walked farther, ignored Mr. Pyebald's insistence that the road had become crowded. Especially when he overstated the situation. There had been but one cart and two horsemen on approach. If he had desired his repast so desperately, he should have stayed behind.

Juliana stared out at the scene before her. The yard was a perfect stage of exaggerated shadows. The well-worn cobblestones reflected the light so truly that the shadows were chiseled, and yet nature was playing a game. For a bucket took on the proportions of a vat, the straw baling a mountain, and the creeping figure was—

Juliana looked again. She could not see the form that created the shape, but she could, indeed, see its distorted shadow.

It looked like a man making his way to the gate in a stealthy, unnatural manner. It practically screamed to be noticed.

Juliana squinted uselessly and stared. She blinked and was rewarded with only marginal clarity. Then the man stepped out from under the cloak of darkness. His back was turned, but something in his build struck her as familiar.

He unbarred the gate, and as he stepped through, two other forms appeared. They gathered and slowly walked beyond Juliana's sight. The gate was left unattended and open. Her heart began to pound.

By this time, Juliana's posture was tense, and her feet had once again found the floor. Her nose almost touched the glass. She wondered if she should alert the house.

That man had left them in danger, exposed. Anyone could enter now and take advantage of a sleeping house. As soon as Juliana had convinced herself of the need to raise the alarm, the man returned to the yard. He rebarred the gate and slipped back into the shadows. Within moments the yard was again a perfect stage of exaggerated shadows. Nothing moved.

Juliana sat back down; she didn't remember rising. She frowned and wondered about what she had seen. It took on less importance the longer she puzzled with it. By the time the lightening sky began to banish all the chiseled shadows, Juliana had convinced herself that the incident was of no significance and none of her business, and she had finally fallen asleep in the chair.

SPENCER STRODE SMARTLY DOWN THE POORLY LIT mews, taking short, shallow breaths, trying to inhale as little of the sour air as possible. He swung his walking stick in such a manner as to reveal any unsavory pile of straw-clinging excrement before encountering it with his highly polished leather boots.

Lawks, he had forgotten the stench of the city, in particular the narrow lanes between the great town houses of Mayfair. Had he not preferred to reach his destination surreptitiously, he would have traversed the wider, marginally cleaner, avenues of the square.

The corner of Spencer's mouth curled up with satisfied amusement at the thought of his uncle's reaction to a jaunt such as this. Uncle James would have joined Spencer in a trice, and plied him with queries from one end of the mews to the other, had he known of Spencer's adventures. Perhaps one day Spencer would be able to reveal his true vocation.

Uncle James was Spencer's guide through boyhood, the father figure that had been missing in his salad days. His sire, Theodore Northam, had yielded to the call of the netherworld while Spencer was just entering adolescence. Spencer's mother had entreated her brother, James, to take Spencer in, if only for a little while.

It proved to be a tremendous gift—far from the banishment he had thought it to be.

James was a busy man, the second son of a great lineage who had turned to law to support his large vivacious brood. But he was also a devoted family man who, without reserve, included Spencer.

Spencer was not a dispirited child when he returned home to Norfield on the anniversary of his father's death. For twelve months he had witnessed what a large family could be: the clashes, the support, the respect, and the frustrations, but most of all the underlying caring. His mother had tried to provide a similar atmosphere in their ancestral home, but to no avail. The halls of Norfield were quiet, the entertainment staid . . . the ennui extreme. It left Spencer at loose ends at the advanced age of eighteen. It was boredom as much as anything that set him on his present course, that and his well-intentioned uncle.

They had been dining at Brooks's; Uncle James castigated him in a kindly fashion for his irresolute life. The mild tirade had been slightly irritating, but Spencer bore it without umbrage. Upon reaching the conclusion that, indeed, his life needed focus, though they had yet to divine in which direction, Spencer waved his uncle off and returned to the gaming tables.

However, as he watched his fellows throwing more blunt about than they could afford, a gentleman known to him only in the periphery approached. It would seem that Lord Winfrith had overheard the conversation with Uncle James and offered a solution.

Spencer was not indoctrinated into the clandestine underworld of the War Office immediately. It was a slow process—taking almost a full three months. His first assignments were light, with little enough to be done and accounted for. He merely needed to keep an ear open to the casual conversations of those about him for anything more than the usual Francophile, anything that could be fodder for the little emperor's purposes.

As Spencer took on duties with more consequences, he found that his life lost its monotony. He no longer knew what to expect from day to day, and he found that exhilarating. He enjoyed a short but dangerous journey to Spain and more recently France, although enjoyment from that one was more in hindsight, after having succeeded at his purpose. His easy personality had carried him through many a troublesome situation, though, at times, it was merely by the skin of his teeth.

Spencer arrived at the Mayfair town house with his boots, thankfully, unsoiled. He rapped sharply at the back door with his cane. He nodded to Raymond as the butler wordlessly guided him through the kitchen, the little hall, and into the front of the house. The man's expression displayed no surprise at Spencer's unorthodox entry.

Lord Winfrith was awaiting him in the study with Mr. Bibury. This chamber was sheathed in the favored oaken paneling of the day and sprinkled with large furniture in deep greens. An insipid fire glowed beneath the tall mantel, and the gentlemen stared fixedly at the uninspired, fading embers.

"Ah, there you are, Northam," Winfrith commented, as if it had not been two months since their last meeting. "What say you to Bibury's preposterous claim?"

Spencer entered the room with comfort and informality.

They knew one another well. Bibury had been the one to indoctrinate Spencer into the grittier aspects of his occupation—such as knife play and surreptitious observation. Lord Winfrith had helped Spencer hone his French and taught him how to navigate the social world of the Ton while listening for traitorous rhetoric tied up in social niceties. While they were of a mind when dealing with governmental issues, they were as contentious a group as any of his majesty's swells when dealing with the ordinary questions of the day.

Spencer took the glass of brandy that Raymond offered and waited until the door had once more sequestered the men from the world. "Which particular preposterous claim would that be?" He swirled the amber liquid around the glass, warming it before taking a gulp.

"That Lord Hart's grays are Carfield stock."

"Well, I must say, Bibury, that is mighty far-fetched. Lord Hart's pockets have been cleaned out for some time. Next you'll be saying that his son is no longer beetle-headed." Lord Hart was a philandering dolt not known in Town for his intelligence, his horses, or his witty offspring.

Bibury shrugged, still staring at the fire. "Perhaps not."

The gentleman sat silent for some moments before inquiring, "So how did you get away from Bobbington so quickly?"

"Usual excuse."

"Ah, visiting your mama. How is she?"

Spencer leaned into the wingback chair and stretched his legs out before him. "Still at Norfield, actually. She seldom leaves the place . . . something that Bobbington seems to have forgotten." His companions nodded.

"I thought avoiding her was your excuse to visit Bobbington in the first place," Winfrith asked, trying to keep the subterfuge straight.

"No, no, escaping Lady Rayne. She likes to collect younger men, and I intimated that I was in the widow's sights. Bobbington didn't even blink when I laid my desertion of London at her feet. As to mothers, well, Bobbington understands them all too well. They do require a nominal visit every now and then to keep them happy." Spencer smiled, distracted as Miss Telford came unbidden to his mind.

"So how goes the hunt?"

It took Spencer a few seconds to realize that his colleague was not referring to Miss Telford. "Pyebald is our man," he finally stated without trying to hide his distaste. "And his son. They may have been cloaked against the weather, but there could be no doubt of their identity. I watched the disembarkation myself, practically on Ryton's doorstep. Quite a tidy job they made of it, too: brought a horse and cart and two men, used a strong English oak for leverage, and winched the crates right up the cliff. Took all of a quarter hour on a foggy dawn. Too well oiled to be anything but routine. Yes, indeed, our source was right about the how and where, even if he was a little havey-cavey on the when."

"So your time was well spent." Bibury continued to stare sightless into the fireplace. "The communiqué was hidden in the brandy."

"Indeed, Pyebald is no ordinary smuggler. He is a traitor as well."

"Knowingly?"

"I saw the marked crate. Watched him place it on the cart's seat while the rest were stowed in back. Too obvious for coincidence."

"I take it that the thing is now in Town or you wouldn't be."

"Nothing buffle-headed about you, Winfrith."

"Thanks ever so." Winfrith stretched his arms out before him and cracked his neck with a studied, casual manner. "And I suppose you will be needing extra eyes for a few days or so."

Spencer smiled. "Would I be here otherwise?"

Winfrith laughed. "No, you would be with your dearest mama."

Spencer joined in the joke with a chuckle of artifice. Given a choice, he would be enjoying the evening with Miss Telford . . . discussing insects of some sort.

CHAPTER

7

In which there are many varied witnesses to the comings
and goings at the Reeves town house

THE REEVES ADDRESS IN MAYFAIR WAS BY NO
means shabby, Juliana mused as she gazed out her
chamber window down into the bustling street below.

The tall, narrow town house was an impressive white affair,
with a multitude of large windows and classical columns that
stretched up three floors. The square was one of the finest in
the city. The center park was of a size that allowed for many a
garden path, providing that necessary breath of greenery in an
otherwise dull, grimy, urban monotony. The persons on the
promenade were either well-heeled gaggles of resplendent gentry
or their hangers-on.

The shuffling of humanity back and forth was quite fascinating. Still, Juliana couldn't help but wish that one of those

mustached gentlemen leaning on the fence would magically turn into the personage of Mr. Northam. The knowledge that he was somewhere out there in that milling mass of denizens was all that kept Juliana from screaming in utter boredom.

Juliana sighed and dropped the curtain; she was expected downstairs. She could not lollygag all morning wishing her time away and observing the city's oddities. The final expedition to the milliner and mantua-maker awaited her. Juliana was excessively tired of visits to shoemakers and glove-makers, not to mention Bond Street shops and cluttered bazaars. She sighed again and turned back to the comfort of her room.

This was probably the smallest of the family bedchambers, but it was hers alone. Carrie was sharing with Vivian, an arrangement that Juliana would not have thrust upon anyone, but it seemed to suit the two girls. They fed off each other in energy and enthusiasm. Vivian's frailty was all but forgotten. Juliana avoided her whenever she could, but it was becoming nigh on impossible; she was now expected to join them on every shopping excursion. It was likely a plot to keep her from exploring the city.

Yesterday, a full five days since their arrival in Town, Juliana had almost made it out of the house unseen. However, Mr. Pyebald had appeared out of nowhere and offered her his arm. He had done it with panache and style, but Juliana was in no way tempted. She suddenly realized that the sunny, warm weather was not really conducive to a casual stroll about the park. It was too . . . sunny and . . . too warm. Mr. Pyebald's agreement and rejoinder that it was in her best interest to remain indoors convinced her that the household had been warned of her wandering tendencies. She would have to outthink them if she was ever going to get to Leadenhall Street.

Juliana's plan to purchase most of her new wardrobe in Lambhurst, thereby freeing her of the time and the need to shop in London, had gone completely awry. Upon their arrival on Cooper Street, Lady Pyebald had asked to see Juliana's presentation gown. It had turned into a moment of high drama.

On first glance of the dress's pretty silver-white loops, the lady had screamed in delicate horror, claiming the gown to be a monumental disaster. She had lain upon the settee, a hand clutched to her ample bosom, and shaken in spasms of disbelief. It would not do, she had whispered in a robust voice, for the chit to be seen beside her jewel, her precious progeny, in a gown such as that. There was nothing else to be done; Juliana would be required to purchase another or all was lost.

Aunt Phyllis had acquiesced to Lady Pyebald without hesitation. It was, of course, Juliana who would be out of pocket, and it was, therefore, of no interest to her aunt other than how it would reflect on the family. The cost was not really Juliana's prime objection; it was the time and waste. But when Juliana suggested that the disaster be remodeled or retrimmed, good Lady Pyebald had wailed that it was worthy of only the scullery maid or the dustheap. It was a gross exaggeration, but Juliana's voice of reason was completely overruled. The gown was begun anew and with all due haste for the presentation was almost upon them.

Thus began the tedious drudgery of fittings and shopping. If listening to the empty-headed prattle on the glories of garlands and ribbons were not enough, Juliana found that she had to endure the indignity of having all her decisions made for her without so much as a by-your-leave. The older women treated her as if she were not capable of rational thought.

Juliana considered informing both ladies that if she were capable of seeing to the running of an estate the size of Hartwell and partnering her father in their research, she was more than able to choose the number of ostrich plumes on her headpiece. They would have been scandalized. That alone might have made the uproar worthwhile.

Still, the most difficult aspect of the busy days had nothing to do with gowns or bustling about the city. It was Juliana's loss of Mr. Northam's company. Lady Pyebald had declared that they were too busy to accept callers until after the presentation. As much as Juliana hated to admit it, they did seem to be inordinately busy.

As the days progressed, Juliana began to understand Aunt Phyllis's acceptance of anything that spilled from the lips of her Ladyship. The woman was well entrenched in the *beau monde*, perhaps merely because of her ancient lineage, but there was no doubt that her eccentric musings and haughty pride were not only tolerated but also appreciated. Notes of welcome; invitations to balls, musicals, and assemblies; and calling cards poured in at the Reeves town house in prodigious numbers.

It was not surprising that when Carrie rushed into Juliana's chamber to drag her downstairs, her words were not a congenial morning greeting but an announcement of their social triumph. With a great deal of pride, Carrie declared that the ball following the presentation was going to be a veritable crush.

"Lady Pyebald has invited all the most eligible bachelors. And it would seem that most are going to see their way to being here. Is that not a delightful start to our careers?"

"Delightful." Juliana didn't try to mask her lack of interest, but Carrie was too involved in her own emotions to notice. Juliana smiled despite herself, for Carrie's expression had taken on a dreamy look, and she was swaying to an unheard melody.

"Silly puss, you will not be able to step out with all of them. There will not be enough dances. You will have to share with Vivian, you know, as well as all the other young ladies vying for the gentlemen's attention."

"And you, Juliana. You, too. Oh, you cannot be as unaffected as you claim. Just imagine the music, the room aglitter with handsomely dressed men and women, and being asked to dance by viscounts and sons of earls, and we will know no one, no one at all." Carrie hooked her elbow through Juliana's, pulling her forward, down the hall to the ever-awaiting assemblage. "No one except Mr. Northam and Lord Bobbington. I made sure that invitations were extended to them."

Juliana quickly glanced to Carrie's profile, trying to understand her comment. Was there a hidden meaning? Had she discerned Juliana's preference already? She would have to be more guarded.

"It would not have been neighborly otherwise," Carrie continued, and then flushed slightly without looking Juliana's way.

Juliana felt a sudden discomfort. The thought of breakfast no longer appealed. Had Carrie already developed a fixation? Oh dear, poor girl. Bobbington was consumed with Vivian; he was not likely to notice Carrie at her side. "No, for I believe you to have known Lord Bobbington for some years."

"Just in passing, at church and such. We have had no occasion to converse at any length before; I do find him quite lively . . . in a staid, neighborly way, of course."

"Yes, of course." Juliana turned her face away, hoping to hide her worried expression.

Her gaze wandered through the open door of the drawing room as they passed. Two very sooty men with brushes stood before the fireplace, staring at the fender. One man glanced over his shoulder and met her look. Juliana stopped in her tracks. The man's eyes were blue—so much like Mr. Northam's that she was instantly drawn to him.

"Juliana?" Carrie tugged her arm.

Juliana started and then frowned.

"We are for the morning room, aren't we?" Carrie sounded hesitant.

"Yes, yes, of course. I don't know why . . . silly me, distracted is all." She glanced again at the chimney sweep and watched him nod.

"Ma'am." His voice was deep and gravelly, not Mr. Northam-like at all.

Juliana shook her head in self-castigation and walked on, returning her mind to the problem at hand. Should she say anything to Carrie about Lord Bobbington's infatuation? No, there was no need; the Season was just starting. Carrie would soon have a bevy of callers.

Juliana squeezed Carrie's arm. "You will have so many conquests before the night is out, old and new, that a journal will be necessary to keep them all straight."

"Really, Juliana? Do you think so?"

"Goose, of course I do. The tragedy this Season will be that the Honorable Miss Reeves will be able to choose only one from her many suitors. You just wait and see. Hearts will break all through Town when you do."

"Oh, that sounds delicious." Carrie giggled. "And you, too, Juliana. You will have admirers, too."

Juliana laughed. "You are sweet, Carrie, to say so."

"I do not jest, for I know of one already."

Juliana was startled. Carrie could not be referring to Northam, as she had not seen him since the short visit at Ryton. Whoever could she mean? "I think your imagination has run away with you, Cousin, for we have yet to meet anyone in Town."

"I do not mean from Town."

Juliana had a horrifying suspicion that Carrie was referring to—"This is an absurd discussion, let us drop—"

"Mr. Pyebald, of course. Mr. Maxwell Pyebald."

"You are quite mistaken." Juliana wanted to steer well away from the topic of Mr. Pyebald.

The man made her uncomfortable. Ever since her misgivings at the inn, she had avoided his attempts at private conversation and ignored his amorous stares. He had made no secret of his interest, and since her aunt had said nothing, Juliana could only assume that he had been deemed worthy. Or, perhaps, she had been deemed worthy of Mr. Pyebald. Whatever the circumstances, she wanted none of it. Even if she were on the lookout for a husband, it would not have been him.

"What are you to wear this afternoon?"

"Do not fob me off, Juliana. Have you not noticed? I am vastly pleased."

Juliana frowned. "Why? Why would Mr. Pyebald's interest in me please you?"

"It is my doing. Oh Juliana, take that frown from your face. I am not cutting shams. If I had not told Vivian about your very comfortable situation at Hartwell and the large inheritance that is to come your way, I am sure Mr. Pyebald would have looked elsewhere. So it is to me that you owe appreciation."

Juliana smiled weakly, breathing deeply through her nose. Her cousin meant well. She didn't realize that she had set Juliana up for an uncomfortable Season. Juliana would have to pull out a full arsenal of set-downs to assure Mr. Pyebald of her utter lack of pleasure at his attentions, and she had to do so with tact and decorum. Not her strong suits.

◦∞◦

SPENCER LEANED ON THE FENCE IN A LANGUID POSTURE, twitching the mustache that was temporarily glued to his upper lip. It itched. He supported an open but unread newspaper before him. His eyes appeared entranced by the latest lurid tale of the city while in fact they never left the Reeves residence.

The large park was proving to be an excellent vantage point. There were plenty of milling people to shield him. On different days this week, Spencer had observed the household while in the guise of a dandy, a tradesman, and a coachman—he had even accompanied a chimney sweep into the house itself. No one had questioned his presence or even given him a second glance . . . though there had been an uneasy moment with Miss Telford. But it had quickly passed.

Winfrith and Bibury were finding the same on their shifts. There was a dearth of curiosity in this neck of the woods, an apathetic menagerie of souls—very convenient for the purposes of the War Office.

Spencer found that the tedium of this vigil was not as overwhelming as it could have been. There was no underlying tension. He was fairly certain when the communiqué would continue its journey. Although it was beyond him as to why there was a delay. He could only hope that it would lead directly to his quarry this time and not to another cat's paw. Spencer was ready to see this game played out. The leak turned to their advantage.

The playbill from the cliff-top had used a rudimentary code, and Spencer had seen the paper whisked from its hiding place in the oak just as the brandy crates had been pulled up the cliff. Spencer expected the communiqué to be passed at the May first performance of *Hamlet* at the Theatre Royal Drury Lane on Catherine Street. Nine days hence. That would be the day of reckoning.

Until then, all he had to do was watch the Pyebalds, who were deeply ensconced in the Reeves household, and note any visitors or appointments—anything unusual that would be worthy of further investigation.

So far he had nothing to show for his diligence. It was a dull business as the women of the household never ventured out but to visit a shop, and the men's rare jaunts took in White's or Brooks's. Only Mr. Pyebald's occasional sojourn into the Hells provided any entertainment, especially as it was to that traitorous highflier's detriment.

It would seem that the man had worn out his welcome in the better clubs and had to resort to the underbelly of the gaming world for sport and entertainment. But here, even the gullgropers found him untouchable. The man was on a decided losing streak, his luck having left him too deep in dun territory. Spencer found that an exceedingly pleasant thought. Social censure rode hard on the man's heels. Yes, very satisfying, indeed.

The animosity that Spencer felt for the traitor far outweighed his calculated distaste for Mr. Pyebald. The reason for this discrepancy was something that Spencer did not want to explore. It might have to do with the comely Miss Telford.

Spencer had been particularly disappointed to learn that the Reeves and Pyebald families were not receiving and would not be doing so until after the three chits' presentation at court. He didn't examine that disappointment too closely, either, on the off chance that it might be Miss Telford's company that he missed and not the opportunity to advance his case.

As it was, the planned complicity with Miss Telford was still going to afford him a more comfortable position for his observations for the better part of a seven-night or two. That was the reason, and none other, that he anticipated their next meeting. Nothing else. At all.

Spencer turned his fixed gaze away from the front of the Reeves town house and glanced around. He was pleased to see that Bibury was about to take up a position by the corner, leaving Spencer free to return to his own apartment and guest. Spencer folded his paper with deliberate, precise moves and noted, as he did so, that the Reeves family's carriage was pulling up in front of the residence. The coachman jumped to the curb, lowered the roof on both sides of the landau, and then stood smartly by the door.

Ah, the ladies were off on another shopping excursion. Spencer could tell by the ramrod stance of the man in livery. That posture was adopted only when Mrs. Reeves was about to appear, and she only appeared when there was shopping afoot. It had been thus for the past six days.

Mrs. Reeves must be a veritable dragon. Spencer chuckled in recollection of Miss Telford's comments on the cliff-side. The more he saw of the family the more the girl made sense.

Spencer glanced up at the closed door of the town house. He had no idea how these delicate creatures could find the interest and energy for such endless shopping. Spencer found it tedious and exhausting.

He had been doing much the same with Bobbington, decking the fellow out so he could preen like a peacock before his Miss Pyebald. And at every opportunity, Spencer tried, without success, to discourage this folly. He pointed out the wonderful qualities of certain pretty, vacuous young women in Town—of whom Bobbington's mother would heartily approve—who had social position and funds and had no intent other than to find a suitable husband with whom to rusticate.

There were many, just like Miss Pyebald. In fact, Spencer could hardly tell them apart. Could Bobbington not settle his affections upon one whose family was not trying to bring about the downfall of Britain? It would seem not. Bobbington remained fixed on Miss Pyebald. Spencer simply did not see the attraction. She had none of Miss Telford's unaffected ways or easy conversation. No, Spencer just did not see it.

On that thought, Spencer glanced once again at the door. His stomach plummeted. Bobbington was standing across the street from the carriage, staring up at the windows in a most indelicate and obvious way. Adoration was written all over his face. He was about to call attention to himself. And he would be seen as a fool.

Spencer sprang into action. He dropped his paper to the ground and then stooped to pick it up. When he rose, his upper lip was no longer covered with hair, although it did sport a red splotch and his eyes were tearing.

Spencer rubbed at the spot unintentionally, making it redder. He swallowed, straightened his shoulders, and tilted his top hat back so that it no longer shaded his eyes. He stepped away from the fence and quickly approached Bobbington from behind.

The tap on the shoulder brought a jerk of surprise, and then his friend whirled around with a look of apprehension on his face. It relaxed upon recognition.

"Northam, why I never—what brings you here?"

"Just passing, old boy." Spencer glanced up at the still-empty stairs of the town house across the street. "Wish I could say the same for you." He had to get Bobbington away before the grand exit.

"I am merely . . . merely taking in the air." Bobbington nodded toward the park. "Lovely area for a stroll, is it not?"

Spencer snorted. "Rot. You are here to see Miss Pyebald. It is patently obvious. You really must learn to control these urges, you know. They are going to make you look completely spoony."

"Well," Bobbington blustered, "I will not be the first. History is full of great tales of the foolish antics that young men go through to win the hearts of their fair maidens."

"Yes, but standing outside her house ogling is nothing like climbing a mountain or scaling a tower. You only look foolish. You do not want Miss Pyebald to look at you with amusement or pity or even apathy. You want to impress her with your manly qualities." It was not that Spencer wanted to give Bobbington advice on how to win Miss Pyebald, quite the opposite; however, it was all that he could think of to remove Bobbington from the area. "Let us away to the boot-maker. I do believe he said they would be done by today." In the corner of his eye, Spencer could see the door opening. He took a step and gestured Bobbington to his side. Now even if the ladies saw them, it would be as if they were, indeed, merely passing.

Bobbington sighed and fell into step. "Yes, you are right, of course. It is always thus. I am just finding it enormously difficult to wait. The ball is not until the day after tomorrow. Such a very long time to—"

"Mr. Northam," called a high, excited voice from across the street.

Spencer looked around Bobbington in time to see Mrs. Reeves and Lady Pyebald waving as they descended. The three girls and Mr. Pyebald followed closely behind them.

Spencer's look of astonishment was not feigned.

Bobbington gave him a smile that smacked of righteousness. It also gave Spencer the sudden desire to plant a fist—"Mrs. Reeves, Lady Pyebald, what a pleasant encounter." The two men crossed the street as he called out his greeting.

Bows were made all around, and Spencer was satisfied to see that Miss Telford looked none the worse for her forced confinement. In fact, she looked rather lovely, even more so than he had recalled. Her eyes were clear, and the way she looked at him—

"So happy to receive your reply." Lady Pyebald talked directly to him, seemingly oblivious to Bobbington's presence. "We are going to have quite the gathering. There will be no room to breathe. Crush, crush, crush."

It took Spencer a moment to bring to mind the invitation to the post-presentation ball. "Yes, I . . . we are greatly looking forward to it." Spencer glanced around at the young ladies and noticed that Miss Pyebald had something stuck in her eye. She was valiantly trying to bat it away with her fluttering eyelashes. Miss Reeves on the other hand seemed to be having problems with her neck as she kept tilting her head first to one side and then the other. Only Miss Telford had any semblance of normality, although her eyes kept wandering to his lips.

Then Spencer recalled the mustache and hoped that there was no glue stuck to his face. He might have known she would notice such a thing. Observant, just as she had said. She would make a fine agent, if she weren't always getting herself into sticky predicaments. Perhaps after this . . . Spencer tried to refocus on the situation at hand.

Lady Pyebald was talking and shepherding the group toward the carriage. "So until then, we must say our good-byes. As you can imagine, there is much to do to make our girls' coming out as successful as possible. I am sure Vivian will be the belle of the ball. Do you not agree, Mr. Northam?"

Spencer could feel the noose of a scheming mama, but he was not so easily led. "I am sure it will be a great success for all concerned." He made a point of glancing at Miss Telford. He was pleased to note the upturn of her lips and the slight flush of her cheeks.

"Yes, well, I am sure it will." Lady Pyebald was less impressed with his retort.

Mr. Pyebald, who had up to this point been quietly standing as an observer, stepped toward the carriage to assist the embarkation. He moved directly between Spencer and Miss Telford.

When Spencer shifted, so did Pyebald. To the casual observer, it was merely a mistake, but to those involved in the posturing, it was a highly charged situation. Pyebald was staking a claim, and Spencer was going to have none of it.

"We, as well, must be off." Bobbington nudged Spencer none too gently on the back. "Well met. Be seeing you all soon." He grabbed at Spencer's arm and left him no choice but to follow.

"What are you about?" Spencer asked when they had put enough distance between the shopping party and themselves.

"Old boy, I seldom have the opportunity to rescue you. I was not about to miss my chance."

"What are you on about?"

"Please, Northam, we have known each other for eons. That devil-may-care attitude only works on strangers. I know when you are about to take umbrage. That blighter was begging you to make a scene, and I did not think it was in your best interest or mine."

Spencer felt his blood cool. He was surprised to realize how quickly it had come to a boil. And then to add insult to almost injury, Bobbington had saved him instead of the other way around. Had the world tipped over? The only thing that could be worse than the damage now done to his ego was if his usually unobservant friend had discerned his true interest in the Pyebalds.

"I have never seen you so taken before."

Spencer frowned. "With what? Whom?"

"Miss Telford."

Spencer let out the breath that he didn't know he had been holding. The game was still on. "I do not take your meaning." He had to protest to make it seem real. Bobbington would not be taken in if he acquiesced too easily. Without meaning to, Spencer glanced behind. The ladies were pulling away, setting off on their jaunt, and the three youngest turned as one to look at him.

Spencer felt uncomfortable, like a beetle under a microscope. He swallowed deeply, smiled mildly, and bowed with no great flourish. He didn't want the complications; Miss Telford was quite enough.

Just before Spencer turned back, he saw that Pyebald was still waiting by the curb, waving amiably at the disappearing vehicle. However, when Pyebald turned, his eye met Spencer's, and it was anything but amiable.

CHAPTER
8

In which the glorious glamor of the beau monde
is fully realized in all its delightful elegance . . .
and surprising intrigue

"WILL YOU MEET ME IN THE GARDEN?" Pyebald whispered ardently into her ear as he stepped closer in the second figure of the country-dance.

Juliana stifled the resounding *no* that almost flew from her lips and smiled. She waited until the next figure to speak, when she was able to utter more than a one-syllable answer.

"Mr. Pyebald, you, more than any man here, know the answer to that question. Were you not in the room when your lady mother admonished us to decorum? I believe you were, for I saw Vivian glance your way when Lady Pyebald insisted that a reputation, and all possibility of a good match, could be lost on something as seemingly trivial as a tryst in the garden." She was not going to mention that she was not after a match, good or otherwise; it was a moot point.

"Yes, but such conventions do not apply to those living under the same roof. I am your protector. No one would see it as an impropriety. Besides, you look overwarm. You must be in need of a breath of air."

Juliana sighed and shook her head slightly. Mr. Pyebald skipped away from her before she could reply. She caught Carrie's eye as the girl danced by with her head held high and a grin on her face that stretched from ear to ear, every step a study in perfection. Juliana smiled back.

It really was a wonderful night, despite the endlessly ridiculous entreaties of Mr. Pyebald. A mere two hours had passed of this glorious merriment. And Mr. Northam had yet to arrive.

Juliana felt immeasurable relief that the worst part of the entire Season was over, the dreaded presentation. It had gone rather well. Perhaps "without calamity" would be a better description, for two young ladies had fainted in anticipation, and one patroness required assistance at the end of the long ceremony. However, the incidents did not overly affect the Pyebalds or the Reeves family, for as much as they might cluck and express sympathy, the afflicted were strangers.

To Juliana, the ceremony earlier that day had been nothing more than an abyss of possible embarrassments. All those lurking disasters, such as tripping, stepping on someone's dress, or forgetting to curtsy, were gone. Her new court gown had been finished on time and to Juliana's mind looked remarkably like the first. Fortunately, this one was declared adequate. Juliana thought it charming and felt rather elegant in the large, out-dated hoops. She did, however, find the numerous ostrich feathers a little over the top. She was also quite aware that *adequate* was a euphemism that meant she would not put anyone to shame or detract from her companions.

Juliana did not mind. She was more than happy to have been adequate at court when her ball gown this evening went far beyond adequate, even without her mother's locket. It was the essence of grace and style, and Juliana could almost imagine herself to be beautiful. The dress had *not* been her aunt's choice.

Juliana had already been flattered, complimented, and introduced to more people than she had ever known. The *beau monde* was not as daunting as she had expected. In fact, London was friendly in a stifling, formal manner.

While Juliana had expected Vivian and Carrie to attract most of the young male attention, she found an equal share doled out in her direction. She had no idea how Vivian felt about it, but Carrie had shown she was vastly pleased with her raised eyebrows and disguised winks. There were more than enough bachelors to go around.

Juliana tripped lightly through the last figures of the dance, thinking that all she needed now was the arrival of Mr. Northam. He would change the complexion of her evening.

This was the beginning of their ruse, and Juliana was full

of anticipation. She knew she would have to hold her growing affection in check, but when it did show through, Spencer would think of it as part of the charade. She need not be overly concerned about a betraying word or glance. He would merely think her a highly skilled actress, which, of course, she was not.

Suddenly, the air felt charged. She turned slowly toward the doorway and swallowed. The noisy chatter of the multitudes of glittering women and elegant gentlemen muted to a whisper; the inane banter of couples and strangers disappeared in the warmth of Spencer's eyes.

The music seemed to swell and the jewels in the room seemed to flash brighter. Juliana laughed heartily at Mr. Pyebald's comment as he passed—not that he was witty, for, in fact, she heard not a word, but it was an expression of her happiness.

At last she had traversed the room, and they were alone in a sea of undulating souls. She waited with bated breath for Spencer's first clever, engaging words.

"Good evening, Miss Telford. You look enchanting."

Well, perhaps what they lacked in originality, they made up for in heat. Or was her imagination running rampant?

"Good evening, Mr. Northam. I have been looking forward to your arrival, as have the rest of my family and friends." She was not going to win any poetry prizes, either.

Juliana watched Spencer glance around, and while she did

not bother to check, she knew by his expression and the direction of his look that the nod was leveled at Vivian, the smile to Carrie, and the puckered brow to Mr. Pyebald. He had undoubtedly met her aunt and uncle as well as the Pyebalds at the entrance. The older couples were lying in wait . . . ready to inform any eligible bachelor of the obvious—that their daughters were worthy and eager for attention. It would have been humiliating if it were not amusing.

A figure on the periphery of her vision hovered at Spencer's side. "Good evening, Lord Bobbington," Juliana added quickly, almost forgetting her manners in the excitement of the moment.

"This is a splendid display, Miss Telford. Quite a change from the first time we met—"

"Yes," Juliana interrupted. "So good of you to recall the quiet gathering at Ryton." She feared he would mention the cliffside if she allowed him to reminisce too long. "Have you had a chance—?" Juliana felt herself propelled forward as two bodies collided with her, none too gently. Spencer caught her arm until her feet were steady beneath her once more. The warmth of his touch permeated their gloves and lingered when he pulled away. It took a concerted effort for Juliana to draw her eyes from his to see who had jostled her.

Vivian and Carrie jockeyed for position beside her. "Good evening, Mr. Northam," they simpered in unison. Carrie added, "and Lord Bobbington."

"The ball is a grand success, is it not?" Vivian's question was rhetorical. "Why, the room is fair to bursting. I have never seen such a spectacle."

"One would assume not, in that you have only just come out." Bobbington, unfortunately, stated the obvious.

Vivian didn't blink or acknowledge his comment. It was as if he hadn't even spoken. She pouted prettily and continued. "The music is entrancing, the cadence so very tempting. One cannot help but sway and move with the rhythm of the orchestra." She began to demonstrate her appreciation of the music, gracefully bumping Juliana as she rocked from side to side. "Do you dance?" Vivian directed her question to Spencer, excluding Bobbington by the slight turn of her body.

It was apparent that Spencer had been placed on the list of possible good matches but Bobbington had not. This charade was not going to be without its share of difficulties.

"Indeed," Spencer answered smoothly. "Miss Telford has just consented to be my partner in the next set." He touched the dance card hanging from her wrist, implying that, if anyone cared to look, they would find his name neatly printed inside. He held his arm out in Juliana's direction, and she laid her glove gently over his.

She couldn't help but smile at the sour line of Vivian's petulant face and the pleased surprise of Carrie's. All knew that no such request had been made, but that his choice had.

Spencer turned Juliana toward the other dancers. They

crossed the room with the required display of indifference, and they positioned themselves in the ready for the dance.

"I HOPE YOU ARE ENJOYING LONDON, Miss Telford," Spencer commented as they waited, knowing it was expected of him. He stared at the couples on the dance floor as if enthralled by the final steps of the country-dance. His formal words were meant to suppress the heated sensations coursing through his body. He was acutely aware of Juliana's proximity.

Juliana laughed. "Really, Mr. Northam. And when would I have done that? You know me to have been in the company of my aunt for the better part of the week."

Spencer felt a hint of discomfort. "We have not had a chance to talk since St. Ives Head." He wondered if his disguises had been penetrated. "I would not hazard a guess about your occupation during these past days." He did not need to guess; they were in his report.

"I am sure you could surmise that I was not out and about doing anything that I would consider of worth. When you saw me last, I was on my way to Oxford Street—shopping yet again."

Spencer turned to face Juliana and was pleased to see that her eyes were sparkling with humor, not the self-pity implied by her words and tone. "Ah, no time to walk unfettered by a large body of water."

"Worse, I was subjected to the most excruciating torture. We were shopping, visiting dressmakers and the like." Her hand touched lightly just above her modest décolletage as if expecting to find something hanging around her neck. It was done without any obvious conscious thought, as if it were a habit.

"Now that would be a most unusual statement coming from any other lady."

"Granted. But believe you me, this country miss was about ready to solicit a chaperone back to Hartwell, posthaste."

"Well, I must say, on behalf of all the gentlemen here tonight, we are delighted that you suffered the torture—for you are a very lovely sight." Spencer wondered if his words were a trifle too warm, for Juliana was flying her colors and staring at the floor. She was the very picture of maidenly modesty.

Lawks, she was a marvelous actress.

"Thank you," she said quietly, then, almost under her breath, added, "but there is no need for such flattery in private conversation."

"There is no such thing in a crowded room, Miss Telford."

When Juliana straightened, she nodded, but her expression was a little wistful; and Spencer realized that he had unintentionally implied that his words were feigned for effect. "However, be that as it may, my comment was not flattery but merely the truth." The wistfulness was still there. She did not believe him.

"And you? How have you been enjoying London?" Juliana changed the subject.

As Spencer smiled at her tactics, the clearing of the floor caught his eye, and he realized that the next set was about to begin. He led Juliana forward to her place. "Much the same as you, I am afraid," he stated quickly. "Bobbington needed to revive his wardrobe as well. And I must say I agree with you, shopping is beyond tedious." He glanced down the line as he secured his position, expecting to see Bobbington staring dolefully at his Miss Pyebald from among the spectators. Spencer was rather surprised to see his friend lead a partner to the end of the line. She was none other than Miss Reeves.

For the next half hour, Spencer and Juliana swirled and stepped to the lively music. They laughed and carried on a very disjointed conversation. It consisted of sentences begun during one figure and completed on the next. There was so much chatter, music, and movement in the room that they could barely understand each other, and their hilarity was as much the nonsensical discourse as it was the intoxication of the dance.

"We will be hiding the lark tomorrow afternoon," Juliana's strange comment came near the end of the dance.

"Is that a card game of some sort? Or—"

"Our whole party will be driving in Hyde Park tomorrow afternoon," she stated with clear enunciation of her consonants, indicating that she was repeating the comment. They waited as the couple beside them stepped forward. "If the weather is conducive."

"Splendid. I do believe Bobbington and I now have the same intentions. And are you to—"

Juliana was caught up in the arms of another dancer as Spencer whirled his partner in a double turn.

Once they were back in their forward positions, Spencer tried his question again. "Are you to enjoy the Kensington assembly or the Strath recital next?"

Juliana stepped to the right as he moved opposite. "Singing ass, I believe," she said with a straight face.

Spencer blinked. "I think it safer to clarify that one with you on the morrow."

Juliana nodded in such a way that Spencer was fairly certain she had heard not a word.

Just as he was about to ask about *Hamlet*, he noticed an abrupt movement behind her back. It was as if there was a scuffle near the doorway. Spencer was not alone in his distraction, for the music trailed off, ending with the long wail of an oblivious violinist. Footfalls pounded briefly, as dancers lagged behind the music's termination, and then they, too, fell silent. All eyes were on the scene at the door.

"I will not have it." Lord Pyebald's shout was clear and succinct in the hushed room. "He is not welcome. Get him out."

Spencer and the rest of the assembly watched as a smirking young man, impeccably dressed, with dark wavy hair was set upon by two large footmen. They grabbed him roughly about the shoulders and pulled him backward out of sight of the company.

No one in the room moved or commented, but everyone

detected the strong aroma of scandal. They waited to see if the whys or wherefores would present themselves, or if it would escalate.

Lord Pyebald raised his beefy arms and smiled an artificial grin. "Young men, they will do anything for a free drink."

The ladies tittered; the men guffawed. No one believed the disagreement was that simple, least of all Spencer.

It was all very intriguing.

"Who was that?" he asked Juliana in a studied, casual way.

The look of puzzlement on her face was more of an answer than her uninformed shrug. It was a matter of which even those close to the family were unaware. This could be worthy of an investigation.

Just as the orchestra's lithe music cut into the tense atmosphere, Spencer glanced around the room to see if anything else was off-kilter. He watched Miss Pyebald glare at her father with a tight jaw and clenched fists and then turn back to her partner with feigned nonchalance. Lady Pyebald, sitting with her cronies by the wall, watched her daughter's faltering steps for a moment, and then she, too, turned a glare on Lord Pyebald— it was returned in kind, and then both peers of the realm allowed themselves to be distracted by their guests. The silent argument had been but an instant and would have been missed by most.

As Spencer continued to assess the crowd, he noticed that Bobbington was not like most—unfortunately, his friend had noted the exchange. Bobbington's face was clouded—likely worried that the young man at the door was a significant rival for his darling's affections. Someone not approved by her papa but who had found an endorsement with her dear mama. What a predicament.

And as Spencer contemplated the mixed emotions swirling in the belly of his friend, his eyes met those of another gentleman, staring unwaveringly at him. Mr. Pyebald's glower held the now-too-familiar hint of hostility. That was not unexplainable; Spencer snickered quietly. He turned from the molten animosity to the gentle, laughing eyes that were circling around him.

"I do not believe Mr. Pyebald appreciates my attentions to you, Miss Telford. He looks quite out of sorts."

Juliana followed his nod, and they both watched the man look away and then stomp off in a pet. "Likely, he believes you will succeed where he has been unable?" she ventured with a laugh in her voice.

"How is that?"

"Mr. Pyebald has been trying to get me into the gardens all evening under the pretense of my needing a respite."

"Most indiscreet."

"Exactly."

Spencer took Juliana's arm and led her to the top of the line. "The gardens cannot be overly large, the possibilities of seclusion few. If you *were* to need a respite, I would be more than happy to accommodate."

Juliana laughed. "Mr. Northam, as we've already agreed, that would be indiscreet."

"I certainly hope so."

Juliana's broad grin was a handsome reward for his tom-foolery. He almost wished he could persuade her to take a turn about the garden. However, at the end of the set, convention dictated a visit to the back of the room for a refreshment.

Spencer had just passed Juliana a glass of lemonade when they heard the swishing approach of Miss Pyebald. Her eyes were veiled and her mouth puckered with concern. She was almost hesitant, certainly solemn.

"Is all well, Vivian?" Juliana asked. She placed her hand on Miss Pyebald's arm.

"I am unsure, Juliana. It is Carrie. She has gone quite pale, almost ashen. I took her out to the balcony for air, to see if that might restore her spirits, but . . . but I believe the excitement of the evening has taxed her overmuch."

"Have you spoken to Aunt Phyllis?"

"No, I have not. Do you think I should? Carrie asked that I fetch you. Should I—" The girl half turned as if she were about to leave immediately.

Juliana tightened her grip on the younger girl's arm. "No, no, dear. That would cause undue distress to my poor aunt. I will do what I can." She turned to Spencer, passing back her glass as she did so. "I am afraid I must see to Carrie." She smiled.

"It is likely nothing. Maidenly nerves or some such. I shall be back presently."

Spencer offered to accompany her, but it was Miss Pyebald who suggested his presence might not calm Carrie's nerves as well as a quiet tête-à-tête with her cousin. Juliana nodded in agreement and asked him to stay inside.

"I shall look for your return." Spencer bowed gallantly, disappointed to see her step through the doorway alone.

"I am sure Juliana will make Carrie feel better. She has a way with people, you may have noticed."

"I have, indeed," Spencer answered warmly.

"As have I," announced Bobbington as he stepped smartly into the place vacated by Juliana.

Spencer had noticed his friend hovering, waiting for his chance to join the conversation.

"Really, Lord Bobbington, I had no idea that you were so well acquainted." Miss Pyebald's eyes were large and innocent, but her smile strained to remain in place. She clearly did not appreciate the interruption.

"Well, I, I do not really know her. That is to say, we have only just met." Bobbington floundered.

"Perhaps it is just the general sense one feels in her presence." Spencer tried to help his friend out of his embarrassment. If he bumbled about too long, the fellow might make reference to their cliff-side meeting. It was information that Spencer did not want in the hands of any Pyebalds. An innocent comment to her father or brother could give the game away.

"Yes, well." Miss Pyebald looked from one gentleman to the other. She tipped her head toward Spencer with the stance of making a private discloser. "She is not quite as . . ." She hesitated as if searching for the right word. "Not as unblemished as she would seem."

"Oh." Spencer felt the muscles of his back constrict.

"No, indeed," the spiteful gossip continued, "she has been known to take long walks, alone."

Spencer trod on Bobbington's instep to keep him from smiling or affirming the comment.

"I have been known to do so myself from time to time." Spencer plastered a guileless look upon his face. "A brisk walk on a fine—"

"Yes, but that is a gentleman's prerogative, whereas a young lady . . . ? Well, perhaps I should say no more."

"Perhaps you should say less."

Miss Pyebald flinched and leaned back as if stung. Her expression was a picture of confusion.

Spencer hadn't meant to speak aloud. He was rather confused himself. Why had he felt so protective when the pretty minx was maligning Juliana? It was not as if their relationship were anything but feigned.

No sooner had the thought crossed his mind than he realized that his reaction would be seen as growing evidence of an attachment. So instead of feeling that he had erred, he now congratulated himself on his quick thinking. He would contemplate the other issue later.

Miss Pyebald must have seen the conviction in his eye, for she beat a hasty retreat, spouting some nonsense about having to talk to her mother. She didn't even glance in poor Bobbington's direction.

"Face it, old boy," Spencer addressed his friend after Miss Pyebald had left. "You are not making any pathways into the heart of Miss Pyebald."

"Well, she certainly sees you as a possible match. She hardly noticed me at all. But I will not give up hope. What kind of lover faces adversity and merely walks away? No, I shall redouble my efforts."

"You do that."

"Just you keep your focus on Miss Telford."

"I intend to."

"Good."

The two men stared at each other in silence. Rivalry had reared its ugly head. Spencer thought a little clarification might help, but just a little. "I am not interested in Miss Pyebald, Bobbington. You can be sure of that."

The tension that had puckered the lines above Bobbington's brows relaxed. "I thought not, but she is such an angel. Who could not be swayed by her captivating eyes?"

"I had not noticed."

"Excuse me, Mr. Northam," a timid voice broke through the thick air of posturing, "but have you seen Juliana? I thought I saw her with you just a moment ago."

"Yes, indeed. That is most amusing. She has gone in search

of you." Spencer nodded to the delicate porcelain doll before them. "Are you feeling better, Miss Reeves?"

Miss Reeves frowned and shook her head slightly. "I am well, Mr. Northam. In fact, never better. All these people, and dancing, it is more than enough to keep one full of energy."

"Were you not feeling poorly just moments ago?"

"No, not at all. Whatever gave you that idea?"

"Miss Pyebald asked Miss Telford to attend you on the balcony. She said that you were unwell."

"Well, that is most strange, for I have not seen Vivian this past hour or been out to the balco—Mr. Northam, wherever are you going?"

Spencer felt as if his heart were galloping. With as much decorum as possible, he quickstepped around the dancers and headed toward the arched doorway of the balcony. It would seem that Maxwell Pyebald was not above compromising innocents and using a gullible girl to do so.

CHAPTER
9

*In which a reprehensible betrayal is brought to fruition
and a delicious awareness is born*

JULIANA STEPPED OUT OF THE DOORWAY AND INTO the refreshing night air. The lively rhythms of the orchestra behind her softened and then dissipated, carried away on the cool breeze that gently swayed her skirts. She glanced down the moonlit balcony, first one way and then the other. It seemed deserted. Even the stone seats by the stairs were empty, eerily so.

"Carrie," she called. She kept her voice hushed, not wanting to draw attention from the revelers on the other side of the threshold. "Carrie, it is I, Juliana. Are you well?"

There was no answer.

Juliana furrowed her brows and glanced back over her shoulder. All appeared as it should within the walls of the town house. The glowing candlelight revealed a room full of elegance and laughter and high-stepping strangers. She turned her gaze back to the emptiness. Why did the night suddenly fill her with such foreboding?

"Carrie," she called again. This time her appeal was more strident as the fear that something terrible had happened to her cousin came unbidden to her mind.

Juliana rushed over to the railing and looked out at the garden. As Spencer had said earlier, it was not overly large. The neighboring houses abutted too closely for anything but a mere suggestion of greenery. And yet the blue moonlight revealed no living soul, only shadowed flora.

Juliana squinted into the half-light, waiting for something to materialize. And then she heard a rustle, such as would be made by a skirt. She leaned over the rail farther and saw movement, not out in the garden but closer to the house. It came from the bottom of the stairs, hidden away from both the moonlight and the candle glow.

Juliana felt great relief. Carrie may not be well, but she knew that there would be the devil to pay if her mother caught her out in the garden alone. Clever girl.

Juliana turned to the stairway and skipped down from the first floor. When she reached the bottom step, she halted and called out to the shadow.

"Carrie, what is the matter?"

Juliana had just enough time to see that it was not Carrie but Mr. Pyebald who awaited her when he pulled her off the step and into the shadows with him. In a flash, she knew that she had been hoaxed.

"Mr. Pyebald, I am so glad to see you," she lied as she tried to disentangle herself from his embrace. "I am looking for my cousin Carrie. It would seem that she is unwell and in need of assistance. Do you think you might help me find her?" Juliana hoped that her appeal to his gallantry would override any other thoughts that might be lurking in his self-involved, beetle-headed mind.

"Miss Telford, Juliana, how I have longed to hold you in my arms."

"Mr. Pyebald—"

"Call me Maxwell," he whispered into the air above her ear as he jerked her against his chest. "How you set my heart aflame."

Juliana heard little more of his blathering nonsense, for she was much too involved in foiling the multitude of hands that he seemed to have sprouted. No sooner had she pulled one from her bodice than another appeared and cupped her bottom. Then his lips decided to demonstrate the sincerity of his words by planting wet kisses reeking of sherry across her face, all the while trying to find her lips.

Juliana was nearly at the end of her strength when she heard a noise on the balcony above. No sooner had a surge of relief flooded her mind than a new fear blossomed. This was a very compromising situation. The last thing she wanted was to be caught in a seemingly passionate embrace. Her Season would be over before it began. She would be sent back to Hartwell in terrible disgrace or married off to this buffoon before she could say do-not-let-him-near-my-inheritance.

This was a particularly sticky predicament. It topped her disreputable list, even above St. Ives Head. Hanging off the cliff was a much more comfortable situation than this. At least there she had a knight to rescue her.

As soon as her thoughts turned to Spencer, Juliana knew he was the last person whom she wanted to encounter. To hear rumors of this seemingly intimate embrace would be terrible enough, but to witness it? He knew her to be less than besotted with Mr. Pyebald, but did he know her well enough to know this scene was not of her making? She prayed it was not Spencer's footfalls thundering down the stairs. She had to escape before anyone caught her with this fumbling fool.

Juliana placed both hands against Mr. Pyebald's chest and shoved. It was like trying to move a brick wall. "Release me at once." Though she knew it was futile, she tried again.

This time Mr. Pyebald flew backward, landing with a thump in a muddy flower bed. His expression was as shocked as hers.

Juliana swallowed and looked up. Mr. Northam, her handsome, congenial knight, stood before her, his face a mask of rage. In his hand was a remnant of Mr. Pyebald's neckcloth.

"Please, it is not what you think. Not what it looked like," she said quietly. She reached her hand toward him in appeal.

"That piece of filth was not accosting you?"

Juliana stared dumbfounded. Perhaps she had been away

from Hartwell too long, among those who always saw the worst in others. She had forgotten that there was still reason in the world.

"Well, yes. Then it was exactly what it looked like. I was so afraid that you would think—"

"Who's down there? Juliana? Juliana, is that you?" Lady Pyebald's voice ricocheted off the walls. "Are you in the garden, alone with a man after I so expressly forbade it?"

Juliana turned and looked up at the blustering woman. The lilac turban squeezed onto her head bobbed with indignation and drama. Her daughter stood demurely at her side.

It was too late to jump back into the shadows. Juliana's lovely white dress reflected the moonlight beautifully. "No, Lady Pyebald, I was simply—"

"No, no? It is obvious that is precisely what you are about. How can you say *no* to me, girl, when I can see a man standing next to you? Show yourself, sir, that I might know who it is that has despoiled this lovely flower."

Juliana was still looking up when Spencer stepped into the light; she knew that he had done so by the surprised look on Lady Pyebald's face. "What is the meaning of this, Mr. Northam? For I thought much better of you." Her voice still carried through the darkness, but it was decidedly softer. "That you would take advantage of a—"

Juliana felt a brush against her skirts and a small hand slide into hers. She turned her head to see that Carrie now stood beside her. A great flood of relief and affection for her cousin filled Juliana.

"Not to worry, Lady Pyebald," Carrie spoke up with a force that surprised Juliana. "We would not come out to the garden alone, quite as you directed. We were very conscious of your advice and only ventured out for air together. Mr. Northam and Lord Bobbington were but escorting us back in before you arrived."

Juliana glanced away from Carrie and saw a man emerging from the shadows. It was, indeed, Lord Bobbington, and he looked decidedly uncomfortable.

"The air was most restorative," Carrie continued, "and we are eager to return to the dance floor."

"Well"— Lady Pyebald's frown subsided —"come inside then." She glanced up at the stars twinkling in a magnificent display high above their heads. "Night air is not good for anyone. Come in before you catch your death. Your dresses are not hearty, you know."

"Yes, Lady Pyebald, of course." Juliana made as if to step toward the stairway.

It was enough to convince Her Ladyship that duty had been done. She turned back to the warmth of the candle glow and disappeared through the threshold with Vivian trailing behind her.

The moment they were gone Juliana whirled around, ready to give Mr. Pyebald a true and proper set-down.

The flower bed was empty. All that remained were trampled and flattened tulips. The coward had skulked off while they had been occupied with his mother.

"Where?" she started to say, but the spitting and hissing of her cousin supplanted her own anger.

"How could she? Never again will she be a friend of mine. Vivian set you up, Juliana. It was a trap."

Juliana glanced at Lord Bobbington and saw that his face was bright red, and he was swallowing convulsively. His discomfort was now extreme. "Yes, dear, but this is not the time to discuss it. Let us go inside, as Lady Pyebald suggested, before these kind gentlemen catch their death."

Carrie nodded. She was mute and only barely mollified, but Juliana knew that the music and dancing would soon put her to rights.

Besides, Juliana needed to move. Her legs were beginning to shake for some reason.

Bobbington offered Carrie his arm. The girl bit her lip, sighed prettily, and glanced up at Juliana. "As you wish," she said, making a valiant attempt to keep her thoughts to herself. She gracefully placed her hand atop Bobbington's, and they stepped in unison to the stairway.

Spencer offered his arm to Juliana, allowing the other couple to gain a modest distance before speaking.

"I hope you are none the worse for this evening's work?" he asked formally, his voice tight and tense.

"I am fine. Thank you, Mr. Northam." Juliana tried to

lighten the atmosphere by taking on a calm demeanor that she did not feel. "Once again you have been my salvation."

"Miss Reeves rendered you more assistance than I."

"As well you know, I was not referring to Lady Pyebald's accusations. It was your timely rescue from Mr. Pyebald for which I owe my thanks."

"His behavior was unpardonable, reprehensible."

"I quite agree. Though I should have expected it."

"It is not to be expected from any gentleman."

"*Gentleman* is not a word that I would have used to describe Mr. Pyebald for quite some time now." It felt like eons since the lecher's hand had wandered at the inn.

"Has he made overtures before? I will not have it. You cannot stay under the same roof as this cad. I will find you another family with whom to spend the Season. I will not have you . . ."

Juliana stopped at the top of the staircase and brought her hand up. It almost touched his lips. "Please, do not take on so. I am well able to take care of myself."

Spencer seemed to have a hard time finding words. "I—" He cleared his throat. "I have seen plenty of evidence to the contrary."

"Mr. Northam, our arrangement was for appearances, nothing else. If I were to vacate these premises for one of your choosing, we would be making an unintended declaration. It would also prevent the very thing that we were trying to accomplish, that of bringing Lord Bobbington into Vivian's company as much as possible."

"But, I—"

"I will take pains to avoid Mr. Pyebald."

"He is more devious than you realize."

"No, I think not. I am well aware of that aspect of his character."

Spencer's brows furrowed, and his gaze went from her hand to her mouth. The singular way in which he was staring made Juliana feel rather heady, as if she were about to float away. Without conscious thought, her body leaned in to him at the moment his seemed to be drawn to her. She dropped her hand and took a deep breath, waiting for his next move. He swallowed and then leaned closer. His lips were mere inches from hers.

"Juliana, are you coming in?" Carrie asked from the doorway.

Juliana looked up quickly. Her cousin motioned for her to hurry across the balcony. She didn't appear to notice Spencer's close proximity.

Juliana turned back and saw why. Spencer stood a respectful distance from her, and his eyes were no longer dark and full of a hunger that Juliana did not quite understand. But it had been exquisite and exciting while it had lasted. She regretted its disappearance.

Once again, Juliana placed her arm on Spencer's. It trembled slightly, but if he noticed, he gave no sign. He would likely assume it to be the residual effect of Pyebald's assault, not the unexplored emotions that coursed through her.

Juliana took a deep breath, lifted her chin, and stepped with

Spencer across the threshold. She could maintain this facade as well as he. A smile here, a little conversation there, and no indication that there was now a tangible link between them, a delicious awareness of each other that they carried throughout the night.

❧

SPENCER YANKED OFF HIS NECKCLOTH, and he tossed it, his top hat, and his gloves onto the stand by the door of his apartment. His man, Karl, picked up the discarded objects with great dignity, waited patiently for Bobbington's hat and gloves, and then silently disappeared into the back rooms.

"God's teeth, I need a drink." Spencer stalked over to a cabinet by the fireplace and splashed a generous amount of port into a glass. He lifted it toward Bobbington in a gesture that asked if he, too, felt the need.

"Not for me. I am not the one who had to dance and smile all night while itching to stretch my fingers around another person's neck." He dropped into a chair by the fireplace and propped his feet up on the grate.

"Oh, you noticed that, did you?" Spencer paced across the room in large predatory strides.

"I am sure everyone noticed that your smile had a sharp edge, even though they had no idea why."

"If he had gone near her again," Spencer sputtered. "If he had even come back into the room, I would—"

"But he didn't, did he? The fellow likely passed out somewhere. You heard Lord Pyebald complaining of his son's inability to hold his drink. He might not even remember trying to kiss Miss Telford."

"You treat this so lightly. It is no joking matter."

"I think you, Northam, have lost perspective. And I have no doubt it is because of your feelings for her."

Spencer ignored the words that were too close to the truth. Instead, he gnawed at another bone. "Listen to you. If your Miss Pyebald had not been complicit in this sordid affair, you would be joining me in my fury. You would not have a young lady treated thus."

"Hold on now. This was not the doing of Miss Pyebald. No, indeed. She was merely the pawn of her brother's entreaties. She said so."

Spencer snorted and shook his head at his friend's gullibility. Bobbington ignored it and continued to blather.

"She thinks Pyebald and Miss Telford well suited. She is such a sweet romantic. She danced with me two sets, you know. Talking all the while about what an excellent match they were.

"This situation is not of her making. She did not know that the man stepped over the line or that Miss Telford's affections are already engaged elsewhere. Pyebald's behavior would have been most distressing to poor Miss Pyebald otherwise."

"Aha. See." Spencer waggled his finger in front of his friend. "You admit he crossed the line."

"All right, all right. He gave his ardor too much rope. He

was a wretch and is deserving of a good thrashing. That being said, there was no doubt he was in his cups. Had you done anything beyond pulling him down, Miss Telford's reputation would be in shreds. And you would not be admitted back into the good graces of Cooper Street. Ever." Bobbington sighed deeply and shrugged his shoulders. "Do not dwell on the matter overly, for it all came to rights. You rescued the damsel, again. And are likely well entrenched in her good books. That can hardly be for nothing."

Spencer stopped pacing and glared at the dying embers in the fireplace. He thought of Miss Telford's tantalizing face, particularly her pert, kissable lips. His pulse quickened as his mind's eye wandered down her invitingly curved body and back up again. He could almost feel the heat that had been generated as they pressed closer and closer.

Spencer allowed his knees to fold, and he dropped with a resounding thump into a chair.

Perhaps the reason he was so angry was that he realized he was no better than the drunken sot he detested. And he had no such excuse. If Miss Reeves had not called out to them, Spencer would most happily have gathered Juliana into his arms and kissed her until her toes curled.

Spencer couldn't remember ever feeling this want or need before. How could he have let himself get into this terrible state? What was he thinking? Despite his best efforts, he couldn't resist this sweet, intelligent innocent who needed a guardian angel at every turn.

 155

He could not lose sight of the fact that he was using her. It was bad enough to manipulate Juliana's position in the family to provide entry into the Pyebalds' affairs; it was reprehensible to make love to her in earnest. He was no better than Pyebald.

The silence stretched on as Spencer and Bobbington both stared with deep concentration at the meager offering of the dwindling fire.

Spencer's thoughts were fixed on the whys and wherefores of Juliana. They volleyed back and forth. One minute, he decided, she was a duped pawn in a traitorous household, the next she was a skilled actress or a lackey or, perhaps, a willing conspirator.

Spencer knew his emotions were running too deep when the thought of Juliana as a confederate of the French was followed by a dismissal that wasn't based on reason. He rubbed at his face and tight jaw.

No. Logic; get back to logic.

Why would a young lady, with no pretensions to marriage, grand or otherwise, stay in a household of unpleasant relatives and predatory acquaintances when she had other options?

Spencer knew his proposal to find Juliana housing had been an ill-conceived notion. It had been made in the passion of the moment. No well-reared young lady could have taken such an offer, certainly not without expecting intense scrutiny and censure. Society would have expected him to make an offer of marriage posthaste. Declining was the right thing to do.

And yet the idea of being associated with Miss Juliana Telford was not as unpleasant a thought as he would have expected. In fact, all those times he had put aside thoughts of Juliana to be considered later had somehow gotten together without his knowledge. They had formed a consensus.

If Spencer were ever to consider the possibility of a marital union, it would be in the form of a young lady somewhat like— if not exactly like—Juliana. Someone with intelligence, humor, and an engaging manner. Someone who made liberal use of his rescuing tendencies and yet fiercely declared independence. Someone with whom to share dreams and ideas—not to mention long, passionate nights.

It was reassuring that Juliana had no inclination in that direction, or Spencer might have had to withdraw himself from her company and rethink his approach to the investigation. Here he was, after having known this perplexing person less than a month, questioning his devotion to the institute of bachelorhood. This was the height of ridiculousness. He would not succumb to such unsophisticated wiles.

That thought brought Spencer full circle. While his ardor might be engaged, common sense asked questions, including the most important query of all: Was it too late to claim back his heart and search hers for truth?

∞

"JULIANA, are you asleep?"

Juliana opened her eyes and squinted toward the doorway

of her bedroom. "Carrie?" She pushed herself up into a half-sitting position. "Is all well?"

"Oh yes, most certainly. I just cannot sleep. The excitement hasn't settled yet." The girl jumped up onto the bed uninvited and jostled Juliana in the ensuing pounce. "My feet are sore from dancing, my mouth aches from smiling and talking, and yet I can hardly lie still. I do not think I will sleep all night long."

"I could. If I were left alone."

"Oh no, Juliana, you cannot mean it. Vivian is already snoring, and I have no one with whom to talk."

"But what is there to say tonight that cannot be said in the morning?"

"Oh Juliana, how can you be so cross? We have to assess every gentleman we met tonight. What they said, what they did, the color of their eyes, and the cut of their coats."

Juliana stretched up further, curled her shoulders, and cracked her neck. "Goose, you know Aunt Phyllis will tell you with whom you are to be enamored and whom to ignore. And it will not be based on the color of their eyes. Now, go to sleep. You will know in the morning. Please, dear, I would like to get a few hours—"

"You are so at ease—so content," Carrie sighed. "By the end of the Season, I will be out of the game, too—just like you."

"I never was *in* the game." Juliana pulled a fluffy feather pillow from beside her and handed it to Carrie. The girl could sleep here.

Carrie grabbed the pillow willingly enough, but rather than

settle in, she plumped it and set it against the headboard. She pulled its mate from under Juliana's elbow and repeated the procedure. She didn't appear to notice Juliana's sour expression.

Juliana sighed, shook her head, and sat up fully. Carrie's words finally penetrated. "Out of the game? Whatever are you talking about?"

"Mr. Pyebald, of course."

"After what happened this evening, Carrie Bertha Reeves, I would think that you would have more sense than to even suggest such a thing. And what happened to your assertion that Vivian was no longer a friend of yours?" Juliana's sudden adrenaline staved off any shadow of sleep that might have been lurking behind her eyes. "She placed me in a very awkward position this evening."

"I know, dearest Juliana. I agree," Carrie crooned. "It really was quite appalling, shameful—despicable . . . we cannot think of any words that Vivian has not used herself. She greatly regrets the whole affair. When she realized that her brother was in his cups, she persuaded Lady Pyebald to take a turn on the balcony. She was coming to chaperone just as Mr. Northam reached you." Carrie leaned toward her cousin. "Can you forgive her?"

"Perhaps I can pardon her, Carrie, but I will no longer trust her. You should not, either. And as to Mr. Pyebald, he will *not* get my forgiveness or good opinion—it is lost forever! You must never—and I mean *never*—leave me alone with that wretched man again."

"I will try not to." Carrie nodded with more conviction than conveyed in her words and then frowned. "But I thought it . . . well, a form of flattery. A compliment. To go to such lengths to secure a few minutes alone with you."

Juliana was not going to explain what transpired in those few moments. "I am not interested in stolen moments with anyone, Carrie. I have said it before, and I will say it again."

"Oh, I am glad to hear you say so. I was starting to worry that you were taken with Mr. Northam, and I was loath to tell you that Mama has other plans." Carrie yawned and slumped back onto the headboard. "Mama thinks he is a better match for Vivian. Though I can see why you might be setting your cap for him—even if I do find him a little overcurious. Quite a handsome fellow."

"Curious?" Juliana frowned. "How do you mean?"

"All throughout our set of country-dances, Mr. Northam plagued me with questions."

"Really?"

"Indeed, most tiresome. Did the Pyebalds have any regular visitors? Who were their particular friends? Oh, and yes, he even wanted to know about Lamar Stamford."

"Who?"

"Lamar Stamford. From Lambhurst. Did you not meet the Stamfords? No, wait; I believe the family to have gone to Town before you arrived. Well, it is not likely that you are to meet them now. It is a shame. They have had to retrench—no one says anything, but I have heard a rumor or two that their debts are enormous." Carrie flushed slightly. "Besides, there seems to have been a falling out between the Stamfords and the Pyebalds, as you saw."

"I did?"

"Oh, yes, everyone did. The great kerfuffle at the door. When Lamar tried to push his way forward. I would have thought him invited, but apparently not."

"I see."

"But he is a good dancer, so I can forgive him."

"Who? Lamar Stamford?"

"Mr. Northam."

Juliana pinched the bridge of her nose and sighed. "I am afraid you are being less than clear, Carrie dear."

Carrie looked over at Juliana with half-closed eyes. "I can forgive Mr. Northam's questions due to the fact that he is an excellent dancer."

"Did he ask any questions about Vivian? Or praise Lord Bobbington? Or say—"

"Please, Juliana." Carrie's eyes were now fully closed. "I am trying to sleep."

Juliana frowned and reexamined Spencer's conversation during the ball. It had, indeed, been sprinkled liberally with questions and curiosity. Why? Was he such a person that had to know all, of friends and neighbors? Or was there a purpose to his questions other than that which he had stated?

Despite the feelings he aroused in her when he was around, Juliana did not really know Mr. Spencer Northam. Their acquaintance had been for such a short duration.

Now upon examination, it did seem rather extreme for a gentleman to set up a grand escapade, such as he had with Juliana, for the purpose of providing a friend with the opportunity to see a young lady. A young lady who was now out in society and at liberty to see anyone of her mother's approval. Perhaps Lord Bobbington was not worthy of this approval and, therefore, needed Spencer's intervention. But why would Lord Bobbington not be acceptable? And why was Mr. Northam interested in Lamar Stamford?

The longer Juliana contemplated, the more uncomfortable she became. Was it possible that she had given her heart to an unqualified rogue? Someone who was using her for his own nefarious and mystifying purposes? Was it too late to claim back her heart and search his for truth?

CHAPTER
10

*In which the all-important ride down Rotten Row
presents the young ladies to their best advantage*

THE NEXT AFTERNOON PROVED TO BE ONE OF THE
finest that Spencer had experienced thus far in the
Season. Faint drifts of harmless white clouds only occasionally
interrupted the bright, clear blue sky. The breeze that gently
lifted the burgeoning leaves was fresh and warm and held a
promise of summer.

The value of such a gift was lost on none of the *beau monde*,
for they went *en masse* to worship the day's beauty at Hyde Park.
Long, endless lines of the most fashionable people, coaches, and
horses surrounded Spencer as the undulating crowds meandered
down the sandy road called Rotten Row.

Spencer guided his tall black stallion into an opening
behind Viscount Petersham's chocolate-colored coach while

Bobbington edged in beside him. The two feasted their eyes on the wild spectacle. It was a menagerie of livery, spotted dogs, yellow and blue waistcoats, ostrich plumes, and parasols. The Ton was here to flirt, greet friends, and fill others with envy. Spencer was here to see Juliana.

Only to ask some pertinent questions, of course. Nothing else.

He would not allow his mind to be distracted by her sweet rose scent. He would only make queries that would further his investigation, and he would refrain from observing her open, guileless expressions. Juliana might have caused him to notice her, but he would let it go no further than that. His resolve was once again in place.

Spencer had eaten heartily that morning, dressed impeccably, and then conversed with some wit. But there had never been a moment in which he hadn't been required to dismiss Juliana from his thoughts. Bobbington had not called him on it, so Spencer could only think that he was hiding his distraction well.

"Sorry, what were you saying?"

Bobbington raised his right eyebrow, and Spencer realized that he had seen this expression several times recently. Perhaps *hiding* wasn't the right word. Being ignored might be more apt.

"I was merely commenting on Hart's grays. His horses appear to be mighty fine."

"Yes, indeed," Spencer said without following Bobbington's gaze. He wasn't really interested. He was acutely aware that he might miss Juliana in the huge crowd. She had said they would be here today if the weather was conducive. And it just didn't get any more conducive.

"Northam. I say, Northam." Bobbington's tone was slightly irritated, as if Spencer hadn't been listening.

"Yes, what is it?" Spencer turned his head and caught the profile of a flaxen-haired woman up ahead. She was resplendent in a flamboyant purple riding costume, surrounded by an animated cluster of young swains. Spencer quickly lowered his gaze. He continued to stare at the ground until he saw the hooves of her roan mare pass.

"I say, Northam, I believe that was Lady Rayne," Bobbington commented most unhelpfully.

"Yes, indeed." Spencer nodded. "I don't think she saw me."

The two riders considered each other. Bobbington was the first to look away. They were silent for several minutes, nodding and bowing to other acquaintances.

But Bobbington could not hold his peace for long. "I don't think it would have mattered, Northam. She has found herself another lapdog—a *litter* of salivating puppies, in fact."

"So it would seem." Spencer half smiled and then turned to his friend and shrugged. "Being out of Town has done the trick."

Bobbington laughed. "It most certainly has." Shaking his head, Bobbington returned his gaze to the crowd. Spencer knew that the Pyebalds had been sighted as Bobbington sighed and a spoony smile spread across his face.

Glancing over his shoulder, Spencer saw that two open carriages approached. The first contained none other than the illustrious figures of Lord and Lady Pyebald, dressed in their finest and looking as disheveled as ever. The second carriage followed closely behind, and while Spencer could see none of the young ladies, he knew them to be in the party if by nothing other than the lifted chests of the bucks parading nearby.

"Mr. Northam," Lady Pyebald squealed. Her greeting allowed Spencer and Bobbington to separate from the long line and approach their carriage for conversation. "How perfectly grand to see you. I do hope you enjoyed yourself at our little gathering last evening?"

It was sad to see a woman of her advancing size and years simpering.

"Yes, Lady Pyebald, it was generous of you to include us in your celebration. I assume none of you fine ladies are feeling any ill effects from the rigors of the ball?"

Spencer glanced about as he addressed the company at large. He wanted to see reassurance in Juliana's eyes, proof that she had not been further subjected to Pyebald's advances.

However, only Miss Pyebald, who sat across from her parents, nodded and fluttered her eyelashes. Her simple white carriage dress was spread out before her in an artful display that was far from spontaneous. With a quick glance to the other carriage, Spencer noted that Miss Reeves occupied the seat facing Mr. and Mrs. Reeves. There was no sign of Juliana. His stomach clenched and was on its way down to his boots when Spencer noticed the pair on horseback waiting patiently on the other side.

Spencer was greatly relieved to see Juliana. He gave her a broader smile and deeper bow than he had intended but saw the tentative hesitance of her nod and wondered at its lackluster nature.

The riding costume she was wearing was not the unflattering affair from St. Ives Head but a becoming style that both accentuated her small waist and brought color to her cheeks, color that deepened the longer their eyes were locked.

Eventually, a snort from the horse beside her broke the spell. And while Spencer could have sworn their greeting was not overlong, the discomfort on Juliana's face seemed to indicate that it was.

Then Spencer noticed the rider beside her and understood, all too well, from where her discomfort issued.

Mr. Pyebald sat rigid on his horse, staring at Spencer with his typical expression of animosity. His proximity to Juliana almost propelled Spencer from his saddle, but a sudden, tight grip on his coattail prevented any such move.

The grip belonged to Bobbington.

Juliana watched the rush of color subside from Spencer's face and wondered if the anger that had spurred it was based on her protection or his pride. She was grateful for Bobbington. He had understood his friend's intent instantly and brought Spencer to his senses with a mere touch. Bobbington hadn't even said anything but continued to converse with Aunt Phyllis in waxing banal tones about the splendor of the previous evening. Spencer had collected his emotions, divested himself of his friend's hand, and then joined in the discourse with witty banter that impressed Carrie and Vivian excessively. He completely ignored Pyebald.

With bated breath, Juliana waited. She might be wrong. All the uncertainty of Spencer's true nature that had plagued her throughout the night might not stand up to the scrutiny of a bright day.

Up to this point he had been the picture of propriety, dividing his attentions evenly among the ladies. He laughed over Lord Pyebald's comment that the Season was already too long, and he shared a prediction with Mr. Reeves regarding the next turf race at Newmarket.

It was all harmless. There was nothing out of the ordinary, and his questions focused on common social subjects, such as the weather and Carrie's favorite novel.

Juliana swallowed and took a deep breath. Her imagination had taken her on a ridiculous journey once again. There was nothing sinister about Spencer Northam and his strange appeal for their comings and goings. It was nothing more than he had stated, a way to bring Bobbington and Vivian together. It was the work of a romantic.

Juliana was relieved that she had not acted on her suspicion, although what she would have done she knew not. It was all water under the bridge. She could take up enjoyment of Spencer's company once again, embed the memories to take home with her, and hoard the pulsing emotions to examine at a later date. She need not see anything behind the questions and curiosity.

"Of course, Mr. Northam, if you wish."

It was the sour tone of Lady Pyebald's comment that drew Juliana from her reverie. The lady's voice had been all honey and sugar to this point.

"Maxwell will accompany you for the sake of propriety. Cannot be remiss in our duties as chaperone, now can we, Mrs. Reeves?"

Aunt Phyllis suggested that Mr. Northam might be better served if he paced their carriage instead of pulling ahead. They might find that they had a lot in common, but Spencer demurred and turned his magnificent stallion in Juliana's direction.

He expertly maneuvered between Pyebald and herself, then set the pace at a trot while leaving the others slightly behind at a walk. Juliana noticed that Bobbington called out to Pyebald just as he was about to encourage his horse to a faster speed.

"Are you well, Miss Telford? You are uncommonly quiet this afternoon," Spencer asked the moment they were out of earshot.

"Am I that much of a gabster, Mr. Northam, that a modicum of silence denotes an ailing disposition?" Her smile took away any pretense of insult.

Spencer returned her smile and then looked over his shoulder to Mr. Pyebald, who was slowly catching up despite Bobbington's efforts to engage him.

"I hope you are not finding your situation too difficult—"

"I am fine, Mr. Northam, in all circumstances," Juliana interrupted quickly. "You need not be concerned."

"But—"

"He has apologized most profusely, as has Vivian. Both are quite contrite and desperate to make amends. Unfortunately, I now find that I am no longer an ignored appendage to the household but something much worse. I am now subjected, at every turn, to flowery, inexhaustible prose on my exceptional qualities and goodness. It is all rather tedious. But nothing worthy of concern; no subsequent rescue is required."

The frown that had entrenched itself between Spencer's brows slowly dissipated. "Are you certain?"

Juliana glanced to the road ahead and then back again. She met his gaze directly. "Mr. Northam, can we ever be certain of anything? Or anybody?"

"No, I suppose not."

Juliana pulled her lips together in disappointment. She would dearly have loved for him to disagree, to claim that they might know each other, eventually, as good friends. It was a future that Juliana knew she would have to forgo, but it would have been pleasant to imagine.

"So what are your plans this evening?" Spencer asked, as one would in a proper discourse.

Bobbington and Pyebald had finally caught up and were within earshot. While the desire to outpace them again made her heels itch, Juliana bowed to convention and slowed. Spencer followed suit.

"I believe it is a private card party. Lady Pyebald supposes it best to spread out the excitements."

"And then?"

Without any encouragement, desire, or need, the thoughts and suspicions of Spencer's motives came flooding back. She tried to drop them back into the abyss of insecurity from which they had sprung, but they would not be moved.

Juliana lifted her hand to pinch the bridge of her nose. She stopped the movement abruptly. It was a telltale sign of discomfort, a state she would rather hide. She dropped her hand, but not before grabbing at the place where her locket should have rested. She sighed with recollection of its loss.

"I am not sure as yet," she hedged. "There was talk of taking in a play."

"*Hamlet*?" Spencer's voice was strangely tight. "I thought you would be going . . . later."

"Really, how so?"

"It was in my mind that your party would be enjoying the festivities on May Day."

"Do you know something that I do not?"

Spencer laughed, but it held no humor. "I must have misunderstood an earlier comment, is all. I am sure that you will enjoy it. I hear it is all-the-crack. Perhaps I will see you there."

That sounded like a bouncer to Juliana and not a well-executed one at that. She frowned and tilted her head, as if by doing so the words would fall into place.

She looked into his handsome face and tried to read his expression. It was almost as if he were puzzled. Or was that disappointment? There was no doubt that whatever Spencer Northam was contemplating, it had made him profoundly miserable. It was there, hidden behind his charming, lopsided smile.

"WHAT ARE YOU ABOUT?" Spencer watched Bobbington shift the large Chinese vase that had been sitting in the right corner of the drawing room window. It was the usual signal to Bibury, an agreed-upon message—meet me at St. James's Church at nine.

"Well, I have seen you moving it about. Can't make up your mind as to where it looks best, eh? Thought I would help." Taking out an overly large handkerchief, his friend dusted the ornate urn and then he proceeded to shake it out in front of the window. As expected, the process did nothing more than send the dust sailing into the air.

Coughing, Spencer tried to nudge Bobbington out of the way, but his friend was quite determined to unsettle every little bit of dust from the large white square before he could be dislodged.

"There. Better, don't you think?" Bobbington looked quite pleased with himself.

"No, I do not think. I will do the deciding . . . and I have decided that I like to move the vase about rather than have a stagnant arrangement. Today, I wish it to be here." Spencer replaced the vase on the right side of the window. "Though I might change my mind tomorrow."

With a shrug, Bobbington turned and picked up a notebook. "Suit yourself," he said as he left the room.

"Indeed." Spencer stared after his friend more annoyed than was warranted; after all, the fellow didn't know he was interfering with a commission of the War Office.

"HE SHOULD NOT HAVE SENT YOU, Miss Telford. There is nothing more I can do for you." The man who uttered these words was small in stature with sharp features that put Juliana in mind of a mouse. His white hair winged out on either side of his head as if it was his habit to pull at it when angered. Juliana could imagine that the hair stood on end by each day's closing.

"As I stated earlier, Mr. Dagmar, my father did not send me. I came on my own." Juliana noticed his eyes wander over to Nancy, who stood patiently by the office door and shook her head. Being alone was a relative term while in Town. "It was my understanding that you might consider publishing our scientific works on the *Coccinellidae*. That is what you declared in your letter of eighteen months ago. We have heard nothing from you since. I took up the correspondence these past five months, and still you have not had the courtesy to reply. Please tell me, are you or are you not going to publish? It is of great importance to my father and to me."

"Yes, but to no one else, I will warrant."

"I beg your pardon?"

"You and your father have attached your names to a common tedious insect. The only ladybirds of interest to the English gentleman these days are those found in Haymarket."

"Mr. Dagmar! Really, that is most unmannerly of you to make such a reference in my hearing. And I will have you know that another scientific journal discussing the lady *beetle* is being shopped around. *You* would have the good fortune to be ahead of the game were you to—"

"Enough of this nonsense. Who would want to read a natural history as observed by a lady? And a young lady at that! Now be off with you. I am an important man with much to do. This is all beyond your understanding. I recommend, most heartily, that you go back to your needlepoint and leave the pursuit of learning to those with the minds to do so."

"I will have our papers back then."

"Be off, I said." He muttered something under his breath that sounded like a derisive comment about women thinking that they could conduct business.

"Not without our research. It is not your property. I wish it returned at once."

The agitated man looked around the cramped room. It was in complete disarray. Papers were strewn one on top of the other, books of various sizes hung out of overstuffed cases, and there was an overall clutter of gadgets and paraphernalia. Juliana was not surprised when he harrumphed and said he had no idea as to where it was.

"Well, it must be found, sir. I will not leave the city without it."

"Fine, come back next week." The man didn't even have the decency to see Juliana to the door. Instead, he waved his hand at her as if she were a fly to be shooed away.

"I will, Mr. Dagmar. You can count on it. And I will not leave your office next time without the research." She stood, straightened her dress, and marched to the door that Nancy now held open. "I will be back."

Juliana made a dramatic exit with her head held high and her posture full of authority, but she was thwarted after all. Mr. Dagmar was not paying the least bit of attention. She had thought she had pulled it off rather well and was disappointed that Nancy was her only witness.

"Oh, Miss, I am that sorry. Will yer Da be troubled?"

Juliana smiled and then laughed lightly at Nancy's surprised expression. She waited until they had gained the street before explaining. "Nancy, I never expected Mr. Dagmar to publish our work. If he truly were interested, he would have written some time ago. No, I just hoped he might do so and save me from the drudgery I must now face."

"I do not rightly understand, Miss."

Juliana pulled a piece of paper from her reticule. She waved it in the air like a flag. "There are at least six other publishing houses in London that print books on the natural sciences. I found their names in the volumes of our Hartwell library. Surely, among them I will find an interested party."

"Six, Miss. That is a lot a walkin'."

"Yes, you are right. And we'd better start sooner rather than later. I am supposed to be picking up a matching ribbon for my latest bonnet, so we will have to include that in our search. We do not want Aunt Phyllis to regret granting me my request."

"You know, Miss. I thought I 'eard Mr. Pyebald callin' after us. Somethin' h'about comin' with. Do you think we shoulda waited?"

Juliana placed an indifferent mask on her face. Lifted her skirts with one hand while perusing the list in her other. "No, I do not recall asking for an escort. You must have been mistaken."

"Yes, Miss."

Juliana thought it best to protect Nancy. Aunt Phyllis might look for a scapegoat for this escapade, and it was better if the girl could honestly say that she knew nothing of Mr. Pyebald's intention to accompany them. And Juliana could argue ignorance as well, being that his company had been implicit in Aunt Phyllis's consent but not stated. She didn't mind looking imprudent if she had accomplished her task.

But the search turned out to be a lot more difficult than

Juliana had envisioned. The three closest publishing houses, still within a block or two from where they began on Northampton Road, employed draconian measures to see her to the door. Only one suggested that she return on another day. The other two required a hackney coach, a great deal of time, and many inquiries to find. When at last Juliana returned to the town house, the family was in an uproar.

She had taken almost three hours to finish what should have taken no more than one. And while Carrie was greatly impressed with the perfect match that Juliana had at last found in her ribbon, the rest of the family was less so.

To make matters worse, and despite the fact that Juliana had arrived with more than enough time to change and prepare for the play, Lady Pyebald flew into vapors and Lord Pyebald suggested postponing the jaunt. Mr. Pyebald was sent to exchange the tickets for a later date, and Aunt Phyllis retired early with a sick headache. Vivian sulked and blamed Juliana for their ruined evening, and the girls decided to play cards in their room, well away from their . . . frustrations.

Juliana was left to sit alone in the drawing room with Uncle Leonard. A dull, quiet night was meant to show her the error of her ways.

Aside from the occasional crack of the fire, delicious silence reigned. Juliana thought it a wonderful respite, but she did not wish to be on bad terms with the man sitting across from her.

"I am sorry for the fuss, Uncle. I really had no idea that I would cause such a disruption. I—" She silenced her blathering when she saw that he was looking over the edge of his book with a bewildered expression.

"My dear, this is the first moment I have had to relax since we arrived. I couldn't be happier. I really do not understand the fuss myself, but then women . . ." He shrugged. "Your shopping might have been a tad overlong, but I know you to have a sensible head upon your shoulders, which is more than I can say about some in this household, and I was not concerned. Not in the least." His smile was calm and soothing. "The strictures of society can be so confining."

Juliana began to feel a lessening of the tension that had built up through all the histrionics.

Uncle Leonard raised his book slightly as if to recommence reading and then lowered it again. "Did you find what you were looking for?"

Juliana recalled the last two publishing houses, which had expressed an interest in the lady beetle research and the one that had given her an appointment for next week. "Yes, it was a most successful excursion. Did you not see the ribbon and how well it matched?"

"Of course, my dear. The ribbon. I had forgotten the reason for your outing."

Just as Uncle Leonard lifted his book back to eye level, he looked at her and smiled.

And Juliana could have sworn that he winked.

CHAPTER
11

In which Mr. Northam mulls over erroneous information while Miss Telford continues to shoulder the blame for . . . pretty much anything that can be laid on her doorstep.

"NO, I WILL NOT." Bobbington fixed Spencer with what was likely meant to be a piercing glare. He looked more like a ruffled pup. "If you had kept to your seat for more than five minutes at a time, you would have enjoyed the play and not feel the need to return. It is upon your own shoulders."

Bobbington sat across from Spencer almost lost in the tall, dark wingback chair that had been placed in the grouping by the fire. There was room for four, but none of the other men in Brooks's at the time seemed inclined to intrude upon the friends' terse discussion.

Spencer allowed it was always best to let a man spill his

spleen before interjecting a little sense. However, Bobbington had been huffing and puffing since breakfast. "It was not my fault." He started to introduce reason, but it was still a little too soon.

"How can you say that? It was most certainly your fault. Indeed, you hardly looked at the stage, jumpy as a Belgian rabbit and more interested in everything around you. It was like being with a ten-year-old."

"It is not my fault," Spencer tried again, "that Miss Pyebald was not there."

Bobbington opened his mouth to disagree and then clamped it shut with a snap. He looked slightly sheepish and then sighed. "It was my understanding that it was a planned outing for the Reeves family and the Pyebalds. I intended to put myself forward. I thought it the perfect place to be noticed. Was I wrong? Did you not tell me that—?"

"Yes, yes," Spencer interrupted in a tone sharper than he had intended. "That was my understanding as well. Miss Telford indicated that they would be attending, although I had had my doubts." He contradicted his severe tone by curling the corners of his lips up and lifting his shoulders.

"Your doubts! Well, you could have had the courtesy to inform me. My heart was set." He glared once more at Spencer; however, his frustration was finally winding down. "Oh devil take it, never mind. I know you must be vastly disappointed as well. I have never known you to take an interest in a lady such as Miss Telford before." He tried to laugh, but it came out as a snort. "Little minx for telling us they would attend."

Spencer shrugged again, as if it truly were not disturbing that Juliana had lied. He knew that she had fibbed the moment the words left her mouth in Hyde Park. She had looked decidedly uncomfortable. He had not expected it of her. He thought her above the common. His only comfort was that she was not practiced at cutting shams. He hoped there was some reason for her subterfuge other than being in league with the Pyebalds.

"I was simply not in the mood for *Hamlet*, is all, a temporary condition. I apologize for my rudeness, and, to make amends, I have sent for new tickets. You will yet witness the solemnity of the graveyard scene. It is unparalleled, I understand."

"Well, perhaps." Bobbington seemed slightly mollified. "I will let you know."

Spencer was not deceived by Bobbington's noncommittal acceptance. He knew that if there were a ghost of a chance to encounter the fair Miss Pyebald, Bobbington would be at the head of the line. "Thank you for your consideration." He didn't even try to hide his tone of sarcasm.

"I found it rather tedious myself."

Spencer glanced up.

Lord Winfrith stood next to Bobbington's chair, leaning against the side. His arm was draped casually over the top. He looked relaxed and a tad bored. It was a skillful disguise. "But then *Hamlet* was never my favorite," he finished.

"Of course, you would find it lacking." Bobbington sniffed. "You were as bad as Northam. Hardly a moment passed that one or the other of you was not up on one pretext or another. I mean really. It was a wonder we were not thrown from the theater."

Lord Winfrith's laugh was loud and hearty. "We were the least rowdy of the bunch, Bobbington," he said at last. "If they start throwing out those of us who find it deadly dull to sit still, what will they do with the catcallers, toss 'em in irons?"

Bobbington shook his head and half turned to Winfrith. "If it will allow the rest of the audience to enjoy the play, I say they should go to it." The chilly tone was meant to be a set-down, but the entrance of a gaggle of young men distracted him. "You will have to excuse me. I see an acquaintance from Lambhurst." Bobbington stood and pulled his waistcoat down with a little more force than was usual. "I will go reacquaint myself." He walked away with his chin lifted.

"It is getting more and more difficult to hide my purpose from Bobbington." Spencer lowered his voice once Winfrith claimed the newly vacated seat. "I believe he has discerned that something is amiss. It is not in his conversation as much as the watchfulness that he has taken on since we arrived in Town. Perhaps I shouldn't have introduced you to him last night— certainly not as a friend of the family."

"Worry not. This game is almost over, that is, if you are right about May Day."

"I expected to know it as a certainty, but Miss Telford is not the reliable source I once thought."

"I do not believe Miss Telford willfully misled you."

Spencer snorted, but Winfrith's raised hand encouraged him to lean closer.

"It was much known at the card party I attended the night before last that the Drury Theatre was, indeed, to be their source of entertainment for the next night. I heard it from Lady Pyebald herself. Something must have happened."

Spencer swallowed, and he felt the quickening of his pulse. "Is Bibury there now?" The possibility of Juliana in another predicament was not hard to imagine. The only surprise was how immediate alarm had displaced suspicion. This was a strange condition.

"Yes, and were it significant, I am sure we would have heard. Fear not, we will soon know what it was."

Spencer leaned back, thinking that Winfrith had read his thoughts. He nodded as if his mind were calm and well ordered, not the chaotic jumble that pitted logic against emotions. "Word has it that the Reeves and Pyebald families will be attending the Strath recital this evening. Lady Strath has included me in her invitation, likely due to the ministrations of the Pyebalds. I believe I will go to hear the dulcet tones of the soprano after all."

"Excellent notion, and perhaps you can learn the point of Miss Telford's jaunt through those unfashionable parts of Town while you are at it. Although if you think it relevant, we can start making quiet inquiries at the premises."

"Perhaps not as yet; if it has nothing to do with our case, we might damage Miss Telford's reputation merely by asking. And if it has, well, we might tip our hand. At this late date, we do not want to have to start anew. Best hold off, at least until I see the lady this evening. I will be able to—"

Spencer's words were cut off by a great guffaw coming from the gaming tables. Looking around, Spencer saw that Bobbington stood with a group of bucks. One young dandy with a pointed nose and a canary-yellow waistcoat was the focus of the men's merriment. He looked nonplussed and annoyed. He raised his quizzing glass to look down on those gathered around him until the laughter died down. "I will see to it directly," he said with such a solemn air that another roar of laughter followed instantly. The young man flinched as if struck. He threw back his shoulders and sashayed to the door. Another young man with dark wavy hair broke away from the crowd and raced after him.

Bobbington turned to see that both Spencer's and Winfrith's eyes were upon him. He grinned largely and patted one of the bucks on the shoulder before crossing back to the other side of the room. Spencer was pleased to see that his friend's expression was much more congenial than it had been when he had headed in the opposite direction.

"Poor Hart," Bobbington said when he reached them. He was smirking and did not look sorry for the young man at all, despite his words. "His father has been marshaling Hart's fine new horses about Town as if they were his own. And young Hart didn't even know it." Bobbington dropped into the seat beside Winfrith. "It has put him in quite a pucker. Can you imagine the set-to there will be tonight? Perhaps I should not have mentioned it." Again, Bobbington looked anything but guilt-struck.

It was good to see the return of his old spirits.

"OH DEAREST CARRIE, I am all atwitter." Juliana glanced at her companion, touching her sleeve to draw attention to the importance of her words. She was about to enter the hallowed halls of the British Museum, where all manner of learning might be anticipated. Could there be any better excursion?

Hooking her arm through that of her cousin, Carrie smiled as they crossed the threshold of Montagu House and stepped into the ornate hall of the graceful—if somewhat French in style—building. "I understand completely. For I find that I, too, am greatly excited."

"Me, too," commented the unwelcome escort at their side. Mr. Pyebald illustrated just how truly in harmony he was by stifling a yawn as he stood looking up at the beautiful painted ceiling.

Leaving him to his ennui, Juliana led Carrie through the arched doors toward the grand staircase. As soon as they turned to proceed up the second flight, Carrie gasped. "What is that?" And then she revised her question. "What are they?"

Standing in a large alcove on the left of the staircase were four stuffed animals: three with spectacularly long necks and mottled hides of orange, brown, and ivory and a completely dissimilar bulky creature of gray, with a horn on its nose. Juliana had never seen anything like them before; she had, however, read about them. "I believe they are giraffes, and that ungainly thing might be a rhinoceros from Africa."

Unfortunately, their overlong pause gave Mr. Pyebald the opportunity to catch up. "Don't go running off like that, my dear girls. I promised to stay at your sides, and that is precisely what I intend to do."

Far from seeing this directive as a state of rule, Juliana took Mr. Pyebald's words as a challenge. It was fortunate that Carrie knew her cousin well; Juliana did not have to explain her tendency to . . . well, dawdle and dash.

The displays in the Mammalian Saloon required a thorough examination, as did those of the Botanical Room and the Gallery of Antiquities. However, upon saturating her mind with details of each of these various subjects, Juliana would then rush to the next room—often as soon as Mr. Pyebald chose to sit or lean . . . or stare at some other female figure. It was somewhat entertaining, if for no other reason than it gave her a sense of thwarting his authority.

It was on one of these dashes that Juliana nearly bumped into an elderly man with the most engaging blue eyes. She came to a halt just in time and apologized for the near collision. The gentleman nodded and then turned away, leaving Juliana wondering why it was that she saw Spencer Northam in the shadow of every man she encountered—no matter what his age.

Shaking her head at her own folly, Juliana watched the elderly gentleman as he leaned over a display of tropical birds and frowned. There was something in the way he held himself, as if he were younger than the years spoken of in his heavily lined face. Turning quickly, to call Carrie's attention to this oddity, Juliana walked straight into another gentleman. Fortunately, this fellow didn't remind her of Spencer but instead—.

"Lord Bobbington, what a great pleasure." Juliana was surprised by the gentleman's rather disheveled look—well, not really disheveled—he was costumed in a far more somber and rugged outfit than was his norm. He wore a cap and was swathed in browns; his boots were soiled . . . and of an inferior quality. In fact, he looked very un-Lord-Bobbington-like, and Juliana might have walked right by him had she not turned at that precise moment.

"Lord Bobbington!" Now it was Carrie's turn to notice the gentleman.

And notice him she did, but Juliana was fairly certain that Carrie could not tell anyone what color Lord Bobbington wore or whether he doffed a cap, for her dear cousin was staring solely at his face. There was a very sweet smile in her expression that brought one of a similar ilk to the lips of the gentleman. And then he ruined the moment entirely.

"Is Miss Pyebald with you?" he asked, and Juliana was hard pressed not to give him a resounding set-down.

Fortunately, Carrie found her voice before Juliana. "No, Vivian claimed to be a little peaked this morning, but I believe she just wanted to avoid the museum."

"Well, more fool she." Lord Bobbington redeemed himself and then some, by spouting those words with great derision and offering Carrie his arm. "I see you have no worthy escort. Please, allow me."

"Oh, but Mr. Pyebald is with us. There, you see . . . sitting in the corner." Carrie used her chin to indicate a figure in the back of the room; it looked as if their attentive companion had closed his eyes and was napping away his duties.

"As I said, Miss Reeves, as I said."

Juliana grinned, much in charity with Lord Bobbington. She allowed Carrie and Lord Bobbington a little distance before following. As she reached the threshold of the next room, Juliana looked back over her shoulder to puzzle out the old man by the bird display case.

It proved to be a pointless exercise; she could make no more observations in his regard. He was gone. With a frown, Juliana scanned the room; the only familiar figure in the crowd was that of Mr. Pyebald, slumped in the corner, looking every inch the ne'er-do-well he was.

"You will not solicit his attention. You will restrict your comments to the commonplace, such as the weather, and under no circumstances will you visit the garden with him." The litany of requirements droned on and on.

Juliana sighed very quietly to herself. She did not want to be accused of insubordination. She was still paying penance for her selfish rebellion, as her afternoon spent ribbon searching had been termed by the older females of the household. An ounce of freedom was apparently worth a long, repetitious list of commandments.

Juliana listened to her aunt with half an ear. Her hands were placed demurely on her lap, her eyes suitably downcast, and only her unseen toes tapped out their impatience.

"Mr. Northam is not to have your sole attention. If he . . ."

Juliana had not seen Spencer in two days. She would be more than happy to give him her sole attention. As it was, she was suffering suitor deprivation, or at least that is what Juliana had termed it.

Suitor deprivation, she had decided, was the condition of missing Spencer so much that she was now seeing his face in everyone. He had driven a dray down the street and stopped to chat with the constable on the corner just yesterday. Dressed in dull grays and a cap pulled over his eyes. He had also been the face of the grocery deliveryman, covered in a soiled apron, leaning on the fence. And she had even seen him in the proud buck strolling the park.

Juliana almost chuckled at herself. But stopped just in time. It would not be understood.

"It is Mr. Pyebald who will receive your attentions."

Juliana was abruptly brought back to the drawing room with those disturbing words. "No, Aunt." She could hold her tongue only so long. "I have told you that I do not see Mr. Pyebald and myself as a match. You may push him in my direction until the heavens drop, but I will never see in him a husband."

"What? Take yourself off that high horse of yours, Juliana. Independence and free thinking are most unattractive in a young girl. These decisions are best made by those who know the ways of the world."

Juliana stood up and walked to the drawing room window. They had been left alone for this little session of harassment, and thankfully that meant she had only one formidable foe to deal with at a time.

"I am already besmirched, Aunt. For I plead guilty to both independence and free thinking. And I say Mr. Pyebald is not the man for me."

"Nonsense, girl, it is a perfectly equitable match. You will have money; he will have a title. What could be more suitable?

If you are thinking on Mr. Northam, I can tell you that Lady Pyebald and I have decided he would be best for Vivian."

Pushing back the curtain, Juliana looked out at the busy street, doing her best to control the amusement that she found in her aunt's proclamation. "Be that as it may, Aunt, I will marry whom I choose, if I choose. As I am certain will Mr. Northam. Your schemes are for naught." And even as his name crossed her lips, Juliana saw Spencer.

Or at least another man who looked just like him. He was chatting up a nurse with a pram, directly across from the town house. Juliana watched as he bent, picked what had to be a very new flower from the bed beside them, and then bowed with little or no finesse. The young woman simpered at his attention. Juliana could almost hear her giggles. It was all rather charming.

Yes, suitor deprivation. She hoped it would be cured this evening. It would be good to see his face in earnest.

"OVER HERE, Mr. Northam. Yes, yes, so good to see you. It has been too long, much too long. Sit with us; do. We shall catch up. Sit here. And you as well, Lord Bobbington. We have plenty of seats. Yes, indeed, one for everyone."

This was the real Spencer, the impeccably dressed, handsome young gentleman with the discerning blue eyes and the friendly, lopsided smile. Gone were the weak imitations from the street, and gone was the dour Spencer from Hyde Park. Here was the man who made her knees weak and her heart pound, and he was making his way through the line of red chairs toward her. Past Lady Pyebald and Aunt Phyllis, then Carrie and Vivian . . . he would soon be at her side.

"Move over, Juliana, and let the gentleman sit." Her aunt's smile was large and toothy.

It was not at all attractive, to Juliana's way of thinking.

She rose and with great dignity placed two empty seats between her and Vivian. She sat again and made a show of smoothing her skirts; it was the only way to keep her hands from snaking out and pulling Spencer to her side.

"Yes, right there. Oh, I thought . . ." Aunt Phyllis's smile wilted slightly when Lord Bobbington sat next to Vivian. "Wouldn't you like to exchange seats, my lord? With your friend? Give you a chance to converse with my niece."

"Thank you, Mrs. Reeves, but I am quite comfortable." Lord Bobbington rose slightly, swished his coattails to the side, and reperched on the chair next to the object of his affection. "I am sure I will be able to entertain Miss Pyebald adequately."

"Yes, of course," came the sour reply. The woman leaned forward and scowled at Juliana, as if the poor seating arrangement were somehow her fault.

Spencer had hovered, waiting politely for everyone to settle. He smiled broadly when it became apparent that he would be keeping company with Juliana. She was very pleased to see him wink.

They were sitting in a line, rather than a group, facing the musicians. Aunt Phyllis had secured the chairs closest to the aisle for herself and Lady Pyebald, to assault passersby, of course. The girls sat beside them and, naturally, Juliana was on the outside edge of their party. Lord Pyebald and his son were not with them as the men had already found the card room, and Mr. Reeves had stayed at home with his book.

It had taken a good part of the afternoon for the grand dames to decide on this perfectly obvious seating arrangement, and Bobbington had just ruined it in mere seconds. Juliana was most delighted.

After all her aunt's stipulations, the one that she could blithely ignore now was the one directing her to refrain from engaging Mr. Northam. To do so while seated next to him would be most uncomfortable for the poor man and downright rude. Juliana would not want to be accused of that.

To make matters worse, in the eyes of her chaperone, not many bachelors were in attendance of this evening's recital. It increased the value of these two gentlemen's presence in their group immensely. But then to have one of the gentlemen wasted on Juliana . . . yes, indeed, this was already shaping up to be a most enjoyable night. No wonder Aunt Phyllis looked so displeased.

The hall of the Strath town house was comfortably large for

a gathering such as this, with a vaulted ceiling and long, heavily draped windows. Wrought-iron floor candelabras had been placed at appropriate intervals between the rows of temporary seats and near the makeshift stage. Thankfully, the Strath recital was not a crowded affair, although it was well attended.

The guests had greeted their host and hostess at the entry and now gathered in their own little cliques about the room. The confusing sound of happy chatter was interspersed with the occasional burst of laughter. The ladies' gowns were grand, elegant affairs with high waists in varying shades of blush, jonquil, and willow-green silk. The men were resplendent in their starched, high neckcloths and colorful waistcoats. It was a room of hushed beauty as they waited with anticipation for the soprano to arrive.

"And how was *Hamlet*?" Spencer asked lightly, after they had finished with the required banal discussion of the weather and the possibility of rain. There was a slight shadow about his eyes that Juliana did not quite understand.

"We did not attend," Juliana replied. "We spent a quiet evening in."

"It wasn't really Juliana's fault." Carrie, who had meandered down the line to hover in front of Spencer, immediately rose to her cousin's defense. "She simply went shopping and—"

"Carrie, dear," her mother called with sweet acidity. "We agreed not to bring that up."

"Sorry, Mama," Carrie called back. She dropped her voice. "I didn't know she could hear me," she said to Juliana.

"Your mother has been gifted with excellent hearing," Juliana said with mock seriousness.

Beside her, Spencer choked slightly and then coughed.

Juliana looked up at Carrie, noticing that her eyebrows were doing acrobatics across her face. She was definitely trying to signal Juliana, but about what she hadn't the faintest idea. "Whatever are you doing, goose?"

Carrie sighed. "Mama thought you might like to switch seats with Vivian. The view is better."

"No, thank you. I am fine."

"Juliana, Mama thinks—"

"Oh, excuse me, Miss Reeves. How remiss of me. I cannot believe I am that obtuse. You wish to view the stage from here. I shall move directly."

"No, no." Carrie glanced sharply at her mother and then back. "No, Mr. Northam, I did not mean to make *you* move. I—"

"Miss Telford, would it be too much to ask if you might take the next seat down? And, let me see, yes, I will move and, voila, all is settled."

Juliana noted that Spencer had maneuvered Carrie so that Lord Bobbington was to her left while he sat on the right. Clever man.

"Did you enjoy *Hamlet*?" Juliana asked, returning to the

subject of their conversation before the seat rearrangement. "For I believe you expressed a desire to go as well."

"We went but didn't see a thing." This time it was Bobbington who answered. He had turned in their direction.

Juliana knew that Vivian would not be giving the young lord much encouragement. Lady Pyebald had struck his name from her possible-match list just today, upon learning of his inadequate funds. Poor man. Matchmaking really was a business.

"How is it that you went to the play but didn't see it?" Carrie laughed slightly.

"Because this . . ." Bobbington lifted his hand but then glanced at his friend and dropped it. "The crowd was rowdy, couldn't hear a blessed thing. We are going back, though, May Day."

"May Day? What a coincidence. We are, too. Mr. Pyebald got the tickets yesterday. Aren't we, Juliana?"

"Yes, what a coincidence." Juliana frowned, remembering Spencer's comment in the park. "May Day."

"Yes, and we shall not let Juliana go shopping for ribbons that afternoon," Carrie needlessly reassured the company, forgetting—yet again—that the subject had been banned.

"Ribbons?" Bobbington asked Carrie.

"Oh yes, they were a perfect match, which, as you know, is so important." Carrie proceeded to explain to him all about the significance of matching a ribbon to a dress, hat, and reticule.

"Ribbons?" Spencer echoed his friend's query with a lot more skepticism.

Juliana dropped her voice, keeping their conversation private. "Yes, that and . . ." She hesitated for a moment.

Spencer was not family; he would not ridicule or mock her determination to find a publisher for her research. And Spencer was no longer the stranger on the cliff with no business in her affairs; they were friends. Friends talked openly, shared worries and concerns. Friends didn't keep secrets; well, not ones such as these. Friends confided in one another, especially when one needed moral support . . . or an inside edge. "I visited a few printers as well. Do you have any influence in that industry, Mr. Northam? Do you know any publishers?"

"No, I am sorry, I do not."

Spencer didn't look sorry. In fact, he had started to smile as soon as she had brought up the subject. It was almost as if he thought her words in jest.

"I am looking to have my research published," she said in a very serious tone.

"Oh yes, you told me about the study of the lady beetle." Spencer nodded; his expression lost the hint of amusement. "A worthy natural history subject, I am very certain."

"Exactly. Though it appears that the process is not going to be as easy as I had thought—"

"Juliana, let Vivian tell Mr. Northam of her day today," Aunt Phyllis interrupted.

"Yes, Aunt." Juliana lifted her eyebrows and shoulders.

Spencer turned dutifully toward Vivian—leaning forward to bypass Carrie and Lord Bobbington. "What is it that you were about earlier, Miss Pyebald?"

Vivian giggled. Not really a pleasant sight, or sound, but then perhaps such girly antics only worked on the male species. As for the eye batting—well, that looked as if she were suffering an affliction, and yet Spencer continued to converse as if there were nothing untoward about Vivian's behavior.

Juliana sat waiting patiently for Spencer to complete his duty and turn back to her. She was quite secure in the fact that he would. He might be playing a role for the sake of helping Bobbington, but Juliana knew that his enjoyment of her company was genuine. She didn't read anything into it. Or at least she tried not to, but it didn't matter right now. For she knew that the man she admired most in the world admired her. It was in his eyes.

It really was a nice evening.

CHAPTER
12

In which there is much contemplation over
Lord Bobbington's campaign to win his fair Vivian
and Mr. Northam is subjected to the awkwardness
of a fainting young lady

SPENCER WAS THOROUGHLY DISTRACTED. Had Lord
Winfrith not followed the male Pyebalds into the card
room, he could even have been accused of dereliction of duty.
It had nothing to do with the cultured ambience of the hall or
the crystal clear range of the soprano, for both hovered somewhere in the background of his awareness. No, his mind was
totally occupied by, every sense conscious of, the proximity of
Juliana Telford.

The chairs upon which they were seated were the height of
elegance and consequently rather diminutive in size. One only
just fit, even at a perch. And Lady Strath, in her infinite wisdom, had seen said chairs placed in fairly close proximity to one
another in order to allow as many guests an unobstructed a view

as possible. That placed Juliana's skirts, thin delicate clinging skirts, mere inches from him. In fact, when he shifted, as he often felt the need, their knees touched. He could almost feel the warmth of her person. Her rose scent filled his nostrils. His eyes could not help but travel from her profile to the slow rise and fall of her bosom. Never had he seen anything so delectable. He had to remind himself to swallow.

Somewhere in the back of Spencer's mind he was aware that Miss Reeves was near as well. But it hardly mattered, so tightly was he strung over the way in which Juliana moved, gestured, laughed, tapped her fingers, listened, and clapped.

Yes, everyone was clapping. Spencer joined in with enthusiasm. At last the intermission had arrived and he could stare at Juliana in truth instead of glancing at her surreptitiously.

After sharing praise for the talents of the musicians, Carrie stood and made her way down the aisle. Bobbington followed.

Spencer neither knew nor cared where it was that others were convening. Juliana hadn't moved, so neither would he.

They stared at each other for hours or a moment or two. When she finally spoke, her tone was light and airy. It alluded to none of the thick emotions that swirled around them.

"I must tell you, sir, or perhaps it would be best in the form of a warning." Juliana leaned back to catch sight of the watchful pair standing at the end of the aisle. "The mamas have bandied your name about as a possible match with one of the young ladies of our party."

"Yourself?"

She sat forward again and laughed as she did so. It was a musical cascade.

"No, indeed, not. I am not at the forefront of their consideration."

"You might mention that I have no title."

"I believe it is your large estate that is drawing their interest."

"Ah, yes, I should have guessed. Have you hinted that I might not be amenable to marriage?"

"I am not sure that would sit well, being that you are spending so much time conversing with me. It would, rightly so, cause them to wonder about your purpose if it is not for matrimony."

"Ah, yes, excellent point."

"That in mind, you might consider limiting our encounters. Perhaps only for a week or two." Her tone was light, but her eyes pleaded with him to deny her.

Spencer found himself almost sinking into the deep pools of her eyes. He forced himself to look away, but when he did so, he encountered her lips. That increased his discomfort, for now he had to fight a sudden urge to pull her into his arms. Spencer yearned to experience the kiss that had not happened on the night of the ball.

Enough. Spencer gave himself a mental shake. He unclenched his taut hands and ordered his pulse to a less riotous pace. It wasn't easy, but he concentrated on the cacophony of voices that surrounded them as well as the bursts of laughter throughout the room. Another deep breath and then he could see properly again.

Spencer straightened and glanced around, nodding to the grand dames, who were watching him so closely. He had not needed Juliana's warning; it was almost comical in its obviousness.

"We should probably . . ." She didn't bother finishing her sentence. They both knew that they could not remain seated too much longer without being noticed by those other than the family. She sighed. "Duty calls."

Juliana rose, nodded, and gracefully wended her way through the chairs toward the female members of her party. She left a vast emptiness in her wake. Her slight stumble at the end of the aisle produced an indulgent smile on Spencer's lips. It brought his attention back to her character and away from the delights of her body. He chuckled softly to himself, and then he, too, rose. He went in search of Winfrith. He had only a few moments before the music would resume and he could once again feel the proximity of Miss Juliana Telford.

❦❦❦

JULIANA WAS LOATH TO BRING UP THE SUBJECT. She sat with the appearance of calm, listening to not a single note of the soprano's second selection of arias. She knew that it was not fair to allow both Bobbington to hope and Spencer to pay court on false pretenses. She had to say something. She had already stated that it might be in Spencer's best matrimonial interest, or lack thereof, to give her company a wider berth, well away from the machinations of Vivian. Thankfully, his expression illustrated just how seriously he took those warnings.

However, this was another matter. This ate at the very heart, the very purpose of his attentions to her. Once spoken, the words could not be withdrawn. She had to tell him that Bobbington had no chance of securing Vivian's affection.

Not only was this going to break Bobbington's heart, but it would also end their lovely charade. Rather effectively. Spencer would look to his other diversions in Town. She would no longer be able to bask in the warmth of his gaze. He would be otherwise occupied.

She glanced at Spencer beside her and was surprised to see that he was already looking her way. His stare was deep and intense, and she was acutely aware of their touching knees. She swallowed.

She would tell him tomorrow.

As it was, Juliana could not tell Spencer anything the next day; the crush at the Rafferty assembly curtailed any attempt at a private conversation. Significant glances were their only means of private discourse, and when Juliana observed the smirk on Bobbington's face, she wondered just how veiled those glances were. Still, the appropriate time to discuss the end of their little conspiracy evaded them.

The same could be said of the Gareth levee. At least that was the excuse Juliana gave herself. It was a trial—not that she felt any true rush to disclose Bobbington's lost campaign, but that Spencer could be so near to her and yet . . . far enough to prevent the least touch, inadvertent touch, of course. No, that was not what she meant . . . she meant conversation—yes, that was it. He was quite near, and yet discussion was impossible.

So distracted by these touching and conversing thoughts, Juliana was surprised and rather pleased when Spencer left his clutch of gentleman companions by the French doors and came rushing over to the ladies lounging on the sofas by the fireplace. However, his face bore a strange expression, and his focus was on her lips.

Only then did Juliana realize that she was the one leading the conversation. And, as she listened to the words spilling out of her mouth, she realized—with some horror—that she had fallen back on a subject that she knew all too well—but that had no place in a circle of gossipy ladies. "The larval stage lasts between twenty and thirty days, which is followed by the pupa—"

"So, Mrs. Gareth, how did you find Brighton this winter past?"

There was a brief silence—in which the word *bluestocking* was whispered into the ether—and then Mrs. Gareth blinked away her shock and answered Spencer with an anecdote pertaining to a windy day and a lost bonnet. Soon, the conversation was flowing again and Juliana smiled her thanks to Spencer.

Unfortunately, he remained only a moment more to ensure that conviviality had been restored, and then he returned to the gentlemen and their important discussion of smuggled French brandy.

It wasn't until the card party at the Maynard town house that Juliana found herself away from prying ears and able at last to address the sorry outcome to Bobbington's affection. It seemed that providence had its own timetable.

"It would appear that our matchmaking efforts have been for naught, Miss Telford," Spencer stated solemnly.

Juliana was standing between the deep-silled windows of the Maynard drawing room, watching the various games in progress. She had been playing a lifeless game of whist just moments earlier, when Bobbington had offered to replace her. Carrie had replaced Spencer at his table just moments before, and it left the two spares the opportunity to converse quietly without drawing anyone's notice.

"Yes, I am afraid it is all too true." Juliana turned to face the room as he was doing, keeping her voice low. "I am so sorry. Will Bobbington be grievously injured?"

They both glanced in the direction of Bobbington's table. He was laughing and joking with Lady Pyebald. He looked comfortable and not at all discontented that his Vivian was casting cow eyes at Spencer from two tables away.

"Somehow, I think he will survive."

"It is so hard to tell who is best suited for whom."

"Well, I am not certain your aunt or Lady Pyebald would agree. I wouldn't be surprised if they could tell you exactly who would match."

"Yes, but their standards are all based on money and title, not an ounce of consideration for character or compatibility."

"Are you saying that were all thoughts of finances and social standing subtracted from the equation, Bobbington and Miss Pyebald would be well matched?"

"Oh dear, no. I actually do not think they are a well-matched pair at all. My disappointment is merely for his sake. I would see him married to a more pliable woman. For all her light, airy looks, Vivian has a very strong will and would ride roughshod over Bobbington for the rest of his life."

"You sound almost wistful, Miss Telford. Tell me: Has your Season, with all its concentration on matrimony, changed your view on the subject?"

"Well, perhaps slightly, but not in the manner you mean."

"Oh." Spencer turned to her with his brows lifted. "What is it I mean?"

"You mean has all this talk caught me, pulled me into the vortex, and persuaded me to long for a suitor of my own."

"Is that what I meant?"

"Yes, indeed, and my answer to that is no. But . . ."

"But?"

"But my Season has helped me see a less jaundiced view of marriage. For instance, the Morleys sitting—Mr. Northam,

I am trying to explain, and if you would stop staring at me and look to the far table—thank you. Now, as I was saying . . . it is couples like the Morleys that have changed my mind. They were telling me earlier that they have been married thirty-five years. Isn't that marvelous? Not for the number of years, so much as the way they keep—there you see. Mr. Morley just winked at his wife, and she touched his sleeve. They care greatly for each other."

"Perhaps they are cheating at the game, the wink and touch are merely codes."

"Hardly, they are losing, and laughing as they do so."

"It might all be an act."

Juliana laughed. "They are not the only couple I have noticed. Did you not observe the closeness of the Straths and the Drakes? Yes, happy, loving couples such as these have convinced me that there is something to be said for this thing called marriage."

"Aha, so you have changed your mind."

"Only in that I understand its worth, whereas I didn't before."

"So this understanding, it has not led you to plans of your own? Have you met no lord on whom you want to ply your wiles? Your heart is not lost on some witless puppy?"

"No, no plans." She tried to ignore his reference to a lost heart, but her mouth betrayed her. "There is, however, one man who has helped me appreciate the heady emotions behind a possible love match." Juliana watched as Spencer turned his head with deliberate slowness back to face her. She wondered just how far this playful banter was going to go. Her heart was thrumming its rhythm in her ears.

"Anyone I know?"

"I think you might know him, well enough."

"A good man?"

"Would I admire a man who was not?"

"He might be deceiving you."

"I think not."

"Would it matter?"

Juliana frowned and tilted her head sideways. She wasn't sure she liked the direction the conversation had taken. "It would depend, would it not? On the deception."

"Such as."

"If the gentleman always wore a hat because he was bald, it would be a forgivable deception."

"What if it were more serious than that?"

Juliana swallowed; she felt very uncomfortable. She could no longer read Spencer's expression, but it was not relaxed. "It matters little. I am still convinced that marriage is not for me. Devoted to my research, as you know." Best to change the subject. "Are you looking forward to tomorrow's play?"

"Yes, indeed." Spencer looked relieved and almost appreciative of the change. "I am expecting it to be a most entertaining night."

"We are to have a box."

A burst of bawdy laughter erupted at Maxwell Pyebald's table. Juliana and Spencer turned to find the man's eyes upon them. She felt Spencer stiffen.

"Indeed. I forgot to inquire of my man where we are placed. However, it matters not. I am sure you will be easy to spot."

"Mr. Northam, I thought we agreed that it was pointless to place Bobbington in Vivian's path. You need not seek us, or me, out any longer. The game cannot be won."

"Some games are worth more in the playing than in the winning."

As they stared at each other, lost in the heady emotions that accompanied such delicious scrutiny, a swish of skirts alerted them to an approaching lady.

"Juliana, be a dear and let me near the window. The heat of the fire is going to my head." Vivian maneuvered herself in between the couple, leaning in Spencer's direction. "I will be so glad, won't you, Mr. Northam, for the truly fine weather of summer, when we can laze about out of doors in the fresh air."

Juliana pulled her scarf more fully around her shoulders to stave off the chill in the room. She looked at Spencer over Vivian's head with a raised eyebrow. There were four windows in the ornately carved room, none of which were open as it was dreary and damp outside. The coal basket in the fireplace had long since reached its peak and was providing limp heat. Vivian's ploy was as transparent as—.

"Oh dear." Vivian suddenly grabbed at Spencer's arm and then collapsed. As expected, the gentleman caught the fainting figure before she suffered the indignity of crumpling to the floor.

Juliana shook her head while Spencer looked decidedly uncomfortable, holding the swooning beauty awkwardly. His jaw tightened, and a hard look stole into his eyes.

"Here, let me help." Juliana reached for Vivian under her arms, lifting the girl's weight off Spencer. "Aunt Phyllis, might I trouble you for assistance," she called over her shoulder.

The sound of a chair scraping back almost eclipsed the protests of the quickly recovering girl. "No, no, I'm fine. Let go." Vivian straightened and yanked her arms from Juliana's hold. "Feeling much better, in fact." She smiled up at Spencer, batting her eyelashes, and leaned closer to him yet again. "Want to take a turn around the room, Mr. Northam?"

Fortunately, Spencer was saved from responding by the ill-timed arrival of Aunt Phyllis. "Is anything amiss, girls?"

"No," Vivian snapped without looking away from the gentleman in her clutches. "What say you, Mr. Northam? A turn around the room?"

Spencer bowed with elegant grace. "Thank you for the offer, Miss Pyebald. However, I agree that the sultriness here is unbearable, so I shall bid you farewell." He lifted his eyes to those of Juliana's. "And I look forward to our next meeting."

The message was so blatant and so flattering that Juliana

could blithely ignore the many aspersions tossed at her head for the remainder of the evening.

⁕⁂⁕

"LAMAR STAMFORD HAS THE REPUTATION OF A SCAPEGRACE, particularly in Lambhurst. Runs with a pack of wild unlicked cubs. Shockingly loose in the haft."

Spencer leaned back against the black leather cushion of the covered landau. Winfrith and Bibury sat across from him, their backs to the horses. As the coachman negotiated the crowded London streets, the vehicle rocked and bumped across the uneven roads. The sharp clop of hooves on cobblestone was muffled inside the carriage, although the smell of horse was unmistakable.

They were headed toward Catherine Street and the Theatre Royal Drury Lane without Bobbington. Conveniently, the fellow had felt a pressing need to visit the tailor and his club that afternoon, and the men had agreed to meet him. It gave Spencer the chance to exchange information with his mentors, put forward theories, and finalize plans without having to invent an excuse for Bobbington's sake.

"Still, the two families were in close society until recently," Bibury continued. "There appears to have been a major falling out, as you saw at the ball."

"Yes, I think a good many people observed that altercation.

If this wastrel were privy to the communiqués, I cannot see that Lord Pyebald would make such a display of throwing the fellow out."

"Perhaps it was an act, designed to redirect anyone who might be watching." The skepticism in Winfrith's voice showed that while he had put the theory forward, he was not at all convinced of it.

Spencer shook his head. "No, I think not. The man was out of sorts for the remainder of the evening. Too elaborate a ruse for a man such as he." He pulled off his top hat and dropped it onto the empty seat beside him. "No, I thought there might have been a connection, but it seems I was taking a side step. Besides, he has no tie with the War Office and its army dealings."

"Actually, he does."

Both Winfrith and Spencer turned sharply to Bibury as he spoke. "Hart."

"Lord William Hart? Assistant to the undersecretary of state for war and the colonies?" Spencer asked.

"Yes, but not directly. Through his son. Milton Hart."

Winfrith nodded. "Yes, right. We saw them together at Brooks's, remember, Northam? Hart was bragging about his new horses. Yes, that is it, came into some money recently, as I recall. That could be it."

"But it makes no sense. While I agree young Hart might have access to information through his father, and it would be an easy matter to pass it all onto Stamford, there it ends. Stamford and Pyebald are not talking. Why would they quarrel when such large stakes were at risk?"

"And likely large sums. No honor among thieves. Perhaps they had a falling out over the payment."

"Perhaps. But this is becoming too convoluted. If Lord Pyebald and his son wanted to exchange information with this wastrel, they would invite their country neighbor for a visit. No one would wonder about its purpose. Or they could simply meet at Brooks's or White's; even the Hells would cover their actions. They certainly wouldn't take pains to appear to be at odds. And they certainly wouldn't set up a public meeting at a play." Spencer absentmindedly flicked at his hat, almost sending it over the cushion's edge and onto the floor. "No, there must be a reason why these parties had to wait to meet."

"Perhaps our traitor is so well placed that a meeting with undistinguished peers—such as Lord Pyebald and Maxwell Pyebald—would bring about comment, no matter where it occurred," Bibury suggested.

"Like who?"

"I couldn't say. It is just a theory."

"Do we know if anyone of importance is coming this evening?"

Both Bibury and Winfrith looked uncomfortable.

"Well, we will know soon enough." Spencer leaned forward to look out the carriage window. "It appears we are almost there."

The rest of the journey was less about theories and more about positioning, guarding, and watching. This was going to be their best, if not only, chance to see who it was that jeopardized the security of England.

JULIANA KNEW SHE WAS NAIVE AND UNWORLDLY, but she was not obtuse. Something was amiss. She felt it.

Since early afternoon there had been a tension in the town house of an unexplainable nature. Juliana had heard the mutterings of a heated discussion between Vivian and her mother, a sharp unwarranted set-down from Lord Pyebald to Maxwell, and plaintive pleas from Carrie to Vivian. All out of the ordinary and all destined to burst the bubble of euphoria that Juliana was trying to maintain. It was Carrie who brought her resoundingly down to earth.

Juliana had chosen her cream-and-blue satin evening gown for the occasion. Its square, low neckline was elaborately decorated with lace, and the cut of the high waist and flowing overskirt flattered her figure, with little subtlety. It was one of her aunt's least favorites, but Juliana thought Spencer might feel otherwise.

When Carrie burst through the door of Juliana's bedchamber, her cousin was wearing an exquisite ivory dress that put Juliana's to shame. But it was not the comparison of gowns that brought trepidation to Juliana's mind but the cloud upon Carrie's face.

"Is something bothering you, dear?"

"Well, you might ask, Juliana. My frustration is at a height that even I thought unattainable. There are times when I truly do not understand her." Carrie flounced to the mirror, stepped in front of Juliana to view her gown, and did not notice that her pout spoiled her pretty looks.

"Has Vivian borrowed your favorite shawl, lost your novel, or ruined your gloves?"

"No, no, and no. Those are such trivialities in comparison."

Juliana was about to dismiss the tirade when Carrie continued.

"She is going to steal your favorite."

"My favorite what?"

"Suitor."

"I don't have a suitor, goose."

"Of course you do. I speak of Mr. Northam."

Juliana did her best to hide the start that Carrie's words had given her. "I do not know what you mean."

Carrie snapped around to look her straight in the eye. "Juliana Rosamond Telford, I have been watching you and Mr. Northam since the Strath recital. You told me you would not have Mr. Pyebald, and I believed you. So I knew there had to be another."

Juliana could not help herself; she smiled. Carrie was such a romantic. "Really, Carrie dear, Mr. Northam and I are simply friends."

"Friends do not look at each other as you two do."

"What has all this to do with Vivian?"

Carrie sighed, "I tried . . . on your behalf. I even begged her not to."

"What, Carrie, what?"

"She means to try again—to gain his interest. She is determined to have him as a suitor. Not that she is in love. Oh, no. She says she needs a handsome young man to hang about, to make a cake of himself, to catch the eye of those with titles and larger fortunes. She has decided that Mr. Northam will do nicely. She does not care that you have developed an attachment to him."

"Carrie."

"I tried, really I did." The pretty doll slumped her shoulders and looked thoroughly dejected.

"Carrie, you goose. All this fuss and worry for nothing. Mr. Northam is not an inexperienced child; he will not be led astray by the amateur maneuverings of a chit." Juliana lifted Carrie's chin and then kissed her on both cheeks. "But I cannot tell you how pleased I am that you came to my defense. Now, be off with you. I must complete my preparations. I will be down directly."

Juliana swiped at Carrie's backside, intentionally missing. Carrie skipped out the door a much happier girl than the one who had entered.

Unfortunately, she left behind a troubled cousin. Juliana's thoughts were no longer focused on the disquiet in the household but the significance of being at *Hamlet* today. Why had Spencer mentioned deceit at the card party? Why did he still want her company when she had told him that their goal was unachievable? Did he really admire her as much as his eyes said?

Not long after she had joined the others in the carriage, Juliana added another query to her list. How much longer was she going to have to sit in this silent, tense coach before she saw his handsome, relaxed face again?

⁕

SPENCER RECOGNIZED JULIANA'S COACH THE MOMENT it pulled to the side of the street. The covered landau disgorged its three passengers into the crowds that were standing under the portico of the Drury's main entrance. Spencer watched as the cocksure Pyebald offered her his arm and was happy to witness the snub as Juliana placed her arm atop that of her uncle. The pair stepped aside to await the next coach, using the milling bodies of strangers as an excuse to ignore Pyebald—politely.

Spencer was snickering when Bobbington found him.

"What are you doing back there, my friend, chortling to yourself?"

Spencer stepped out from behind the column and into the lantern light. "I thought we were to meet in the vestibule."

"Yes, so did I." Bobbington turned at the sound of a familiar laugh.

They both saw that the second coach had arrived. Miss

Reeves was the first to be handed out by the liveried footman. She laughed at Mr. Pyebald's offered arm, waving it off, and waited for her mother's descent. As soon as the lady had climbed down from the carriage, Miss Reeves lifted her skirts, as did her mother, and they paraded into the building behind Mr. Reeves and Juliana. Pyebald rushed ahead, to be a gallant at the door. Lady Pyebald and Miss Pyebald followed in their wake, greeting and nodding at as many peers as possible in a short space of time. Lord Pyebald followed, ignoring everyone.

"Shall we?" Bobbington swept his arm toward the door, and they filed into the large, noisy vestibule behind a tall lady with an even taller ostrich-plume headband and a jowly gentleman with a dangling quizzing glass. The entrance was overflowing with conversation, elegant gowns, and smartly cut dress coats—patrons of the arts of every size and shape and social position.

Spencer watched Juliana's party slowly make its way toward the left side of the double staircase. He purposefully led Bobbington to the right. It gave him a better vantage point. He saw that Winfrith was not far behind their quarry and that Bibury was watching from above.

Scanning the crowd as he ascended, Spencer noticed a rather animated group of young bucks laughing uproariously and generally making cakes of themselves; they were in complete oblivion to the delicate sensibilities of those standing next to them. Spencer was not surprised to see Lamar Stamford enfolded in their ranks. Nor was he surprised to see the young man's eye staring in the direction of the Pyebalds.

Finally, the great moving mass entered the striking domed Corinthian rotunda of the Theatre Royal Drury Lane.

"I see we are in good company this evening," Bobbington commented as they headed toward the stairs leading to their box. He nodded in the opposite direction to a group of somber-faced politicians and their ladies.

Robert Stewart, Lord Castlereagh, stood talking intently with a man whose face was hidden, at first, from Spencer. He tried not to stare, but curiosity held his eyes in place a little longer than customary. Bobbington must have noticed.

"It's Frederick Robinson, Viscount Goderich," he said. His tone was almost bored.

Spencer nodded without comment. He caught Winfrith's eye and nodded in the direction of the Foreign Secretary and the Junior Lord of the Treasury. He doubted that either was in cahoots with the Pyebalds, for both were well-respected men; however, the theory of a high-level traitor had been put forward, and it had to be explored.

The two friends continued to nod their way to their box with no conversation between them and little more than pleas-antries shared with the other beautiful people of the Ton. Spencer was surprised when Bobbington showed that he had a few acquaintances in the less illustrious ranks. The fellow had stopped to chat with a short man in a barely adequate topcoat and poorly tied neckcloth. An unanimated, red-haired man with a droopy mustache stood next to him.

Spencer snorted and shook his head. He continued to the box, leaving Bobbington to come at his own pace.

Spencer stepped through the curtains of the reserved box and was eminently pleased with the view. Not of the stage, naturally, but of the audience. He could easily see into the three tiers of balconies and boxes facing the stage. His last visit had required a great deal of neck craning into the higher boxes, but this time his man had found seats in the middle tier. Spencer could see into all but a few if he stood to the front of the box. And he could see down into the stalls if he just leaned a little across the railing.

Yes, excellent view. He would have liked it if the candelabras had been placed slightly lower, thereby casting fewer shadows, but Benjamin Wyatt had not consulted him when the theater had been rebuilt last year. And surveillance was not likely one of his considerations.

Bibury had taken a position opposite and should be able to see the remainder of the audience. Winfrith would remain mobile to wait for movement of the suspected parties.

Excellent.

As he continued to scan the audience, Spencer raised his eyes to an angled box on his left. Within its enclosure, Juliana waited, looking radiant, innocent, and extremely alluring. The Pyebald and Reeves families were there, too, and as much as Spencer knew his concentration should be on the Pyebald men, he found it difficult to look away from the pert figure. A pearl among . . . he smiled and left the adage incomplete.

There seemed to be a discussion about seating as he watched Juliana shift twice before settling her skirts. She really was quite lovely and fresh. Then she looked over and caught his eye. Her smile was dazzling and without artifice.

"I have a rather strange request of you, my friend." Bobbington had finally joined him in the box and at the rail.

Spencer turned a furrowed brow to Bobbington. However, the man was not looking at him but into the box of the Pyebalds, just as Spencer had been doing. The expression chiseled on his face was more serious than Spencer had ever seen on his friend before.

"Is something amiss?"

"No, not as yet. However, if there is a to-do this evening, a commotion of some sort that involves the Pyebalds, could you quickly and quietly escort the ladies—"

"What are you on about, Bobbington? What have you gotten yourself into?"

Finally, Bobbington met Spencer's questioning gaze.

"I'd rather not explain right now, but if you could just—"

"No. I will not just anything. You cannot ask it of me without some sort of explanation."

Bobbington sighed and bit his lip. "Why can you not simply do as I ask?"

Spencer's heartbeat had started a steady escalation. "Bobbington, what is going to happen this evening?"

Bobbington pulled Spencer to the back of the box and lowered his voice to a whisper. "We believe that there is going to be a transfer of money or information by a large smuggling organization that we have been following."

"What! Who is we?"

"The Home Office."

"You work with the Home Office? In what capacity? The Home Office deals with domestic problems not—oh, yes. Free-traders. That's it; you are chasing smugglers. Lawks, why didn't you say so earlier?"

"Because it is nothing to you. I only mention it now as I know you have feelings for Miss Telford. I do not want her or Miss Reeves to get caught up in the wave of scandal that will likely ensue. The Pyebalds are in too deep—"

"Tell me you are not planning to arrest Lord Pyebald."

"We are hoping to catch the man he is meeting and then—"

"No." Spencer's voice was sharp and barely above a whisper, but Bobbington recognized the desperation.

"I am sorry, Northam, but—"

"You cannot do this, Bobbington. It is now my turn to impose upon our friendship and beg you to call off your men." He looked quickly to the stage and saw that they were getting ever closer to the opening act. They needed to be in their seats by then or they would attract notice. "I have been working for over four months to put misinformation in the hands of the French. Vital misdirection to help our war efforts! I need the Pyebalds free and ignorant if this scheme is to work. Call off your men, or better yet add their eyes to ours, and we are sure to catch the traitor."

Bobbington stared at him for some moments. "I have men in the stalls." He swallowed hard. "You get to Banks, he's in the back, red hair and mustache. I will reach Richards. And I want answers when we get back."

"As do I."

Bobbington slipped through the back curtain of the box, followed immediately by Spencer. They were racing against time.

CHAPTER

13

*In which a sedate evening at the theater
is full of revelations*

SPENCER THUNDERED DOWN THE STAIRS BUT caught himself at the bottom. Running into the stalls would attract more attention than not being in his seat. Fortunately, the staircase had been empty, and when he emerged from the stairwell, with no apparent haste, the heads that turned in his direction were only mildly interested.

He nodded to a couple seated in the closest row and casually sauntered to where Banks was watching him. Spencer offered his hand. In quiet conversation, he did not greet the man with social niceties—as anyone watching would assume—but quickly informed the man of the change of plans and enlisted his help. Banks looked over Spencer's shoulder to Bobbington, who was on the other side of the theater talking just as casually to Richards. The nod between them was barely perceptible.

Bobbington smiled an amiable dismissal to Richards and then sauntered over to the stairwell, where Spencer met him.

"I believe the curtain is about to rise." Spencer could not keep the tension totally from his voice. They both turned toward the stage, ostensibly to gauge the opening of the evening's entertainment while in fact they were assessing the repositioning of the men. For the first time that evening, Spencer felt that success might be at hand. Six pairs of eyes would definitely see the job done.

Both men casually entered the stairwell, rushed up the steps two at a time, ran down the deserted inner hall to their box, and arrived just as another figure approached with haste from the opposite direction. He was a portly man with a sprinkling of gray in his side-whiskers and a friendly expression plastered on his face.

"Northam, Bobbington," Winfrith greeted them cheerfully with a voice that was slightly breathless and unusually high. "So good to see you." He held out his hand toward Bobbington.

Spencer glanced around; the hall was empty of patrons. They could talk without the chance of being overheard.

Winfrith waited for Spencer's nod before he spoke quickly and quietly. "Just bumped into Lord Ash, my counterpart at the Home Office. It would appear that we have a disaster in the making. Bobbington, you must call off your men—"

"We are ahead of you, Winfrith. Banks and Richards have been ordered to observe, not to arrest. And . . ." Spencer heard the loud squeak as the wheels that drew up the stage curtain began to move. "We had better get to our seats. Did you apprise Lord Ash as to what we were about?"

"Yes, indeed. And I recommend doing the same with Bobbington before there are any more oversights." His voice lowered until it was all but a mutter, and Spencer had to strain to hear. "There should have been a sharing of information long before this. Could have worked together. Bloody incompetence." Winfrith shook his head, rolled his eyes, and then smoothed the furrow on his brow. He plastered his smile back on his face, straightened his shoulders, and marched off.

Spencer and Bobbington entered the box just in time to see the thick red velvet curtain reach its zenith. Spencer nonchalantly swept his tails out from under as he slowly sat down in the plush chair with deliberate ease. He positioned himself so that he could view the stage and the Pyebald box without turning his head. He noted that Bobbington had done the same.

Spencer was conscious of Juliana's fascinated stare directed solely toward the stage. She seemed unaware of his return.

"Now, I believe we need to get things straight," Spencer said as the last of the applause for the entering actors died away. He kept his voice very low, and his lips hardly moved.

"I will allow you the honor of going first. After all, I have just pulled my men from a case that was weeks in the making. I need reassurance that I did so wisely."

Spencer almost smiled, but months of practice kept his lips from curling. "It was in the best interest of the country."

"So you said, but I would appreciate some details."

The audience laughed, and Spencer did, too. Bobbington nodded and grinned. Neither had any idea what had caused the hilarity, but it hardly mattered. They only had to appear as if they were attending.

Spencer began to recount the evolution of his assignment, starting with his trip to France. He described how he had infiltrated the lair of their enemies and eventually gained access to a communiqué being sent to England. The original message had come from one of Napoleon's lieutenants waiting in Erfurt. Spencer explained how he had embellished the vague request, seeking more specific information regarding troop movements and giving it a sense of urgency. He wanted to track the communiqué quickly and feed erroneous facts to the traitor at the other end. The misinformation had to reach Napoleon before the French marched on Leipzig.

Spencer had accompanied the messenger overland but had then been forced—by a suspicious captain—to find his own way across the Channel. Fortunately, the drunken, distrusting fool had already divulged the landing point in England, as well as the approximate length of the journey. It had not been hard to secure a boat that allowed him to beat the slow scow and be lying in wait for the smugglers to arrive at St. Ives Head. Spencer's distrust of the Pyebalds had begun not long after.

Spencer glanced sideways at his friend. Bobbington's expression hadn't changed. "I am afraid there is no doubt that the family is involved."

"I knew as much." Bobbington lifted his chin and smirked, albeit in the direction of the stage. "That is why I developed such a devotion to Miss Pyebald."

Spencer was nonplussed. "It was an act? For my benefit?"

"Yes, indeed, how else could I explain my interest without divulging my assignment? Rumors of the Pyebalds' involvement in smuggling had been circulating for some time. This looked to be a perfect opportunity to catch them, and then you showed up on my doorstep . . . well, I thought I had no choice."

Spencer snorted. "Well done, my friend; you had me completely taken in. I did not twig to your may game at all."

"Well, the compliment can be returned, for I had no idea that you were with the War Office. But now that I think about it, it makes perfect sense. Yes, perfect sense."

Both were silent for a moment.

Bobbington's train of thought was obviously running in the same direction as Spencer's when he finally stated. "As best as we can figure, the Reeves family is not involved, and neither is Miss Telford."

Spencer bridled inside but nodded calmly. He couldn't believe that Bobbington had the audacity to speculate about

Juliana's loyalty. He did his best to forget that he, as well, had harbored doubts not so long ago.

⚜

Juliana stared at the stage, trying not to gape like the green chit she was. She smiled when Carrie did and clapped when she saw a like movement with her aunt's hands. Above all, she tried to take in every sight and sound that enveloped her.

The actors were marvelous, the costumes as bold and ornate as ever she had seen, and the background painting looked straight from that of a storybook. She had no idea why the audience tittered when Hamlet hiccuped and almost dropped the skull—it was rather rude of them. Or why they booed when Ophelia tripped while trying to glide across the stage. It was such magical drama.

Then there was the theater playing out in the stalls and boxes. Lady Pyebald regaled Aunt Phyllis with a cornucopia of titillating tales of shock and woe in a voice loud enough to apprise the entire group: The friendly, fat-cheeked gentleman in the box next to them was, indeed, showering favors upon his companion, but she was not the daughter that she appeared to be. The tightly trussed woman in a bright red gown with the plunging décolletage seated across from them was not a cheap, light skirt but a countess of ancient noble lineage. The tense white-faced young dandy sitting below with a group of chortling friends had just lost his fortune at the gambling tables of

White's. Lady Pyebald barely paused for breath and hardly looked at the stage.

Glancing toward Spencer's box, Juliana noted that Spencer was regaining his seat as Bobbington vacated his, again. It seemed that they were restless tonight and not greatly interested in the entertainment, at least not that on the stage.

And they weren't the only ones. Twice, Lord Pyebald and Maxwell had risen without a word and disappeared through the curtain. In fact, they were gone now. No one had mentioned it, and it would seem that only Spencer shared her puzzlement. On each occasion, he had glanced from her smiling face to the empty seats. Juliana was pleased to note that his eyes never wandered to Vivian. So much for her wiles and preening.

Juliana tried not to gloat, but perhaps there was a smallness in her after all, for she greatly enjoyed Vivian's inability to distract Spencer.

"I think I will get some air," the pretty schemer whispered into Juliana's ear. She stood and straightened her skirt into an artful display.

"Should you not wait for your father? Or perhaps your brother?"

"No, just let Mama know that I will be back presently. That is, if she ever comes up for a breath."

"You will not. Vivian, sit down!" The woman was apparently adept at talking and listening at the same time.

"But, Mama," Vivian said smoothly, "we have discussed this."

"Indeed, we have, and you know my feelings perfectly. A scene is the last thing that we need right now, and if Lord Pyebald were to—well, as you said, we have discussed this. You will not wander about without my company."

Vivian smiled at her mother. She stepped behind Lady Pyebald's chair and whispered in her ear.

"Very well." The corpulent woman disentangled her daughter's arms from around her neck, grabbed her reticule, and pushed her chair back. "I apologize." She nodded toward Aunt Phyllis and Carrie, who were pretending not to be interested in the disagreement.

The ladies, however, did not make it out of the box. Just as they approached the back, Mr. Stamford and a foppish young man with a canary-yellow waistcoat pushed the curtain back and entered.

"Lamar."

Juliana heard breathy excitement in Vivian's reaction.

The four standing in the shadows stared at one another for some moments before the conversation began.

"See, Vivian, I was sure Mr. Stamford would not neglect his friends." Lady Pyebald's smile was tight. With a reluctant nod to propriety, she turned to the company. "You recall Mr. and Mrs. Reeves and their daughter."

Juliana was not acknowledged, but then neither was Mr. Stamford's friend.

"Yes, of course." Mr. Stamford hesitated for an instant then stepped forward and inclined his head. As he did so, Juliana noticed that his eyes swept past her aunt and uncle and into the audience. As soon as the greeting was complete, he stepped back into the dim light.

"We haven't seen you in so long." Vivian had yet to take her eyes from Mr. Stamford's face.

"Yes, indeed, it has been some time." His voice had lost its edge as he addressed her. "Too long."

"Yes, and if you wish to see the inside of Ryton Manor again, I suggest a little boot licking, my boy." Lady Pyebald reached into her reticule and pulled out a sealed paper. "Until then, I wanted to issue you an invitation." She passed the paper to Mr. Stamford.

He bowed, but when his eyes were once again level, there was a decided sparkle in them. "I thank you, but I am not yet ready to dangle after Lord Pyebald's good opinion."

"Still high in the instep, I see. Well, then I recommend a hasty retreat. His Lordship will be returning presently."

"Yes, yes, I will be go—"

"Oh no, stay," Vivian interrupted.

Juliana had never seen the usually calm, conniving girl in such a state. There was no denying that Mr. Stamford had made an impression on her.

"Please—" Vivian started to say.

"I must go," he said softly. He used his chin to point his companion through the curtain while keeping his eyes fixed on Vivian.

Juliana hoped that Lady Pyebald had not seen the wink as the two men disappeared. She would not like it.

Vivian glared at her mother, then lifted her chin, and sashayed to her chair. She lowered herself with great aplomb and turned her gaze back to the stage. Suddenly, *Hamlet* was of more interest to her than it had been all night.

"Are we entertaining?" Aunt Phyllis asked Lady Pyebald once she, too, had regained her seat.

Lady Pyebald's brow puckered into fleshy folds. "No, Mrs. Reeves, why do you ask?"

"You extended an invitation to Mr. Stamford."

"Ah, yes, that. I was hoping to see his mother, Emily Stamford, when we return to Lambhurst."

"In the summer?"

"Exactly."

"But that is two months from—"

"Please, Mrs. Reeves, I am trying to hear. If you did not wish to see the play, you should have stayed home. Really."

Juliana actually heard Aunt Phyllis's jaw snap shut. It was rather pleasurable to witness such an unabridged set-down. She smiled and looked to Carrie, hoping to enjoy the moment, but the final scenes of *Hamlet* enwrapped the girl.

Juliana turned to Spencer, hoping that he was not once again traipsing around the theater. She was pleased to see that he wasn't. He was comfortably ensconced in his box and staring in their direction. He was smiling. It was a broad, contagious

smile that made Juliana's cheeks lift even farther. She knew that
Spencer could not have heard the set-down, but he seemed to
have caught her mood, for the tension that she had seen in him
earlier had disappeared. In fact, if she were to describe the look
on his face, she could only say that he looked like a cat that had
swallowed a canary. It was a strange expression for a sedate
evening at the theater.

SPENCER RUBBED THE SMILE FROM HIS FACE. His initial
reaction upon realizing the true identity of the traitors was surprise, followed immediately by a sense of victory. But, in fact,
the mission was far from complete. While it was now apparent
that the French messages were passed through Lady Pyebald by
way of Miss Vivian, Stamford, and Hart—not Lord Pyebald
and his feckless son—it had to be determined how Hart received
the information he dispatched and whether Lord Hart was involved. Victory was still a distant figure running in and out of
shadows.

Bobbington returned from his vigil—watching the nomi-
nally guiltless Lord Pyebald and his son—not long after
Stamford and Hart had quit Juliana's box. The news of the
ladies' duplicity had not surprised Bobbington as much as it
had Spencer. Bobbington had merely nodded and explained
that the need for power and money shone brighter in Lady
Pyebald's eyes than it ever had in Lord Pyebald's. Bobbing-

ton should know; he had lived in the same town with them all his life.

Spencer wished that his reticence had abated earlier. It might have saved a lot of conjecture, not to mention legwork.

And so Spencer stewed with undefined impatience. The Pyebald men remained restless throughout the evening, and eventually Maxwell Pyebald led Bibury outside and into the dark backstreets. Bibury had yet to report in, but Spencer was not concerned. Pyebald was no longer a threat to the security of the Commonwealth. He was more of a nuisance, and they would not be watching his comings and goings hereafter.

Spencer did not have much of an opportunity to enjoy Juliana's company following the curtain drop. They met in the vestibule for smiles, nods, and benign praises of Shakespeare. Then Mr. Reeves, who apparently had more than his fill of merriment, rushed her off to the carriage. It left Spencer and Bobbington to the clutches of Lady Pyebald and Mrs. Reeves. Fortunately, they were distracted. The women figuratively and literally bumped into as many of the aristocracy as they could, introducing the beautiful innocents at their sides as they did so.

❧

"WELL, this was certainly a night of surprises." Bobbington stood next to the fireplace in the drawing room of Spencer's apartment, staring through the cut crystal of his wineglass at the mesmerizing deep burgundy liquid.

The atmosphere in the room eased Spencer's tension and allowed him a modicum of relaxation. For the first time in some weeks, it did not reek of artifice.

Spencer downed his port and rose from his chair. "I can't believe I missed it." He shook his head as he pulled the stopper from the decanter and poured himself another stiff drink.

"Well, they fooled the lot of us. Do not be so hard on yourself."

"The capes," Spencer muttered. "I should have realized. Their hoods were up. How many men do you know conduct business hooded? Caped, yes, but hooded? Cold spring night be damned." He waggled his finger in Bobbington's general direction and then sat again. "It does make a perverse kind of sense. A lady of good repute and a chit in her first Season are not the first suspects of treason. They would think themselves safe from detection. If I had not seen the exchange myself, I would not have believed it."

"As I said earlier, I have lived in Lambhurst all my life. The woman's ploys are legendary. Her tastes run to champagne and fine silk, where the family coffers can barely afford mutton. It is not hard to imagine Lady Pyebald seeing the financial benefits of free-trading, let alone betraying the very soil she stands on. Likely sell out her soul, that one."

"Yes, but Miss Vivian. How could Lady Pyebald draw her own daughter into something this sordid?"

"Do not underestimate Stamford. He might have been the one to make the connections. He could have charmed Miss Vivian into participating. The girl could have drawn in her mother, rather than the other way around. An inexperienced chit like that, she likely fancied herself in love."

"To a confirmed rake with no funds. No wonder Lord Pyebald tossed him out on his ear."

"Yes, indeed, that would explain the necessity of a public meet." Bobbington dropped down into the chair beside his friend and loosened his neckcloth. "So what happens now?"

"Well, now we feed Hart the wrong numbers and locales of our troops until he takes the bait and misleads Boney."

"Are you going to arrest everyone involved?"

"Not until they are no longer of use."

"You do realize that Miss Telford is likely to be tainted by proximity. People are judged by the company they keep."

"Yes, in fact, now that we have determined that it is the women of the Pyebald household, not the men, she is in more danger of being ruined by their avarice." Spencer swallowed hard, forcing the bile back into his stomach. "She will be painted with the same brush of scandal." She needed to go; somehow he had to make her see that it was in her best interest to leave . . . without ever telling her why. He would use all his powers of persuasion to send her home. The only problem was that she might listen.

Spencer needed a drink. Where was his glass? "Karl," he called.

"Yes, sir," the man answered almost immediately.

Spencer looked over his shoulder. Karl stood in the doorway with Bibury at his side.

"Sir, you have a visitor."

"Come in, Bibury. You may go, Karl." He flicked his hand toward the hall. "Oh yes, before you go too far, can you bring us some fresh glasses?" He glanced at the almost-empty decanter. "And some more port, too."

Karl bowed with great dignity. "Very good, sir."

Spencer rose to greet Bibury properly and stopped halfway to the door.

Bibury's lip was swollen and split; dried blood crusted his chin. "Bibury, whatever—Karl, forget the port. See if you can get us some ice, will you?"

Spencer heard a murmur of assent from the back of the apartment. "Whatever did you get yourself into?" he addressed Bibury once more.

"Do I look that poorly?" the man asked with wide-eyed innocence, before grinning and resplitting his lip. "I am sure that I will not be complaining as much as Pyebald come morning."

"Lord Pyebald?"

"No, indeed. Maxwell in-deep-with-the-money-lenders Pyebald. I followed the bugger to a Hell, but he no sooner stepped across the threshold of The Pigeon Hole when he was drug out for a thumpin'. I thought they were going to kill the prig, so I jumped in. The bugger didn't even stop to thank me. Simply run off like the sapskull he is. A fine gentleman."

"Indeed." Spencer shook his head. "A fine gentleman."

He had to get Juliana out of that house.

CHAPTER
14

*In which Uncle Leonard takes it upon himself to
aid his niece in scholastic matters*

JULIANA SHIFTED IN HER CHAIR AND LIFTED THE letter slightly, only sufficiently to get it out of the glare of the early-afternoon sun streaming in her window. Her father's hen-scratch hand was hard enough to read as it was, without adding the overbrightness of the day to her straining eyes. She sighed and read the last few words again.

Yes, indeed. There it was. Despite his stoic references to doing quite fine without her, and his assurances that all was well, he mentioned twice—not once but twice—that Miss Gilson had asked the curate to dine at Hartwell. Juliana could feel anxiety emanating from the pages. The possibility of her old governess and the curate forming an attachment fairly screamed horror in the ink. They would be running away together any day now.

"Poor Father," she said to the empty room. "He is so afraid that life will change. And he is putting on a brave face for my sake." She neatly refolded the page and then held it on her lap while staring into space. She could almost see his furrowed brow as he wrote the letter: her gentle, graying father with a ready smile, who relied so heavily on his routine.

Oh well, if all went as planned, if their research was accepted and then published, life was going to change no matter what, as life was meant to do. But it would not be a tremendous alteration—simply a shift of their focus: onto the next stage in development of the fascinating *Coccinellidae*. This change, he would welcome . . . he just didn't know it yet.

Juliana felt that she had no choice; it was publish or lose the recognition of their research. Her father had advocated a delay, always wanting to add, to clarify, and to elucidate further. Juliana would have been content to let it be, for a few more years at least, had it not been for Mr. Redmond, Mr. Thurstan Redmond. A Friday-faced cad with earnest questions—cutting shams about his research, all the while intending to use *their* discoveries for *his* book. It was hard to imagine the devious nature of some people.

No, the Telford research had to be under the Telford name. There was no going around it.

The tap of footsteps approaching her half-open door pulled Juliana from her trance. She pulled her foot out from under her and dropped it to the floor. It was a comfortable position but not seemly, and heaven forbid in this correct household that one be caught sitting on one's leg.

Another set of feet approached, and Juliana listened—more with resignation than interest—to the muttered exchange. It had been a topsy-turvy day, and she had no inkling as to what other histrionics were waiting. It almost made her not want to leave her room. There was an exception, of course, and it went by the name of Mr. Northam.

Carrie burst through the door with her eyes sparkling. Naturally, she hadn't knocked.

"Oh Juliana, we have guests. Nancy just came up to let us know."

"Goose, we cannot receive without either your mother or Lady Pyebald. And as far as I know, they are still indisposed." That was a polite euphemism for Lady Pyebald's hysterics upon discovering the ruination of her son's face and person.

Maxwell Pyebald had walked into the morning room with a faltering step, a cloth around his arm, and the look of suffering written across his motley-colored face. It was very dramatic and well staged. Last night's actors could have taken lessons.

But Juliana thought he got much more of a fuss than he had expected. Granted, it was the worst black eye that she had seen, but it would heal, as would the split lip, cut knuckles, and pulled elbow.

But Lady Pyebald had used Maxwell's sorry appearance as an excuse to throw the household into a frenzy, screaming for a physician and cursing the evil men who partook in such un-civilized behavior. That they could cut down a young man in the prime of his life was tragic. The world was a vile, vile place. It was almost as if Maxwell had died as opposed to coming out on the wrong end of a scrape.

Naturally, Maxwell had been sent to bed. Poor man didn't even get a nibble of the hearty breakfast he had served himself. It was declared dangerous. Juliana smiled. She had seen a cup of chocolate and a large bowl of broth being carried to his room. He would not find either very filling.

"As far as I know, Lady Pyebald is still with Mr. Pyebald, as is Vivian. And your mother is lying down with a sick head-ache."

"But Papa is downstairs."

Juliana laughed. "Since when does your father entertain guests? No, best inform Nancy . . ."

"Lord Bobbington and Mr. Northam."

That silenced any argument Juliana was going to make.

"Apparently, they are in the library."

Juliana stood and quickly crossed to the looking glass. She had to make sure that her dress was not rumpled. It had nothing to do whatsoever with checking that her hair was in place and flattering. No, no. That was not her intent . . . at all. She swept her arm toward the door. "We best not keep them waiting. The library will likely be very quiet until we get there."

"Poor Papa. He is not a talker." Carrie's eyes were bright, and her color had grown slightly in the past few minutes. "We had better rescue him . . . them." She jumped ahead of Juliana and fairly skipped down the stairs.

But upon arriving in front of the library door, they were greeted with enough voices and laughter for a gathering of many.

"Do we have other guests, Chester?" Juliana asked just before he pulled the door to.

"Yes, Miss. Lord Bobbington and Mr. Northam."

"No, besides—" Juliana didn't continue as the door was now wide open and showed quite clearly that, indeed, there were only three men. They were talking, laughing, and chortling about someone called Tom Cribb, and they did not immediately realize that their male bastion had been invaded. Words such as *facer*, *ropes*, and *prizefighting* leaped out of the jumble.

Chester cleared his throat twice before the men looked toward the hall. Then all three looked guilty, like little boys caught with their fingers in the honey.

"Ah, yes, there you are." Uncle Leonard came forward to greet them as if they had not been in his company just a few hours ago. "Lord Bobbington and Mr. Northam are here," he added needlessly.

Carrie advanced ahead of her, and Juliana noticed the shy underlash look she gave Lord Bobbington before she sat down. By the sudden flush on his cheeks, Juliana thought he might have noticed, too.

The library was not a large room, more on the order of a study and likely would be called such by any but her aunt. However, the size was of no consequence; it was a comfortable room.

Tall, dark oaken shelves lined the walls; they were filled to overflowing with tomes of various sizes and colors. The sweet smell of paper and ink wafted through the air, and the atmosphere was relaxed. A large, inlaid desk sat catercornered from the windows, next to the fireplace, and a grouping of chairs was positioned cozily across from it. There was seating for all, but Uncle Leonard declined. He leaned, instead, on the mantel of the unlit fireplace.

It was a congenial gathering, and there was a lightness in the conversation that was unexpected. Sympathy was expressed for the astonishing plight of Mr. Pyebald—although Juliana could see no surprise in the eyes of their guests—and the proper topics of the weather, the previous evening's entertainment, and Mrs. Reeves's health were dispensed with in short order.

Juliana's earlier lethargy quickly disappeared and was replaced with an acute awareness and feeling of pent-up energy. She met Spencer's eyes on several occasions and had trouble looking away.

Spencer was excessively handsome; she found it most amazing that his looks improved every day. No sooner had she decided that he could not possibly get any more handsome, he did. And then there was that scent he wore, dark and musky and dreamy. It made her knees weak. Thank heavens she was sitting down.

Juliana smiled at Carrie's teasing comment to Lord Bobbington regarding his lack of appreciation for the arts, and then she glanced back to Spencer and caught him staring at her.

There was a slight lull in the conversation, and Spencer opened his mouth twice as if to speak. Finally, he formed his question.

"Will you be in London much longer, Miss Telford?"

It was a startling deviation.

"I actually have not given it much thought lately."

"I believe at one time you said that you would not be in London overlong. You mentioned something about needing to get back to your father, if I recall."

"Yes, you are quite right."

"No, Juliana. You cannot be serious." Carrie pouted. But she did it very prettily. "You have not seen and done nearly enough to consider for a moment returning to stuffy Hartwell."

"Hartwell is not stuffy, Carrie," Uncle Leonard diplomatically countered.

"Indeed not, for I have the windows thrown open on sunny days and the rooms dusted regularly," Juliana replied in defense of her beloved manor.

"No, no. Not that sense of stuffy. There is nothing to do. Too much . . . thinking, not enough frolicking, like here in London. You must stay the Season."

Juliana laughed. "I beg to differ, Carrie. I do believe the people of Compton Green frolic as much as Londoners do, just in a different manner. But I have always said that I came to London with a purpose besides enjoying the Season." Her hand unintentionally clutched at the spot above her bosom where her locket used to sit.

"I believe I know what that purpose is." Uncle Leonard nodded, and she had no doubt that he did. "Do you need any assistance?"

"Excellent idea, sir," Spencer encouraged.

Juliana glanced his way with a puzzled frown affixed firmly between her brows. But he was not looking at her; his gaze was still on her uncle.

"Thank you, Uncle. I would indeed."

"Capital. I was wondering when I could step in. Shall we say early next week?"

"Or perhaps even earlier."

The words were not from her mouth but Spencer's. Juliana looked at him again, and this time he met her eyes and held them. He was trying to relay a message to her, but she didn't quite understand it. There was a sudden atmosphere of urgency surrounding him. Juliana swallowed the lump in her throat.

"Would Tuesday be too soon?" Uncle Leonard asked as his eyes darted from Spencer to Juliana and back again.

"No," answered Spencer.

Yes, screamed Juliana's mind.

"Yes," said Carrie aloud. "We are to visit the Faredells Tuesday afternoon."

"Very well. The day after?"

"No, we are to go to Almack's that evening."

"Carrie, my dear, I do not believe Juliana will need the whole day to prepare. I am sure she could find a few free hours in the afternoon."

"Yes," Spencer agreed for her.

Juliana's eyes widened at his presumption, and she tried to give him a pointed look. He refused to meet her eye. Finally, she sighed and agreed on her own. "Thank you, Uncle. The day after tomorrow will do nicely."

"I say, Miss Reeves. Perhaps you should visit Compton Green as well," Lord Bobbington interjected. "I hear that part of the country is lovely this time of year. I am sure Miss Telford would greatly enjoy your company."

Carrie laughed. "Lord Bobbington, I have absolutely no intention of leaving Town until I can well and truly say that I have seen it all." Her eyes sparkled, and she tilted her head to the side.

Juliana was sure she saw Carrie flutter her eyelashes. The look on Lord Bobbington's face indicated that he was aware of her flirtation as well. And liked it.

Juliana smiled. It would seem that Lord Bobbington was no longer interested in Vivian. She glanced over to Spencer, hoping he, too, had seen the transfer of affection. But while his face was turned toward the pair, he was obviously lost in thought—for his expression was pained.

Juliana felt uneasy. Something was going on. Its undercurrent was apparent, but the cause was as clouded as Spencer's countenance. She would have to ask him in a private moment.

They knew each other well enough to do that. Perhaps, at Almack's on Wednesday. She would simply have to be patient— never one of her strong suits.

Spencer was exhausted. He had not slept all night, not a wink. Tossing and turning, he had heard the clock strike every hour until the sun had begun to seep through the heavy draperies. And still, he didn't sleep.

Now, he stood on the threshold of his cousin's town house banging the knocker at the ungodly hour of ten. It was likely that the family would not even be up yet. But Jason would be. That was all he needed.

"Good morning, Mr. Northam," Jason's butler said formally, as though they were not well acquainted. He held the door wider and gestured him in.

"Good morning, Clarence. Is Mr. Grafton up?"

"Yes, I believe he is already in the dining room, sir."

"Excellent. I shall announce myself."

"Very good, sir."

When Spencer stepped into the dining room, he found it occupied by two men, not one. The short, stocky blond was his cousin Jason, and the balding, portly gentleman, his Uncle James.

"When did you come to Town?" Spencer asked the older man after the jubilant greetings had subsided. "I had no word."

Uncle James slapped him on the back and handed him a plate. "Eat, my boy, you look wretched. I only arrived last eve. I was going to send you a note this morning. Business called me to Town, so I shall not be here long."

Spencer looked at the laden sideboard with a churning stomach. He put a couple of bread slices on his plate and then joined the others at the table.

Jason and Uncle James looked from him to his plate and then back again.

"Are you ill, my boy?"

"He is either ill or in love. You look as if you have not slept, Spencer."

"I am not ill, thank you very little. And although my appearance is due to lack of sleep, there is nothing in that which would—"

"Lordy, he is in love. Listen to him, Father. I have never heard such a huff." Jason hooted with laughter.

"It is not love. It is a quandary."

Jason thumped the table with his flat hand and hooted again.

Spencer discovered that his head was throbbing as well as everything else, and he began to regret coming to speak to his cousin.

Perhaps he should just go back to his apartment. Let Juliana return to Compton Green and forget ever meeting her. If he felt this uncomfortable admitting his emotions to those he was closest to, how would he ever explain it to her? Besides, it was not fair; he had always avowed that Jason was his heir. How could he yank that rug out from under his cousin?

Spencer rose. "I believe that I am not in the best of moods to converse, right now. I think I shall—"

"Sit yourself back down." His uncle smiled with the order. Although his grin was not nearly as broad as that of his cousin, it held the same smirk. "You are not leaving this house until you tell all."

"Yes, indeed." Jason nodded with enthusiasm. "Who is she? Have we met her? When is the wedding? Are you going to name your first son after me?"

Spencer shook his head in resignation, slid back into his chair, and smiled. "Well, that answers one of my questions."

"Which was?"

"If it would cause you any grief were I to marry. You are my heir as it is now and—" Spencer was hit in the face with a crumpled table napkin.

Jason was reaching for another projectile, in the form of buttered toast, when his father put a stop to it.

"I had to ask," Spencer explained.

Jason lifted one eyebrow and inquired, "What was the other question? I hope it is not as asinine."

"If I have gone mad?"

This brought an immediate reaction. Both men burst into laughter and, in between their guffaws and snorts, nodded and tried to say yes. It all became too much for Spencer; he either had to join in the hilarity or leave. He chose to stay.

Within no time at all, he was telling them about Miss Juliana Telford, from the mundane facts of her family and where she lived to the fascinating facts about the way the sunlight cast a glow around her head and that her eyes were deep enough to dive in. He skirted her aversion to marriage and concentrated on her interest in natural science. And her lips—well, he didn't tell them everything.

"My boy, I can tell you have been well and truly bitten. Oh, do not frown so. It is not a terrible affliction. It has its pleasant moments." The older man drew in a deep breath and slowly exhaled. "Won't your mother be pleased. She will make a happy grandmamma."

Spencer smiled; his thoughts lingered on the enticing aspects that would produce said progeny.

He was hit in the face with another table napkin . . . or was it the same one.

∽∞∾

"WHAT IS THAT?" Uncle Leonard asked, surveying the lumbering travel coach that pulled up before them.

Juliana was as unimpressed as her uncle by the old, worn, and dingy appearance of the vehicle. It had four horses and an expansive interior. It was a little much for a Town excursion.

"The coach I ordered, Mr. Reeves," Maxwell Pyebald said with excessive brightness.

"And what, pray tell, is wrong with the landau?"

"Mama and Mrs. Reeves had to do some shopping this afternoon, so I took the liberty of procuring another carriage."

"You might want to frequent another stable, Mr. Pyebald. This coach has seen better days, much better. However, the horses look well enough. What do you think, my dear, shall we risk it?"

Juliana knew that it was a question of mere courtesy. Had he seen anything amiss, besides dirt, Uncle Leonard would simply have sent the coach back. What he really was asking was if she still wanted to continue on their outing in the company of the manipulative Mr. Pyebald. Somehow, the man had attached himself to their small party. "It is fine, Uncle. I do not mind as long as it gets us from one point to another. It cannot matter how pretty it is."

"Very well said, especially when we are going into a more industrial part of Town. Perhaps a sturdier carriage will be the better answer. Very well, let us be off. Let me help you up. No, thank you, Mr. Pyebald. As you can see, I am helping Juliana in."

Juliana was pleased to note that at least the inside of the coach was presentable. Also, being larger meant that there would be fewer chances for Mr. Pyebald to touch her knees with his own. By accident, of course.

"So where are we off to?" Maxwell Pyebald asked as soon as he was seated across from Juliana and her uncle.

Uncle Leonard looked at him speculatively. "Are you sure

you want to join us, Pyebald? Should you not be resting? This is not a pleasure outing but one of business."

"Any outing in Juliana's company, and yours, too, of course, sir, is a pleasant excursion." He lifted his arm as if to show off the fact that it was no longer immobile. "Besides, I'm practically right as rain."

"Indeed. Well, we are going to Leadenhall Street first. Could you instruct the driver?"

Mr. Pyebald nodded and did as he was asked, and they were off.

The trip to Mr. Dagmar's office didn't take as long as Juliana remembered. Still, the staircase was just as steep, the office as overstuffed, and Mr. Dagmar as welcoming. Although he was marginally more conciliatory than she had experienced thus far, now that her uncle had been introduced.

"Were you not here yesterday?" the publisher asked with more than a touch of acidity.

"No, it was, in fact, over a week ago. I wish for the return of my research."

It was amazing how much more confident one could feel with the silent support of an uncle. Even Maxwell Pyebald, with his multicolored complexion, lent an air of intimidation.

"But, my dear girl, I did tell you, quite clearly, that I could not find it."

"And, sir, I did tell you, quite clearly, to rectify that oversight."

"But . . . but . . ." he stammered, looking around the room at the very helter-skelter piles of paper. "I would not know where to begin."

The poor man truly looked overwhelmed.

"There are four of us, Mr. Dagmar. We will help."

"What?" Mr. Dagmar threw a protective arm around the closest haphazard pile. "I do not think that wise, my girl. Things might get . . . they might get . . . confused."

"They are already so, Mr. Dagmar. We are not likely to make a particle of difference. Now, Mr. Pyebald, if you would you start at the back, my father's papers are bound in a red—"

"No, you can't," Mr. Dagmar practically wailed.

"Settle, sir, settle." Uncle Leonard's tone was that of a man to a naughty child. He turned to her. "Juliana? May I? I have a thought."

"Absolutely, Uncle, be my guest."

"Mr. Dagmar, could you call in your secretary?"

"My what? Well, I suppose." Mr. Dagmar called out through the open door, "Mr. Pottie." His squeaky shout matched his mouselike appearance.

The young man that came to the door had a friendly, freckled face and intelligent eyes. "Yes, sir."

"Mr. Pottie," her uncle addressed the secretary. "Would you be able to locate the Telford research? It was on the subject of the lady beetle."

"Oh, yes, sir, the one in the red folder. I remember it 'cause lady beetles are red an' it put me in mind o' 'em. You know, all fat in da middle an' it had bits a string holdin' it together like little legs." The young man walked over to one of the piles, rooted around for a moment, and then pulled it out from underneath. "This one, sir?"

Juliana squealed with delight. "Yes, indeed, that is it. Thank you so much."

"No problem, Miss." He smiled and blushed slightly as he passed the large pile of papers to her. "It were a good read, too, Miss. I rather liked it."

"Pottie. That is enough. You may go," Mr. Dagmar interrupted.

Juliana clutched the assorted paper pile to her bosom and smiled brightly. She was suddenly feeling ever so much more charitable to Mr. Dagmar. "Thank you so much for all your trouble." She turned—ignoring the man's muttered comment of good riddance to bad rubbish—and followed Mr. Pottie out the door. She practically flew down the stairs in her excitement, well ahead of everyone.

However, Mr. Pyebald stepped before her as they approached the coach. He pulled himself into it, turned, and held out his hand. It was a unique method of helping a lady into a coach, to say the least.

Juliana had just settled her skirts and secured the red folder on her lap when her uncle put his foot on the coach step.

"Oh bother," Mr. Pyebald sighed dramatically. "Mr. Reeves, I have left my cane behind. Could I trouble you?"

Juliana almost gasped. Could the man truly be so insensitive that he would ask an elder to be his lackey?

"Of course, Mr. Pyebald." Uncle Leonard took his foot off the step and moved aside. "We will wait for you."

"That is not what I meant."

"Yes," replied Uncle Leonard, "I am sure it is." He gestured for Mr. Pyebald to alight and then joined Juliana in the coach.

They could hear the man stomp all the way back up the stairs.

"I do believe the young man is trying to contrive some time alone with you. Would you like me to fall in with those plans, my dear, or not?"

"Oh please, Uncle, I want no time alone with Mr. Pyebald."

"I thought not." He patted her hand. "You have much better taste."

Juliana turned and looked at her uncle. A gentle smile tugged at the corners of his mouth, and his eyes flashed with mischief. And then he winked. Juliana's smile grew wider.

"Well, this is capital, capital indeed. Now that we have the return of the learned Telford papers, I can tell you my good news."

"Good news?"

"Yes, I did some inquiring yesterday, while you were visiting the Faredells. I have an acquaintance in the publishing business. He does not print natural sciences himself, but he knows a man who does. Mr. Henley is going to meet us at The Crank House and introduce us to Mr. Crank."

"Oh, Uncle." Juliana threw her arms around his neck. "This is marvelous; why did you not say so earlier?"

"I did not want to get your hopes up, my dear, if Mr. Dagmar could not find the papers."

When Mr. Pyebald returned with his cane, they set off again. He was strangely sullen and silent, tapping without rhythm on the top hat in his hand. He kept his eyes on the view from the window and made no comment until the carriage pulled up in front of The Crank House.

"Is this our next stop?" he asked intelligently.

"We are a wee bit early." Uncle Leonard pulled his pocket watch from his waistcoat and ignored Mr. Pyebald. "I expected a longer delay with Dagmar. However, Mr. Henley might be here already. Shall we?"

Juliana shifted across the seat as her uncle stepped down to the road. She was about to take his offered assistance when she felt a hand on her arm.

"Perhaps, it would be best for Miss Telford and me to wait here for your inquiry, sir. Do not want to disturb or disrupt without necessity."

Juliana looked pointedly at the hand still fixed around her arm. It didn't move. "Unhand me, Mr. Pyebald," she said quietly but with conviction. It was immediately released. Juliana gathered her skirts and joined her uncle by the coach.

Mr. Pyebald protested even as he, too, stepped down. "But, I say, sir, should we not abide? I do not mind in the least. I will see to Miss Telford."

"Really, Mr. Pyebald, I did not know you to be so hen-hearted. It would seem that your encounter has left you timid."

"No, sir."

"We will go in." Uncle Leonard offered Juliana his arm.

Juliana took it with as much pomp as it was offered, and the two paraded into the offices of The Crank House. It was a considerably larger establishment than Mr. Dagmar's. The offices were on the ground floor rather than the first, and there was a sense of order about the place—greatly lacking on Leadenhall Street.

The secretary who greeted them, while appearing to be of an age with Mr. Pottie, spoke with perfect elocution. And he was exceedingly efficient, for they had hardly stepped through the door before he notified Mr. Crank of their arrival.

A tall, thin man with a pronounced limp and large, dark whiskers came out of an inner office to welcome them. It appeared that Mr. Henley had yet to arrive, but that did not mean that they should be kept waiting. His smile was directed to them all.

The inner sanctum of The Crank House was a sizable, neat room with lots of natural light and a large mahogany desk covered from one end to the other in carefully delineated piles. A hollow in the center had been left bare. The one chair sitting before it was rearranged with two others, and the company sat.

They briefly exchanged niceties, and then Mr. Crank accepted the large collection of papers from Juliana. He immediately laid them out on his desk and proceeded to flip the pages, running his finger down them as he did so.

The room was still. Juliana could hear a clock ticking and the muffled noises from the street. She wondered if she should suggest that they leave the papers and come back for the decision at another time.

"Crank, my friend, whatever are you doing?" a loud voice chortled from the doorway. "You cannot be thinking of making these poor people sit while you read." He was a jolly-looking soul with a wide smile and a ready laugh.

Mr. Crank looked up from his desk. Juliana recognized the blurry, otherworldly look in his eye. She saw it whenever her father was absorbed in their work. "Well . . . no . . . I . . ." Then Mr. Crank smiled as if he had just remembered that he had a room full of clients. He looked at Juliana and smiled. "Fascinating, simply fascinating. I shall have to finish, of course, but I must say the observations are quite remarkable. Very . . ." He looked down, stopped midsentence, and was lost again.

It took Mr. Henley two more interventions before Mr. Crank pulled himself away. The publisher promised to let Juliana know what he thought within the week and nodded with such enthusiasm that Juliana could not help but entertain hopes of success.

Mr. Henley was introduced to the party, and Juliana saw why it was that the gentleman had a wide array of friends; he was such a happy fellow. His smiles were contagious, and he could speak on a wide variety of topics. Mr. Henley even related an amusing anecdote about his run-in with ruffians some years back. It was an obvious attempt to make Mr. Pyebald feel comfortable about his less-than-healthy look, but it was not appreciated.

Eventually the group meandered toward the door, leaving Mr. Crank back at his desk, and Uncle Leonard and Mr. Henley sharing a good laugh in the wake of Juliana and Mr. Pyebald.

The two older men paused at the threshold to draw their conversation to a close, and Mr. Pyebald helped Juliana into the coach. He stepped up after her, slammed the door shut, and raised his cane to thump on the ceiling of the coach.

Juliana reached across, knocking the silver-tipped walking stick from Pyebald's hand, sending it clattering to the floor. "What are you doing, Mr. Pyebald? You cannot signal to the coachman. Mr. Reeves is not yet on board."

The question was rhetorical—it was obvious that leaving Uncle behind had been the bounder's plan. Juliana threw the door open and exited the carriage with much more haste than grace; she had no intention of being alone with Pyebald in a closed coach. Whatever his purpose, it would not be to her good.

"Juliana?" There was surprise in Uncle's tone as he frowned at her from the doorway. He nodded to Mr. Henley in farewell and then approached. "Is anything amiss?"

Glancing over her shoulder, Juliana watched Pyebald step back to the ground, and she shuddered as she looked into the shadowed interior.

Misinterpreting, Uncle chuckled. "A spider? The pitfalls of an aged coach and in such rough shape. I'm afraid it was inevitable. Though I am surprised. Thought you would want to study a spider, my dear, not run from it."

"Yes, Uncle. But not the two-legged variety. I prefer to stay away from those kinds of creepy-crawlies."

Uncle's frown returned, and he turned toward Pyebald. "What is this about, Mr. Pyebald?"

"Miss Telford has an active imagination, Mr. Reeves. Seeing more in an oversight than is warranted. And this jaunt is the epitome of tedium. I will make my own way back." Sending Juliana a pointed glare, Pyebald straightened his shoulders and stomped away.

Juliana and her uncle stared after him.

"He has been trying to get you alone all afternoon, my dear. I'm not sure that he is an honorable young man."

"No, I don't think he is."

"I am beginning to regret offering our hospitality to the Pyebalds this Season, but short of throwing out the whole family, there is nothing I can do. You will have to be vigilant, Juliana. Mark my words, that boy is up to no good."

CHAPTER
15

In which silver candlesticks are prevented from gadding about Town

ESPITE THE SERIOUS NATURE OF HIS VIGIL, Spencer had a difficult time tamping his euphoria. He had left his cousin's town house a happy man—a decided man. He had walked the tree-lined avenues almost skipping. He had twirled his cane and nodded to anyone and everyone he passed. He had noticed that the birdcalls were sweeter and the air smelled better . . . well, less pungent . . . and the day was brighter.

Even now, as he waited for Hart's arrival at Brooks's, Spencer had a difficult time focusing on the task at hand. Stamford was playing cards with his cronies in the far corner and required no interference. There was nothing to distract him from his distraction.

Bobbington had been assigned to follow Milton Hart as soon as the false troop movements and list of imaginary weaponry were safely placed in the traitor's hands. In the meantime, Spencer followed Stamford; at some point, the communiqué would be passed between them, and it would be witnessed. It hardly mattered when, as the players had all been identified, the traitors labeled and put to use by the War Office. The directive of the mission now was to see the erroneous information on its way—off to France, straight to Boney. It was a waiting game, just as it had always been.

A familiar, but surprising, figure dropped into the wingback chair next to him. "Northam."

"Lord Winfrith?" Spencer frowned, casually glancing around to verify that no one was within hearing. "I didn't expect you for some hours—I believe my shift lasts until midnight."

"Yes, indeed. Thought we might have a discussion while we were waiting."

Spencer didn't like the sound of that. "About?"

"Hypotheticals, my boy, hypotheticals."

"Indeed?"

Lord Winfrith glanced toward Stamford, nodded to some inner thought, and then relaxed into his chair. "It has come to my attention that a certain young man is enamored with a certain young lady, but there seems to be a hesitation on the part of the young man, and I thought that I might know the reason. You understand?"

"No, not at all."

"Well, I know this young man fairly well, worked with him on several occasions; and I have always known that one day he would be distracted from his duties—it could be a permanent condition or a mere interlude. But it is all very natural and not to be wondered at. Right?"

"Perhaps." Spencer chuckled, finally realizing the direction of Winfrith's vague topic. Hypotheticals, indeed!

"So what I am saying is that if this young man were of a mind to—let us say hypothetically—marry, I would wish to assure the young man that there are no impediments to any actions he might wish to take in regard to this young lady—*if* he wishes to take any actions, that is. It would be extremely disconcerting to learn that this young man might make his decision about this young lady thinking that his duties were all or nothing . . . which they are not. Certainly not an either-or situation. The current, um, *undertaking* would have to be dealt with first, of course, but after that, it would be up to the young man as to whether or not he continued to accommodate . . . yes, to accommodate. There is many a married person within the . . . well, I just wanted to make that clear."

Laughing outright, Spencer thanked Winfrith for his reassurances all the while wondering what had given him away. Spencer still had so much to learn about this espionage business.

Winfrith looked relieved and placed both hands on the chair arms as if bracing to stand up. But he did not move; he stared for some minutes over Spencer's shoulder and then settled back down. Crossing his legs, Winfrith yawned and reached for a copy of *The Times* lying on a small table next to him. "Here comes Hart. Shall we watch?" he whispered without moving his lips.

Juliana was on her way to the drawing room when a loud clang startled her from her thoughts. That sound was followed almost directly by raised voices—two male voices, given the timbre—but who or what was being said was near impossible to discern. They seemed to be shouting, and the resulting reverberation distorted their words. The echoes built into a cacophony until unladylike curiosity and a need to put an end to the dreadful noise united and sent Juliana rushing to the front hall.

Halfway down the stairs, Juliana caught a most unusual sight, and she hesitated for a moment—perhaps not even that long—before continuing.

"What is this about, Chester?" Juliana addressed the footman, ignoring Mr. Pyebald completely. They seemed to be tussling over a candlestick—a type of tug-of-war. Chester was winning.

"Well, Miss. I can't rightly say, except . . . I believe these here silver candlesticks are best suited to stay in the dining room, where they have lived for the better part of two decades. Don't believe they need to gad about Town with this here gentleman."

"Mr. Pyebald! You are trying to steal the silver? How could you!"

"No, no," Pyebald argued, grunting as he tried to wrest the etched holder back. "These belong to my mother. She brought them with us from Lambhurst so that I might use them for cash if there was a need. And believe me, there is a need."

In a sudden capitulation, Pyebald released the candlestick, sending Chester tumbling backward. Then, taking advantage of the footman's surprise and hard landing on the marble tile, Pyebald scooped up the second candlestick at his feet. Opening his coat, he moved as if to tuck it under his arm.

"Mr. Pyebald!"

Juliana turned to see that she had not been the only person drawn by the shouting. Mr. Reeves emerged from his study with a book in hand and a frown deeply entrenched on his forehead. "What are you doing with my grandmother's candlestick?"

"This?" Pyebald glanced down and then gasped. "This is yours? Oh, I do apologize. What a terrible mistake. Thank heaven you stopped me."

"Those particular candlesticks are of great sentimental value to our family, Mr. Pyebald. And there can be no mistaking the engraved *R* etched into the base. It is quite distinct. You were trying to steal them."

"Never. Never would I betray your trust in such a way, Mr. Reeves. You have been so generous, opening up your house to us. No, sir, I would never do such a thing."

"Really? Your actions say otherwise. The evidence is in your hand." Uncle's voice was deceptively calm.

"My, my, what a lot of drama, Mr. Reeves." Lady Pyebald wandered into the emotionally charged hall with a breezy step despite her size. "My son is a good boy. There is a reasonable explanation for everything. We must not make wild accusations."

"Madam, your good son was trying to steal my silver."

Lady Pyebald continued to stare at Uncle Leonard. Her expression didn't change—no surprise, no dismay. "If he was," she said, casting her eyes demurely at the ground for a moment, "who can blame him, really. His debts are extreme—violence threatened against his person. I'm sure he would have brought them back . . . after."

"After? After giving them to the gullgropers? Are you truly that witless, Madam, or do you think I am?"

"There is no need to be insulting."

"I think there is every need."

"Now, now." Aunt Phyllis joined the argument in the increasingly crowded entrance. "Calmer heads must prevail. I'm sure this is all just a misunderstanding."

"You are late to the party, Mrs. Reeves. We have already established that Mr. Pyebald's act was not a mistake but out-and-out theft." Uncle glanced briefly at his wife and then returned his glare to the Pyebalds, doling it out equally.

"I think it best if I leave for now." Mr. Pyebald bowed respectfully. It required a deeper dip than was his norm and offset his balance. As he righted himself, a strange clink emanated from the general direction of his feet. All eyes looked down and watched as one, two, and then three silver spoons slid out from Mr. Pyebald's trouser leg and landed beside his shoe.

With a nervous laugh, Mr. Pyebald reached down. "Oh, there they are."

Mr. Reeves was faster; he grabbed the spoons, looking at each in turn. "Chester," he said, finally, in a quiet, understated tone. "Give Mr. Pyebald a shake, if you would. See if there are any other pieces of my silver being taken off the premises."

Doing as he was bid, Chester stepped behind Mr. Pyebald, wrapping his arms around him.

"Get your hands off me!" Pyebald's protest was loud and ignored.

"Mr. Reeves, call off your dog. Leave my son be. You are treating him like a common criminal. And I am finding it increasingly difficult not to find offense in your attitude."

No sooner were her words spoken than the tiles proved to be rather musical as knives, forks, and even more spoons dropped onto the marble.

Uncle Leonard took a deep, audible breath and turned to his wife. "You will ask your friends to leave this house. They are no longer welcome. You will see them out within the hour."

"But, sir—"

"Do not even attempt to thwart me in this, Madam. I want them out, now!"

"Come, Mr. Reeves, you must listen to reason." Lady Pyebald's voice had a simpering quality to it. It was most unattractive.

"Mrs. Reeves, will you kindly get this riffraff out of my sight?"

"Now see here! I will not be referred to as such. I will not stand for—"

"Chester!"

"Yes, sir."

"Remove the Pyebalds from my presence."

"You will do no—"

"And, Chester, if any Pyebald possession remains within this house one hour from this moment, you will throw it out onto the street. Including any persons of that name still on the premises. And you may use as many men as you deem necessary to get the job done."

"Yes, sir."

The footman started toward Lady Pyebald. She gave a shriek and rushed up the stairs.

The plaintive, whining apologies of Mrs. Reeves echoed

in the hallway until Mr. Reeves returned to the library, slamming the door shut.

⌘

ALL HAD NOT GONE WELL FOR BOBBINGTON.

"Stamford noticed me."

"Of course he noticed you, Bobbington. You have known each other since you were in leading strings."

"Yes, but it was the expression he wore. I can't explain it. I saw him make a connection with Hart's arrival . . . and mine. Or at least he seemed bewildered and leery—as to why I might be at Brooks's at that precise moment."

"You didn't enter directly but waited a full ten minutes."

"Yes, but he looked over upon my entrance . . . and . . . well, there was something in his eyes. I believe he will be watchful from now on. Looking out for me."

"I believe you to have the right of it." Lord Winfrith nodded, though staring at the fireplace rather than at either Spencer or Bobbington. "I noticed the puzzlement, too. Just after the message was passed."

They were relaxing midafternoon the next day in the Winfrith study, tea at their elbows, tarts on their plates, and woeful expressions on their faces. They had met to assess, scheme, and discuss an uncomfortable subject: the possibility of failure.

It was not a pleasant conversation.

Winfrith glanced at Spencer and then back to the embers.

"Rather an artful job—smooth as silk. Stamford calling for the betting book and Hart passing the message to him as if it were all part of a gamble." He shook his head. "Gambling with lives."

With a great, heaving sigh, Winfrith sat up straight and turned to his fellows. "Bibury is presently keeping an eye on Stamford, and I believe you will have to forgo your next watch or two, Bobbington. Best, instead, to be seen around Town over the next few days . . . at sporting events or riding down Rotten Row. You know, something of that ilk. Frivolous." Winfrith nodded, agreeing with himself. "We can't have Stamford spooked. Or too fearful to pass the message to Lady Pyebald."

Bobbington's brow furrowed into deep ruts. "He has to know this is a hanging offense. Why would he do it?"

Spencer shook his head and shifted, staring sightless out the window. "Money. Perhaps power as well. All self-interest. Try not to think on it . . . he might get transportation instead. He has connections."

"Yes, I suppose that would be better." Bobbington put his plate on the table beside him, tart untouched.

" 'Fraid it means we'll have longer shifts again, Northam."

Spencer shrugged, suppressing a sigh. Hours spent peeking around corners in disguise, waiting for Stamford to devise a surreptitious method to contact Lady Pyebald, was not high on his list of pleasant pastimes. No, not when those hours could be spent in the company of Miss Juliana Telford.

Luckily, he did not have to be vigilant overly long; the French communiqué was passed with flamboyance and verve within the huge crowds of Ascot Heath just a few days later. The *crème de la crème* of the *beau monde* were in attendance for their first horse race of the season. All were atwitter—in a dignified manner, of course—and all were dressed in their finest, top hats and beautiful bonnets required.

Spencer, no stranger to these environs, had no need of a disguise and could meet and greet and observe as openly as he wished. It proved to be a great boon, as the milling crowd offered cover, and the number of acquaintances supplied the reason to flit back and forth.

Unaware of the scrutiny, Stamford approached Lady Pyebald when Lord Pyebald briefly left the ladies to their own devices—likely to visit the necessary. A polite bow, a dropped program, and, voilà, the one retrieved from the dirt had extra pieces of paper added. Neatly done.

The look of relief on Stamford's face as the Pyebalds disappeared back into the crowds was clear even from where Spencer was standing. Unfortunately, Stamford turned just at the wrong moment and saw Spencer watching. Their eyes met, they bowed their heads slightly, very slightly, in acknowledgment of each other, and then they went about their business.

Spencer dove back into the throng and found Winfrith hovering on the periphery of the Pyebald entourage. Their conversation was of short duration and would have confused anyone listening.

"Have you seen the latest *program*, Winfrith? I'm thinking there's more in it than meets the eye."

"Indeed. Young Pup has had a good run, but I think Skirts has come into her own."

"You could be right. But I wouldn't bet too heavily as Young Pup might still have some life—certainly has the eye. Won't be overshadowed, I'm thinking."

"Probably best to leave well enough alone."

"I agree."

Spencer left Ascot Heath with a sense of foreboding. He would do his best over the next few days to reclaim his reputation for easy living and hope that the gossip filtered back through the Ton—and to Stamford. It would be no small disaster if the traitor were to shout a warning to Lady Pyebald, just as the communiqué was about to cross the Channel.

CHAPTER
16

*In which a leisurely stroll through the Vauxhall Gardens
is most rudely interrupted by a deadly chase*

"I CANNOT DO THIS ANYMORE," Aunt Phyllis wailed. It
wasn't a loud lament; in fact, it was all the more pitiable
for its lack of resonance. "I have done all you have asked,
Mr. Reeves. Have I not? I have smiled, I have nodded, and I
have strolled. May we not retire? If I see another back turned
upon me, I will melt into a puddle right here."

"Yes, my dear, you have done admirably." Uncle Leonard
raised his voice ever so slightly to indicate that he no longer addressed his wife, but instead the couple walking in front as well
as the couple walking behind, although the group proceeded
in such a tight knot that he need not have bothered. "I believe
that the evening's frivolity must come to a close, children. Shall
we take the Grand Walk to the front gates?"

"Oh, no, perhaps the South Walk or the Dark Walk would be better. It will be quieter, less peopled," Aunt Phyllis almost whined.

"That would defeat the purpose of the evening, my dear. We are here to show how unaffected we are by the Pyebalds' vicious gossip. To scuttle away on one of the lesser walks would ruin the effect that we have built up all night. No, my dear, we are going to snub as many as we can from here to the gate."

"I thought they were snubbing us."

Uncle Leonard turned his head and looked behind him. He winked at Juliana, who was walking sedately on Spencer's arm. "No, indeed, there is your mistake." Once again he faced forward. "We want nothing to do with them, not the other way around."

Juliana smiled; it was almost as if Uncle Leonard was enjoying himself. But this parading through Vauxhall Gardens among the Ton's finest—was it really necessary?

Juliana glanced up at Spencer. Their eyes met. The tension that she had observed in him just a few days ago had disappeared. He had regained his affable nature, no longer suggesting that she leave Town. It was both enlightening and confusing in equal measure, for she was almost certain it had to do with the lack of Pyebalds in the Reeves town house.

"Poor Aunt Phyllis," Juliana kept her voice very low. "This is extremely difficult for her."

"It will not last long. I can almost guarantee that this time next year, the *beau monde* will know the truth about the Pye-balds, and your family will no longer be in shame."

Juliana heard the conviction in Spencer's voice as well as the veiled meaning. She slowed her steps, allowing some distance to grow between them and the Reeves family—but not too much. "Could you elucidate, Mr. Northam?"

Spencer opened his mouth as if he would do just that, but then a frown flashed across his face. Had Juliana not been watching closely, she would have missed it.

"Yes, I would very much like to explain, but now might not be the best time." He glanced toward her aunt and uncle, mak-ing the reason for his hesitation quite plain. "There is *many* a discussion that needs to take place, and to do so in privacy."

The grin and decided excitement in his eyes nearly took Juliana's breath away. She smiled back, wishing that they could find that privacy immediately . . . for without said privacy, she could not even ask why he needed it.

"Well, some other time then." Juliana nodded as if content, when she was anything but. That, however, had much more to do with their heated stares than the strange comments about the Pyebalds. Eventually, Spencer would explain about that hor-rid family, but for now it was sufficient to imagine the exclu-sion of that beastly group by the same nasty gossips that hung now on Lady Pyebald's every lying word.

Poor Aunt Phyllis. It had been a week of canceled invita-tions and withdrawn support. The Ton was captivated by the surprising expulsion of the Pyebalds from the Reeves town house.

Only this morning, Nancy had come giggling to Juliana's bedchamber with another lurid tale of why the Pyebalds were now taking up residence in Cheapside with Mr. and Mrs. Smith, fourth cousins on his mother's side. This one had to do with drunken boot boys running naked through the halls. Honestly, some people simply did not have enough to do to keep themselves occupied.

The constantly changing saga had already provided a large helping of hilarity both above and below stairs. The only person not enjoying the ridiculous nature of it all was poor Aunt Phyllis. She really did care what strangers thought of her.

Juliana kicked at one of the larger pebbles on the Grand Walk and watched it skitter across the path and stop in front of a gaggle of well-dressed matriarchs and their daughters watching their approach. It was amazing that they could see anything before them, as their noses were so high in the air. Juliana snickered quietly, but not quietly enough as she saw Carrie turn on Lord Bobbington's arm and peek back at her. They shared a look of exasperation and mutual sympathy.

"Spence, my boy," a loud booming voice with great dramatic appeal addressed them from the Grove.

Spencer turned slightly and then stopped. "Uncle James," Spencer greeted a portly man in an elegant burgundy waistcoat striding purposefully toward them.

A couple, somewhat younger than the man Spencer addressed as uncle, stepped smartly forward, also showing eager enthusiasm for the meeting. They were dressed in the height of sophisticated fashion. The lady's large feather bonnet alone would have put a healthy dent into anyone's purse.

"Well met, my boy." Uncle James's voice still boomed despite the close proximity. "Sorry we were tardy; last-minute papers to deal with, you know. But never you mind, we are here now. And what a trail of happy gossips you have left meandering through the Gardens. You were easy to find. We simply followed the blathering nonsense and listened for the indignant harrumphs."

"Thank you, Uncle. I am so glad you could make it. Mrs. Reeves is in a bad way, I'm afraid."

"Oh dear me. Introductions, nephew. Quick, before she melts before our very eyes."

Juliana laughed. She couldn't help it. James Grafton had a contagious friendliness about him, as did Cousin Jason and his wife, Evelyn. With twinkling eyes and bright smiles, Spencer introduced the two groups to each other. The members of Spencer's family made it perfectly clear that they welcomed the association. If they noticed the speculative looks cast their way by the others on the Grand Walk, they hid it very well. In a matter of moments, Aunt Phyllis left her dejected shadow persona behind and transformed into the vivacious socialite they knew so well. Uncle Leonard smiled his appreciation to Spencer.

As the swirl of amiability settled about them, Juliana felt a disquieting tension grow. What would these kind people think if they knew that Spencer had singled her out for attention? Would they still be here, at the Gardens, showing moral support to this ragtag family with problems? Or would they regret the connection?

Juliana looked up at Evelyn. The woman was not as young as she first appeared; little laugh lines decorated the corners of her eyes. She was tall and slim and had the carriage of a woman comfortable with herself and the world around her. She was the kind of woman whom Juliana tried to emulate.

Evelyn met Juliana's eyes and frowned slightly. She subtly maneuvered away from the chatting group and beckoned Juliana to do the same.

"Is all well, Miss Telford? The brightness has suddenly left your pretty eyes."

Juliana was taken aback. Such plain speaking. "Yes, thank you. I . . . I was merely thinking, no, wondering." What was she going to say? "Lovely weather we are having. Are you enjoying London?"

Evelyn laughed.

Who could blame her? The question was insipid and had no relevance. Juliana swallowed and took a half step back—trying to escape her discomfort.

"I am, indeed. London has many diversions . . . but I much prefer the calm environs of verdant fields to the bustle of cobblestone streets, as do you, Miss Telford, from what I understand.

Much easier to study insects in the country." Evelyn glanced at Spencer for a moment before continuing.

Juliana blinked. Evelyn knew, or at least she had guessed, that there was an attachment of some sort. So involved in her relief, Juliana almost missed her next comment.

"In fact, I believe there is to be a journey to the country fairly soon. Will you be returning to Lambhurst as well?"

"Lambhurst?" Juliana turned to look at Spencer and saw him looking speculatively at them. He raised both his eyebrows in a mute query and stepped forward.

"Mrs. Grafton mentioned Lambhurst." Was this then the reason for urging her to end her Season? Spencer wanted her closer at hand . . . to continue their association. Juliana tried to keep the grin from her face. "Are you leaving London, Mr. Northam?"

Spencer shrugged and breathed deeply, almost a sigh. "Unfortunately, Bobbington has been called home on some business matters, and I will accompany him. I'm not sure how long I will be away."

"Oh." Juliana did her best to not look disappointed. Trying to guess the direction of Mr. Spencer Northam's train of thought was proving to be rather difficult. As soon as she decided, definitively, which way his was going, he would head off in the opposite direction.

Mired in her own thoughts, Juliana considered for what must have been too long, for when she rejoined the conversation, it wasn't a conversation at all. Both Evelyn and Spencer were staring at her, their expressions nonplussed.

"Pardon?"

"I wondered about Lambhurst," Evelyn clarified. "Whether you were going to quit London as well?"

Juliana smiled. "I was just mulling over such a possibility; my purpose for being in Town is all but secure now. Publishing my research with my father, as you probably know."

Evelyn nodded, proving that she did, indeed, know.

"And I believe the family has lost its interest in the frivolity of the Season for the time being. Yes, the more I think on it, the more I find it a most acceptable notion. There are many lovely *private* spaces in Grays Hill Park—particularly in the gardens." Juliana met Spencer's gaze and watched as his bright, lopsided smile returned in full force.

"Excellent plan!"

Though she was not certain, Juliana thought she heard him add. "And at St. Ives Head." She must have been mistaken . . . for his lips never moved.

 ❧

LOST IN THOUGHT, Spencer enjoyed the relaxed, convivial atmosphere of this family gathering and imagined it as a template of the future. Holidays and hot summers spent at his estate in Somerset with all these lovely people filling his manor with laughter and bringing that marvelous sparkle to Juliana's eyes. With a benign smile tugging at his lips, Spencer caught an abrupt movement, or rather, an abrupt pause.

A significant collection of dandies had come to a sudden halt in the center of the path facing their party. Talking behind their hands, and all but pointing, the young men shook their heads, squared their shoulders, and made a show of stepping out of the way. Only Lamar Stamford was left standing in the center of the path, staring from Bobbington to Spencer with an expression of growing horror.

This was a pretty pickle: a lose-lose situation. Stamford had made the connection; he was going to run. But would the traitor just run fast and far or would he try to head off the Pyebalds? And if Spencer gave chase, would the gossipmongers do the job instead?

"We should be going, Bobbington." Spencer grabbed his friend by the arm, pulling him out from the inner sanctum of the company. He really had no choice. Gossip could be countered . . . refuted . . . twisted; the warning of a confederate could not.

"What? Whatever for—" Then he noticed Stamford standing agape not twenty feet away. Bobbington's appraisal of the situation was similar to Spencer's. "Lawks!"

The happy chatter was silenced by the vulgar exclamation, and all heads turned their way.

But there was time neither to explain nor to apologize for the rough language—Stamford had turned on his heels and was now hightailing it toward the Dark Walk.

Spencer rushed after him. Gesturing Bobbington to the right, Spencer directed his friend up the Grand Walk; they would trap Stamford between them. The pleasure garden was built on a grid, and they could easily guess Stamford's direction—out. The traitor wanted to escape. He knew the jig was up—if he wanted to survive, he had to get away.

The race was not easily won.

Stamford took to the greenery, where there were no obstacles of the people kind but trees and shrubbery aplenty. Still, despite the stitch in his side and the inability to breathe properly, Spencer gradually caught up to Stamford. Inch by inch. Closer and closer he approached, until the villain suddenly veered behind a huge rhododendron and disappeared.

Spencer slowed and came to a halt. Bobbington reached his side, and they stared at the tangled branches.

"Done for now . . . trapped himself," Spencer panted.

"The side entrance!" The shout from behind was none other than Lord Winfrith, gesturing wildly to the left.

Startled, Bobbington and Spencer recovered quickly and ran in the general direction of Winfrith's flapping hands. It was blind faith, for Spencer had no idea that there was a side entrance to Vauxhall. It was fortunate that Winfrith knew what he was about.

No sooner had they raced down the path than the swinging

gates of the smaller entrance and the surprised expressions on patrons' faces told Spencer that Stamford had, indeed, run this way. Increasing his speed in a surge of desperation, Spencer beat Bobbington through the gate.

Just as he burst through, he heard a loud pop and saw a puff of smoke up ahead—wafting out from behind a tree. Rushing over, he found Stamford trying to hide behind a narrow trunk with a two-shot pistol in his hand—aimed directly at Spencer's chest. Without a great deal of consideration, Spencer chose not to check his momentum but allowed his speed to send him careering into Stamford. The pistol fired—safely into the sky.

It was all over in a trice.

Bobbington helped turn Stamford facedown on the ground, and—though there was much complaining and cursing—they sat on him. They did not have to use Stamford as a settee for too long as Winfrith quickly arrived with two burly constables; they dragged the traitor away posthaste before any of the *beau monde* deigned to inquire too closely about this most irregular behavior.

By the time Juliana and family came rushing through the gate to join them under the leafy canopy of Kennington Lane, Stamford was gone. Bobbington and Spencer looked up, did their best to wear expressions of surprise, and acted as if nothing untoward had occurred—at all.

Spencer fobbed off questions with an unlikely excuse of seeing a friend who owed him money. Bobbington merely nodded—he was still a little winded.

Passing off the incident as a bag of moonshine fooled no one, least of all Juliana.

"If it was all for naught, then why has your wardrobe undergone a significant alteration?"

"Alteration?"

"Yes, you now appear to have a hole in your jacket." She met his look with a raised eyebrow. Then gesturing toward his shoulder, Juliana indicated the cotton padding and bullet-sized tunnel that had passed through mere fractions of an inch above flesh and bone.

"Oh, that is disappointing." Spencer glared at the offending threads. Then, he took Juliana's arm, crooking it through his. "We'll have to talk about this some other time."

Juliana smiled affably. "In private, of course."

Spencer nodded and led Juliana back into the park toward the main gate, where the Reeves carriage awaited.

⁂

Juliana stifled a yawn as she found her way to the morning room of Grays Hill Park. After having been on the road for two days, it was expected that the ladies of the household would need some time to recover. However, dawdling in bed, when she would much rather visit St. Ives Head—where there was a possibility of a handsome young gentleman waiting in the vicinity—was practically criminal. After all, it had been . . . well, two days since she had seen Spencer last.

Not long after returning from Vauxhall Gardens, Juliana had broached the subject of returning to Lambhurst. Uncle Leonard and even Aunt Phyllis agreed that Town had lost its vibrancy; no mention was made of the rescinded invitations, but there was no need. Having been cast aside by society, Carrie was quite prepared to walk away with chin held high. However, upon being told that Lord Bobbington was going to remove to Lambhurst as well, she couldn't pack fast enough.

With an inkling of the reason for Juliana's enthusiasm for the countryside of Dorset, not Devon, Uncle Leonard sent a letter to Compton Green. If Papa joined them at Grays Hill Park, there would be no rush for her to return home. They could while away the summer breathing in the fresh ocean breezes. Juliana's greatest fear was that Papa would not be stirred from his studies and that she would be forced to continue her journey, leaving St. Ives Head—and private spaces—behind.

Juliana slipped across the threshold of the morning room, her hunger heightened by the delicious aromas of kippers and bacon. Juliana needed to feast on a hearty meal before disappearing into the thicket. Calling for a horse was out of the question after having just arrived the night before. As such, she anticipated a lengthy ramble—with the reward of Spencer's person at the end. A perfect way to begin the day.

Juliana had yet to work out why Spencer found the need to visit St. Ives Head regularly, but she liked to flatter herself that she might be part of the reason. Where else could they meet without overly interested parties interfering, or judging, or generally mucking about in her affairs? Though . . . that would not explain why Bobbington might accompany him. It was a puzzle, and one best solved in a direct manner. She would ask him—perhaps today.

With Spencer on horseback while Juliana was confined to a carriage, there was no doubt that he would have reached Lamb-hurst ahead of them—in Bobbington's company, of course. And while there was no guarantee that the gentlemen would be whiling their morning away on the cliffs of St. Ives Head, it was her only option. She could hardly walk over to Shelsley Hall.

"Good morning, Juliana." Seated demurely across the table from her father, Carrie looked bright-eyed and . . . ready for a jaunt, if one looked closely at her gown.

"Carrie dear, you are up. What a lovely surprise."

"Yes, we have places to go, people to see."

Uncle Leonard lowered his newspaper and glanced from one girl to the other. "We do?"

Carrie laughed, waving her toast at him. "Not you, Papa. You may sit here and revel in the joy of being back in Lamb-hurst. No, Juliana and I have plans to take our exercise this morning up on St. Ives Head."

They had arranged no such thing, but Carrie—sweet Carrie—knew Juliana planned to make a beeline for the cliff. Carrie also knew that visiting St. Ives Head for the express pur-pose of seeing Spencer was most improper. And while Aunt Phyllis was still locked in her own misery, she could insist that Juliana stay within the grounds of Grays Hill Park or be sent back to Hartwell. Though Uncle Leonard would likely veto that threat.

There was, of course, another possible purpose to Carrie's early rise and eager anticipation of a long ramble: Lord Randolph Bobbington. Had her cousin reasoned that Bobbington would accompany Spencer to the cliff? It seemed quite likely. And if it were so, then Carrie would prove to be an excellent distraction . . . perhaps even allowing a private conversation.

The slight lift of Uncle's lips, his casual nod, and his return to *The Times* revealed his awareness of her ruse. "You could ask Cook for a basket. Might want to take a small repast with you."

Juliana laughed, whispering to Carrie as she made her way to the sideboard, "Already done."

"Splendid. Most splendid."

"Hmmm, what was that?" Uncle didn't bother to look up this time.

"Nothing of concern." Carrie glanced in Juliana's direction and smiled.

Taking her laden plate to the table, Juliana saw that Carrie was ahead of her by a fair margin, if one was to take into account her nearly completed breakfast. Amazing. Carrie had risen early. Bobbington's presence was calling to her just as Spencer's was calling to Juliana.

Calling to her . . . yes, someone was calling to her. Not Carrie or Spencer but—

"Juliana! Juliana!"

Surprise left Juliana's mouth agape for a moment, perhaps

two. "Father?" Standing, Juliana rushed to the door and would have hastened into the hall had she not collided with the man running toward her. "Father?" she said, her voice muffled as her face was now pressed into the man's shoulder.

After allowing a moment of calm to settle back into the room, Juliana pushed the figure away, far enough to ascertain that it was, indeed, he. Juliana observed a worrying change in her father's countenance. His person was somewhat more unkempt than she would expect; his thick white hair was wild and pulled about, his chin covered with gray stubble. "Father, are you well?"

Rather than answer, her father laughed, tightened his hug, and dipped her from side to side. It was rather disconcerting.

"Um, Father, could you, please, release . . . ? Thank you, that's better. Now, what is this about?"

"About? About? My dear girl, your news, of course. I had it from your uncle." He shifted to the right to look around Juliana and nodded, presumably to her uncle seated at the table.

"News?" Her uncle had told Father about Spencer?

"Yes, yes, of course." Father reached toward her, seemingly intent on another dipping session.

Juliana stepped back, away from the circle of his arms. Oblivious, or simply unconcerned, her father danced to the other side of the room.

"Good morning, Carrie," he said, giving his niece's fingers an affectionate squeeze. "Enjoy London?" Again, the answer seemed of little consequence, for he immediately turned back to Uncle Leonard. "Sorry for the early arrival. Couldn't help myself. Been too excited since getting your letter. I mean, well, look at me. Here I am! This is so exciting. Couldn't imagine leaving Compton Green, ever. But this news, I just had to see my girl." Meeting her gaze, Father rushed back to Juliana. "Well done, my dear. You are a marvel."

"Father, I don't understand. Why am I a marvel?"

"Our research, of course. You found a publisher. I will admit to you now that I never thought it likely—so few are interested in natural sciences, let alone research of an insect as observed by a young lady. Thought that there might be some issue over your gender . . . yes, terrible to think so, but there it is. No, no. This is beyond my expectations."

Juliana laughed and shook the thoughts of Spencer from her head. "Father, you never said so."

"Didn't want to discourage you, my dear. What kind of father would I be to extinguish your hopes and dreams? No, no, couldn't do that. And so this is all the more satisfying that you proved me wrong . . . even though you did not know it. Oh yes, what an outcome. Thought London would be good for you . . . you know, the dancing, the theater, and glittering people. But this, well, now we can start the second stage of our research. Yes, yes."

"I am very glad that you are happy. I am just so surprised to see you here."

"Well, it certainly got me out of Hartwell in a rush. Haven't you been saying you wanted me to travel?"

Juliana smiled and patted his arm affectionately. "And now that you are here, might we not stay awhile? There is a diverse array of insects to study as well as a plethora of *Coccinellidae*. A few weeks of rest and relaxation in the balmy breezes of Lambhurst will do us all the world of good. Don't you think?"

And, it would give Juliana the opportunity to introduce Spencer to Father.

CHAPTER
17

In which Miss Telford and Mr. Northam deal with
boredom and peril in quick succession

SPENCER STIFLED A YAWN AND STRETCHED HIS
right arm in front of him. He swatted haphazardly at
the fly buzzing between the oak branches and lifted his eyes
to assess the position of the sun halfway up the eastern sky.
A breeze blowing across the land from the south brought warmth
with it and the spicy scent of daylilies. Spencer was disinclined
to abandon his vigil, though there seemed little reason to remain.

"Not today, I would guess," Bobbington said—not even
bothering to hush his voice.

Looking toward the shrubbery opposite, Spencer watched
Bobbington's head appear as his friend got to his feet. "No smugglers this late in the morning, especially as Lady Deceiver is

not yet in residence." He glanced out over the rolling fields to the Great-House looming and formidable in the near distance.

Spencer followed his gaze and squinted. There was still little movement at Ryton Manor—none of the hustle and bustle that one could associate with the return of the family.

It was a concern.

Had the Pyebalds gotten wind of Stamford's incarceration? Winfrith would try to keep the news from leaking, but there would be cracks—there always were. A whispered word in the right ear and the Pyebalds would stoke the fire with the communiqué and take a long holiday in Italy.

"I'd want to get rid of it as fast as possible," Bobbington addressed their shared foreboding. "But she's as cool as a cucumber—fancies herself protected by her position in society . . . ancient lineage and all that."

"Protected by the very thing that she is trying to destroy." Spencer shrugged—more from habit than resignation. "Winfrith will let us know if they make any sudden moves. All we can do is wait and watch."

They stared in silence for some minutes—listening to the rumble of the waves pounding at the base of the cliff.

"We could vary our vigil a little," Bobbington snorted. "Tonight, *I* could take the tree and *you* could sit on the ground."

Before Spencer could dissuade his friend of the notion, they heard a twig snap, leaves rustle, and the unmistakable swish of material. Skirts? Bobbington glanced at Spencer and then lowered himself into the grass. Spencer slowly sat back, hiding behind the cover of the gnarled oak.

Staring in the direction of the irregular sounds, Spencer relaxed into a motionless state and waited. Two pretty girls in flowered dresses and bonnets skipped out of the woods carrying a basket, looking lovely and fresh and most appealing. With a grin, Spencer stepped out of the shadows.

"Mr. Northam."

Spencer quite liked the sound of his name as articulated by Miss Juliana Telford. It somehow seemed more rounded and infinitely more enticing than when pronounced by anyone else in the world. Bowing with solemn formality, he ruined the effect by grinning and staring overlong into her beautiful hazel eyes. Unfortunately, his gaze wandered to her mouth, and he was transfixed. The sound of a throat being cleared—noisily— brought Spencer out of his stupor.

"Should I take the basket?" someone asked.

Juliana started, looking down at the object in her hand; it was listing severely, threatening to spill its contents. "Oh dear." She righted the basket and then laughed. "No, no. Not to worry, Lord Bobbington. Thank you all the same."

Prying his eyes away from Juliana, Spencer looked across to where Bobbington and the diminutive figure of Miss Reeves stood, fairly close together. He greeted her with a more casual bow than the one he had just offered Juliana.

"And what brings you ladies to St. Ives Head on this lovely morning?" Bobbington truly looked puzzled.

Spencer smiled, fairly certain his whispered comment in Vauxhall Gardens had done the trick.

"Why, this is the very best place for a picnic," Miss Reeves replied with a wide grin. "It is not surprising to find it occupied."

Catching Juliana's eye, Spencer winked. As expected, she winked back.

Gesturing to a small clearing nearby—well away from the cliff's edge—Juliana placed her basket on the ground. "A little early for elevenses, but we can soldier through, don't you think?" There was no dissent among the ranks, and soon the four were sitting comfortably and close as they enjoyed their alfresco meal.

While Spencer was distracted by Juliana's presence, he was not so far gone that he was oblivious to the amorous glances being shared between Miss Reeves and Bobbington. He thought it an inestimable match. He sincerely hoped that Mr. Telford would feel the same about his imminent proposal to his daughter.

As if she knew where his thoughts had wandered, Juliana addressed the source of his discomfort. "Father has arrived in Lambhurst."

"Pardon?"

"Yes. Papa wrote to Uncle Andrew about Juliana's successful search for a publisher." Miss Reeves nodded in a jerky staccato. "And asked if he wished to join us here in Lambhurst."

"I didn't think anything could pry him away from Hartwell . . . but it would seem that I was wrong." Juliana lifted her shoulder in a half shrug. "It is a most advantageous event—for I will be able to visit Carrie longer . . . perhaps most of the summer. And you, Mr. Northam? How long are you planning to stay in Lambhurst?"

Spencer could feel the weight of the question; though stated in a light tone, it was laden with meaning. "It's hard to say at this point." His eyes slid to the building in the distance and then back again. He couldn't make plans, or proposals, until the situation with the Pyebalds was resolved.

Juliana glanced over her shoulder toward Ryton Manor and sighed, "Yes, of course." Turning back, she stared for some minutes at his coat. Then she leaned closer, and Spencer could no longer consider anything other than the smell of roses and the heat of her body. All clear thought disappeared completely as she lifted her hand toward him and he waited completely befuddled . . . waited to feel the touch of her fingers. On his coat lapel?

"What a lovely specimen," she said just before capturing something between her cupped palms. "Look, an emperor dragonfly." She spread her fingers for Spencer to see, apparently oblivious of the disappointment in his expression.

"A what?"

"An *Anax imperator*. You know, of the *Aeshnidae* family." She looked up with a smile. "Isn't he a beautiful bright blue?"

"Dragonfly, Mr. Northam. Don't worry about the Latin. It's a dragonfly." Miss Reeves laughed.

Juliana looked over to her cousin and nodded emphatically. "Do you want to see? Oh—"

Following her gaze, Spencer saw that she was staring at Ryton Manor. "Oh?"

"The Pyebalds will be here soon."

Bobbington shifted, looking over his shoulder. "Why do you say that?"

"The drapes in the drawing room have been opened."

Spencer frowned. "How can you tell? It's too far away."

"The draperies—the red ones in the drawing room. You can barely see any red now, just the smallest line—see. They are no longer pulled across the length of the windows. A good house steward will direct the maids to keep them drawn, you know. To keep the sun from fading the material when the room is not in use. But now they are open . . . yes, and you can see by the reflection that the windows have been thrown open—to air it out no doubt. Yes, I expect the Pyebalds will be back . . . tomorrow at the latest."

Spencer smiled, impressed with Juliana's observation skills— she had declared this to be an unequivocal truth on this very cliff, and Spencer was quite prepared to believe it.

"It's rather strange," she continued. "I would think that they would have stayed longer in Town. After all, their unwarranted expulsion was placed entirely upon our shoulders."

"Perhaps their new address in Cheapside was not up to their standards." Miss Reeves laughed with hidden meaning. "Not enough silver."

The conversation lapsed for some minutes as looks were

shared between the girls, and Spencer nodded to Bobbington. There was now purpose to their vigil.

The game was on.

❧

GLANCING AT THE SUN, Juliana heaved a sigh. Soon, it would be at its zenith—time to head back to Grays Hill Park. As Juliana packed up the basket, she tried to devise an elegant and surreptitious way to sequester Spencer. Privacy was still in short supply.

She might meander to the cliff-side—ostensibly to enjoy the view. No, she was still uncomfortable about getting too close to that treacherous abyss. Could she ask Carrie to go ahead? That might be pointless, as Bobbington was still within earshot. Could she . . . ?

"Might I speak with you a moment, Miss Telford?"

Juliana lifted her head from her labors and her scenarios. She took Spencer's hand as he assisted her to her feet. Yes, well, the direct way would also work. She allowed him to hook her arm through his, and they began to stroll along the path—away from Carrie and Bobbington.

The silence between them was companionable, their gait matching perfectly, and yet there was a sense of discomfort in the air. Juliana turned to see that Spencer's expression was clouded, his mouth tight.

"Is something amiss, Mr. Northam?"

"No, no. Just lost in thought is all. Trying to figure . . . the best time . . . well, I am heartily glad to learn that you will be abiding in Lambhurst for a while."

"Yes . . . ? Indeed . . . ?"

"Indeed, yes. I would very much like to meet your father." He squeezed her arm gently and, finally, looked down to meet her eyes. "And spend more time with you. However, I am under an obligation that might take some time to be resolved. I cannot come to call until then."

"Does this obligation have to do with the Pyebalds?"

"I'm afraid so."

As they stepped together over a particularly deep rut in the path, Juliana was put in mind of the day that they had first met. On this very cliff. Spencer had never explained his presence. Juliana hesitated, pulling Spencer to a halt with her. She half turned, verifying that Carrie and Bobbington were enjoying their own conversation—not interested and unable to participate in theirs.

"You have been watching the Pyebalds ever since I met you, I believe."

"Yes." Spencer nodded slowly.

Glancing out over the water, Juliana stared east—in the direction of France. "Smuggling or something more serious?"

"Both."

"I should be surprised, but I am not. A more devious family, I have never encountered. There is no honor in them. Are you assisting the War Office?"

Spencer nodded again.

"So, Bobbington was never interested in Vivian."

This time he laughed. "No."

Juliana swallowed with some difficulty, and her heart beat faster. But it was the rhythm of fear, not excitement. Could it be that Spencer's interest in her was insincere as well? "And our pretense—to feign an attraction. Was that for *king and country*, too?"

Much to her distress, Spencer smiled—as if her query were in jest.

"Mr. Northam? Please . . . I . . ."

"That was the purpose, Miss Telford, originally, of course. But, as we both know, the pretense has long since subsided."

Lifting her hand to her bodice, Juliana giggled. At a time like this, one would hope to retain some dignity, but no . . . her immense relief had pushed out a giggle. Most unbecoming. But Spencer did not seem to notice, for he was staring . . . at her hand?

"Why do you do that?" he asked. "As if you are reaching for an object of some sort."

It took Juliana a moment to understand his question. "Habit, I suppose, and a new one at that. I had my mother's locket for only five months or so and yet . . . well, I wore it every day and felt a connection with her because of it. I lost it. Here, in fact. The day I went over the cliff."

"A locket? With a fleur-de-lis?"

"Yes." Juliana was taken aback. "Have you seen it?"

"Indeed. I found it some weeks ago." Reaching into the pocket of his waistcoat, Spencer pulled the etched silver locket out and draped it across her palm. "I have carried it ever since. You'll have to have the clasp fixed, but other than that, it is no worse for wear."

"I can't believe it. I thought it was gone for good. This is marvelous." She turned toward Carrie, holding it aloft, but her cousin merely squinted in her direction. Juliana would show her later.

Spencer grinned. "Pray tell me, why does it sport a *fleur-de-lis*?"

"Mama was French, you know," she said, holding the locket tight against her bodice again.

"I didn't. In fact, I thought it might have been dropped by someone with nefarious intents."

His tone was light and teasing, but a sudden foreboding drained Juliana's euphoria.

"Mr. Northam?"

Spencer's lovely, lopsided smile disappeared. "Yes."

"Is your *obligation* dangerous?"

"No, of course not," he answered much too quickly.

❧

THE NEXT FEW DAYS PROVED TO BE DIFFICULT FOR Juliana as her Spencer-time was not at all adequate. Disappearing for an hour . . . or two required a significant amount of subterfuge. Fortunately, Carrie devised a multitude of reasons for Juliana's absences, ranging from the plausible—lost in a good book—to the more unlikely—sleeping until the day was half gone. Apparently, there were *bug*-hunting excursions as well. Juliana tried not to cringe at that excuse.

She would sneak off early in the morning to sit with Spencer as he and Bobbington whiled away the foggy mornings. Propriety would force her home before too long . . . with only the occasional jaunt back to the cliff with perhaps a cushion or two for comfort, a sheaf of papers to note various fascinating insects—if Spencer was so inclined—or a light snack around teatime.

Spencer had explained that now that Lord Winfrith was in the vicinity, his needs were met—but Juliana saw no evidence of it: no blanket to prevent the seeping damp, no pastries to fill grumbling bellies, and no novel to provide entertainment . . . well, perhaps the book was not wise. It mattered not, she had brought it back.

Father's company proved to be a great distraction, as Juliana could not spend every waking hour with Spencer—and Bobbington—on St. Ives Head, as much as she would have been pleased to do so. Fortunately, a bevy of lady beetles was discovered behind the potting shed. Father and Juliana spent their afternoons in quiet mutual contemplation, as had been their habit at Hartwell. At last Juliana could think of something other than Spencer.

"Somerset is known to be a beautiful part of the country,

Father." Juliana nodded to herself as she sketched a busy beetle stalking an aphid.

"Hmmm. So you have said."

"And Fells, the lovely village of Fells—I have heard that they have *Coccinellidae* aplenty."

"Really? Have you been there?"

"No, Father, of course not." Juliana lifted her head, turning toward St. Ives Head. She could see nothing, naturally; the cliffs were too far away. She tried not to worry, but recollection of Spencer's ruined coat prevented any complacency on her part. Smugglers and traitors were not the nicest of people and could lash out when cornered. Her greatest fear was that next time someone aimed for Spencer, he or she would not miss.

With a deep sigh, Juliana returned to her sketch. "Bath is in Somerset, you know." She looked up when there was no reply and met her father's questioning gaze.

"Is that relevant, Juliana?"

Lifting her cheeks, Juliana tried to smile. "No, I suppose not." She dropped her eyes back to her paper, surprised to see that she had not been sketching the lady beetle at all but a mouth with a lopsided smile.

"I think I will go with you on your beetle hunt tomorrow morning. Perhaps we will have more success if we go together."

Juliana's stomach plummeted; she didn't want to lose those precious moments spent with Spencer. "No need, Father. It's far too early. I'm sure I will find us another place to study on my own."

"I'll come with you."

"No, no, there is no need."

"I'm coming with you."

Juliana tried not to grit her teeth, but the effort forced a sigh from her.

"Is all well?" dearest, most frustrating Father asked.

"Absolutely." Flipping her paper over, Juliana began her sketch anew. "Cheddar comes from Somerset, you know."

"I didn't."

Juliana sighed again and tried not to think of Spencer.

JULIANA ROSE EARLIER THAN HAD BEEN HER CUSTOM for the past four days. The sky was full of promise, but the sun had not yet peeked over the horizon, which was obscured by a band of heavy fog. As the sun climbed higher, the thick mist would dissipate, but for now it clung to the coast, offering Juliana the prospect of a dreary walk to St. Ives Head.

Much too early to expect any kind of breakfast, Juliana was surprised to find Chester waiting by the front door. "I'm going to walk in the garden," she told him as she yawned, using her usual excuse.

The footman reached for the door handle as he spoke in a hushed tone. "Of course, Miss. Though I must warn you—"

"Well met, Juliana. I wondered if the hour was too early, but I see not."

Juliana closed her eyes and took a deep breath—the sound could have been mistaken for a groan. Then, with eyes open and bright, she turned.

"Father, what a lovely surprise."

"Surprise? No, my dear girl, we had an appointment." His smile was boyish and at any other time would have been contagious. "We are off on an adventure."

"Right." Juliana stepped across the threshold, smoothing her skirts with a little more force than necessary and nodding her thanks to Chester. Glaring and staring through the haze, she started to cross the front lawn. There was a bed of roses near the main entrance that could be counted on to have a lively colony of aphids—and, therefore, a gorging lady beetle or two.

"No, Juliana, I had it in mind that we should look in a wilder setting. That might have been your problem, looking in all the same places. I would like to discern the differences with the woodland variety. To understand what it is that *they* eat."

And then without a by-your-leave, he left.

Juliana raced after her father, trying to coax him in the other direction—away from the woodland path that led to St. Ives Head, but he would not be swayed. He rounded the manor in jig time and veered away from the formal beds closest to the house. He trudged toward the informal garden, and Juliana relaxed until she realized that he was going to tramp right through the meadow.

"It's too dark to enter the woods yet, Father."

"Don't be afraid, Juliana. There is nothing to worry about.

See the sun is up enough now—there, there, see. I can make out the path just fine."

Disturbingly, his words were true. Not only was the light increasing with each passing minute, but the path was also clearly defined. And it was a path of her own making; it had not even existed before she had begun her daily—twice daily . . . thrice daily treks to the cliff. Juliana was sick—her father was walking into trouble and she had provided the means.

"Father, Father, please. Stop." Juliana could not let her father continue; she had to tell him. He was putting not only himself but also Spencer, Bobbington, and their mission in jeopardy. "Father, please. Stop and listen to me. We can go no farther." It was not a literal statement, for they were advancing even as she spoke. Juliana's only glimmer of success was that he had slowed. Then, he turned, frowning.

"What is going on? Juliana, are you mixed up in something . . . something havey-cavey?"

Juliana laughed, softly—with little exhalation, as she was very conscious of their nearing proximity to the end of the thicket. "No, Father. You need not fear that I would do something untoward. It is just that we—well, we need to be quieter. We don't want to attract attention or make too much noise."

"I don't think you need to be overly concerned, my dear. I can barely hear you over the racket as it is."

And with that comment, Juliana understood that her anxiety for her father had rendered her deaf to the sounds surging through the shrubbery. There were screams and shouts and . . . the sound of a pistol firing.

"Oh no." Grabbing her skirts with both hands, Juliana lifted them well above her ankles and ran. Horrible visions involving blood and dying breaths leaped into her mind. Her eyes blurred with tears, and her lungs complained about the lack of air. She ran, tripped, picked herself up, and ran again.

When she burst out of the thicket, a chaotic scene met her panic. There were many players, far more than she had expected. A portly gentleman held a struggling Lady Pyebald—who was shouting some very unladylike words. A short man, dressed in brown, stared at the grappling pair as he lowered a smoking pistol. Vivian, scuffling with Bobbington, continued to scream senseless drivel in the midst of the mayhem, and Spencer— wonderful, whole, undamaged Spencer—stood near the cliff's edge staring out to sea through an eyeglass. The corners of his mouth were curved up.

All was right with the world.

And even as that thought passed through her mind, the world convulsed.

Vivian broke from Bobbington's grasp and rushed toward Spencer, arms outstretched. In an instant, Spencer was gone. Vivian had pushed him off the cliff.

CHAPTER
12

In which a young gentleman lying on a ledge will eventually accept a young lady's help

A SHRIEK RENT THE AIR—SO LOUD AND SO FULL of anguish that it cut through every other sound, leaving an eerie silence in its wake. All eyes turned toward the edge of the abyss. Expressions of horror crossed the men's faces, and Juliana felt on the verge of collapse. Forcing her way across the clearing, on trembling and yet stiff legs, Juliana approached the cliff. She had to see, she had to . . .

With a gasp, Juliana allowed the tears to stream down her face, and then she laughed. It was a pathetic display of relief, but it was the best that she could muster in the circumstances. Bobbington, unaware of what Juliana had seen, reached out for her.

"Miss Telford, come away. Please, come away."

"Well, I like her just where she is," Spencer said, pushing himself up onto his elbows. He looked down at his muddied trousers with disgust. "I must say, this business is playing havoc with my wardrobe." He looked up at Juliana with mischief in his eyes, ignoring the shouts and whoops echoing across the clearing. "I am rather glad that I didn't stand over there." He pointed to that tiny, fateful ledge that Juliana had clung to on their first meeting. "This ledge, well, being four feet wide and only two feet down will make it easier to climb back up onto terra firma. Rather embarrassing."

"Oh, I don't know, sir. Your situation looks more dangerous than embarrassing to me. Would you like some assistance?"

Spencer's expression became pensive. "I would hate for you to ruin that lovely gown of yours, Miss. Could you, perhaps, find a farmer or a fisherman who might render me that service?"

Juliana made a show of looking around and then shook her head in mock despair. "I am afraid, sir, that there are no farmers or fishermen about—not even a shopkeep."

"Oh dear, that does put me in a bit of a sticky situation. I shall be considered completely beyond the pale if I am dashed upon the rocks."

"Best not do any dashing then. Merely a suggestion. You can, of course, do as you wish."

"Well, perhaps I *will* take you up on your very generous offer of assistance." Spencer hopped to his feet.

Laughing, she reached her hand down, almost tipping over when he grabbed her wrist. Once raised to the same level, Spencer paid no heed to anyone else and stood facing her at a very improper distance.

"I am so sorry to have frightened you, my sweet Miss Telford." He lifted a muddy hand to her cheek, brushing away her tears—likely leaving a dirty smudge in its wake.

"It was not your doing. There was no doubt of Vivian's intent—we were just very lucky."

"Yes, in many ways." Spencer turned to look out to sea and pointed to a small boat shrinking in the distance. "That means success, and it also means we can now concentrate on other matters—more personal matters."

"Oh!" With a start, Juliana remembered her father, and she whirled around. She swallowed with some difficulty when she saw that Father had followed her to the cliff's edge and now stood a mere ten feet away. She could not read his expression as it kept changing—surprise, puzzlement, concern?

"Oh, Father. I'm . . ."

"Juliana, I believe there to be a reasonable explanation for all this—" Father gestured in the direction of the foulmouthed Lady Pyebald, but he continued to stare at Spencer. "Shall we begin with an introduction?"

Juliana felt a warm rush to her face, and she stepped away from Spencer to establish a respectable distance. "Yes, of course, Father. I would like to introduce you to Mr. Spencer Northam."

"Pleased to meet you, Mr. Northam," her father said as if they were bowing to each other in a drawing room. He paused, considered, and volleyed his eyes back and forth between

Juliana and Spencer. He seemed to be on the verge of saying something . . . and yet the minutes continued to pass without his doing so.

Juliana felt the tension of the moment; it grew tighter and stretched to an unbearable point until she realized that the strain was hers and hers alone. Neither of the gentlemen was bristling. In fact, they looked quite relaxed, and if they were sizing each other up, they appeared to like what they saw.

Finally, Father spoke. "Would I be correct in assuming that you have an estate in Somerset, Mr. Northam? Near the village of Fells."

Spencer laughed. "Indeed, sir. Lovely part of the country."

"As I have been told." Father winked at Juliana. "I also have it on good authority that Fells has a fine colony of beetles that requires a lengthy study."

Spencer's expression became serious—though a hint of humor threatened to reestablish his grin. "It might take years," he sighed with great drama.

Father jerked his head in agreement to some unexpressed question, and he smiled . . . somewhat sadly. "Come, my dear. This has been far too much excitement for me this morning. Feel an irresistible urge to stare at some roses and make notations." He gestured for Juliana to join him but set off before she had done so.

"I must go." Juliana felt she had no choice. "Will you come to Grays Hill soon?"

"As soon as I can."

With a nod, Juliana glanced again at the small boat disappearing over the horizon and then hastened to her father's side.

EARLY THE NEXT MORNING, a knock at her bedroom door roused Juliana from a trancelike state. She had woken at her usual time only to realize that she no longer needed to rush out to see Spencer. He would not be waiting on St. Ives Head; he would soon be coming to Grays Hill. *Soon* being a relative term, as he would likely wait until early afternoon to call—though certainly before three.

With a sigh, Juliana regretted the necessity of waiting Spencer-less all morning—and not for the first time wondered who it was that had thought up all the rules of propriety and etiquette, and why they had to be obeyed so absolutely. Really, it was outside of enough.

In fact, she considered persuading Carrie to join her for a carriage ride . . . in the general direction of Lord Bobbington's manor. You never know whom you might meet while . . .

"Oh, Miss, I have a note for you," Nancy announced as she entered the bedroom. "From an admirer, I would think."

Juliana jumped up from the window seat and grabbed—in the most polite fashion, of course—the fluttering paper from Nancy's hand.

Can't wait to see you. Meet me on Jerkins Lane, next to the old cemetery, at nine. S

Juliana grinned and held the note tightly to the vicinity of her heart. A tingle of bliss started at her toes and raced up through her body. She pretended to swoon against her bedpost, but Nancy chuckled, and soon they were laughing together.

"Better get you dressed, Miss." Nancy glanced at the clock on the mantel. "Don't want you to be late."

"Oh, no, definitely not . . . though he will wait. I need not be anxious on that account."

Despite her words, Juliana rushed to her wardrobe and threw open the doors. She considered one dress after another and then settled on her light Pomona green gown with Vandyke points. However, once that was on, Juliana decided that her cerulean-blue gown would be a better choice. Yes, the ribbons on her bonnet were an excellent contrast with her pelisse and reticule. Indeed, the strings of her purse were the exact color of the pleated trim. Quite pretty—and she very much wanted to impress.

Juliana dropped her cheerful green gown into a puddle and kicked it away. She immediately stepped into the more elegant blue dress that Nancy held for her. She shimmied it up over her hips and attempted to fasten the front buttons. "I am all atwitter." Juliana laughed at her own clumsiness.

"About what?" Carrie asked as she yawned her way into the

room, still in her dressing gown. "What are you up to now, cousin?"

"Spencer wants to meet me." Juliana gestured toward the note on the bedside table. "I must suppose he finds the wait as difficult as I do."

Carrie nodded as she read the short missive. "You'll have to give me fifteen . . . perhaps twenty minutes to get dressed," she said, dropping the note and starting toward the door.

"Carrie!" Juliana waited until her cousin looked back. "Carrie, would it be a catastrophe, really, if I were to . . . to see Mr. Northam on my own? I don't want to wait . . . and he has proved time and time again that he will behave with the most decorum—in the most gentlemanly fashion. I do not have to worry on that account."

"No, I would agree. But there is your reputation to think about. It is most improper, Juliana."

"Yes, I know. But that is likely why he suggested the cemetery. A public venue, though presumably deserted at this hour. Out of doors with the possibility of prying eyes . . . which means there could be a chaperone."

"What? In the bushes? Behind the gravestones?"

Juliana laughed. "Well, I suppose not. But no one need know if we keep it to ourselves."

"Hold still, Miss. I'll never get you done up if'n you don't stay still."

"What would I tell Uncle Andrew?" Carrie asked. "I have run out of excuses."

"Oh dear, you are right. You need something new. Though I don't imagine I will be gone overlong. Still, if my absence *is* noticed . . . well, I have gone to pay my respects to . . . do we have any family in the graveyard?"

"Great Aunt Elva. But she was a tyrant who no one liked."

"Doesn't matter. That's where I have gone."

Juliana stood before the looking glass, verifying that her bonnet was affixed at a jaunty angle and her reticule hung at the perfect length. And they were; the reflection grinned.

Carrie laughed. "Fine. Have a lovely time. Oh, and you had best use the service entrance. Mama is already up and looking rather fractious."

With a peck on Carrie's cheek and a quick hug from Nancy, Juliana skipped down the back stairs. She waved at the startled scullery maid and ignored Cook's complaints about her invasion. Within minutes, she was trotting down the drive toward Lambhurst. The cemetery sat just before the bridge that led into the town. A mere ten or so minutes—yes, soon she would see her Mr. Northam.

Not wanting to arrive disheveled and out of breath, Juliana slowed as soon as the cemetery came into sight. She pushed her way through the rusty main gate and followed the path to Jerkins Lane. However, as she approached the back gate, Juliana saw a large travel coach over the stone wall. Puzzled, Juliana stepped out of the graveyard and looked around for Spencer. He was not in sight. But the big lumbering vehicle did take up most of the lane.

Circling to the other side of the coach, Juliana continued

her search, but Spencer was conspicuous in his absence. With no one sitting on the bench behind the horses, Juliana's queries were temporarily stymied. Perhaps she was early . . . or Spencer meant the end of the lane. He would certainly not have given up his vigil. She had seen him settle for hours.

A movement caught Juliana's eye. The coach's curtain fluttered, as if shifted for a quick glance. Was there someone within? Might a tall, dark-haired, handsome gentleman with a lopsided smile have been spotted from the higher vantage point?

"Excuse me?" Juliana knocked and was pleased to see the door opening. "Have you—"

Juliana's question ended in a gasp. She was seized and unceremoniously hauled into the coach. Mr. Pyebald held her tightly on his lap with one hand, his other over her mouth.

"Go," he shouted, and Juliana felt the jerk of the carriage as it started with more speed than sense would ever recommend.

JULIANA SAT CALMLY AND STILL, watching the conniving, arrogant weasel who mistakenly called himself a gentleman, as he slept. The coach bounced across the rutted country road with tooth-jarring rapidity that sent his head bobbling from one side to the other. His yellowing bruises painted his face in a clownish fashion.

And yet the situation was nothing to laugh at. The longer she sat in this coach, the farther the distance away from safety, security, and Spencer. She had to do something . . . but how, with her wrists bound by the strings of her own purse?

How could the idiot sleep as though nothing was amiss? How could his conscience allow his lids to close? Did he feel no remorse? Did he not know that Spencer, not to mention her father, would not sit idly by while he carried out his despicable plot? What was the despicable plot? What was he planning? He certainly felt no need to explain himself, for when she had demanded just that, he had smiled.

Simply smiled. The villain.

It was not difficult to guess the reason for his villainy. In fact, she had spent the past hour trying to convince herself that the man had *not* swept her away with the intention of dragging her to the altar for her money. But there was no getting around it; with his mother and sister incarcerated and soon to stand trial for treason, Pyebald would have almost no possibility of paying off his debts without resorting to some sort of criminal activity. And he had already proved himself to be an inadequate thief.

Juliana watched the head bobble again and surveyed the once handsome face. It wasn't just the discoloration that marred his looks but also the sneer that hovered around his mouth, even in repose. Juliana had never noticed it before. It was the face of a cruel, self-centered man. No, she could not appeal to his soft side. He likely didn't have one.

Still, while her inheritance was reasonable, it was not in hand. Even if he did marry her, he could not touch it. Her father still lived.

Yes, that was the approach.

"You cannot touch any of my moneys, you do realize."

Instantly, Mr. Pyebald was awake. His eyes met hers, and his sneer turned into a smirk.

"Please, there is no need to be so coarse. Money is not a subject to be discussed between a gentleman and his lady. My man will discuss it with your father's man. I am sure they will be able to come to an agreement after the wedding."

Well, that answered that question.

"My father will not be coerced."

"Worry not, I am not a greedy man. I am patient. There are only a few accounts that require some sort of payment. A token from the marriage settlement will tide them over." He glanced above Juliana's head to where the coachman sat outside and then dropped his eyes back to hers. "It is amazing how much the *promise* of money will still a hand."

Juliana looked at the motley-colored face and understood. Maxwell Pyebald was a coward. He would rather tear a woman from her home and steal her inheritance than risk the fists of a ruffian in a dark alley.

"Perhaps if I were to offer a token without a marriage contract, it would be enough." She knew Maxwell was unlikely to agree, but she thought it worth the try.

He laughed without mirth. "No, I am too deep into dun territory for that ploy. Only the promise of more will save me."

"I will not marry you, Mr. Pyebald. I will simply deny you at the altar."

"Miss Telford, or shall I call you Juliana, now that we are going to be such intimates—"

"Miss Telford is fine."

"You have no choice. I have neither the time for banns nor the blunt for a special license. My only option is, of course, Gretna Green. The town is a full six days from Lambhurst. Six days in the company of a man who is not your husband, no chaperone, no one to see to your honor. Your reputation will be in tatters; no man will ever think to make you an offer. So, you see, we will stand before the witness, and you will accept me. You will have no choice."

"Not all men will see me as a lost cause. A gentleman of true affection would be able to see this as a charade."

"I know you refer to Mr. Northam, but I am confident he will see you as a pariah, as will all of good society."

"You are wrong. And he will see you brought to justice. This is kidnapping, and I will charge you with it, make no mistake about that."

The loathsome snake closed his eyes again and smiled sleepily. "Oh Juliana, so innocent. So ignorant of the ways of the world. No one will believe you—no one will take your word against a peer of the realm. You are a nobody, and I will be a lord."

❧

SPENCER'S NERVOUSNESS WAS UNWARRANTED. He knew it, and yet he could not control the roiling of his insides, the tension in his shoulders, and the urge to visit Grays Hill Park immediately. There was no need. Juliana had made no secret of her attraction to him despite her assertion that marriage was of no interest to her. That proclamation had been made a lifetime ago . . . almost two months. He was almost certain that she was more amenable to the idea of matrimony now . . . fairly certain. . . . well, reasonably certain. Nor had her father shown any animosity on St. Ives Head.

And still, here he was knocking on the front door of Grays Hill Park feeling decidedly uncomfortable—as if something were wrong. It could not be the timing, as arriving earlier than two would have been gauche. Unfortunately, the sense of foreboding did not dissipate when the door was flung open and Miss Reeves, looking wild with anger, confronted him.

"Of all the inconsiderate beings I have met, you, Mr. Northam, take the cake. How could you have done this to us? We were about to send out the grooms looking for you. We have been fretting for hours."

"Pardon."

The confusion must have shown on his face as Miss Reeves blinked and her mouth moved soundlessly for a moment. Then she swallowed and leaned forward to see past the threshold. "Where is Juliana?"

Spencer felt an overwhelming stillness settle about his heart. "I have no idea, Miss Reeves. She was walking into the thicket yesterday, when last I saw her."

"Nonsense. You sent her a note . . . why are you shaking

your head; I saw it. You asked to see her by the cemetery . . . oh no. You didn't, did you?"

"Indeed, I did not. What has happened?"

Rather than answer, Miss Reeves turned and yelled. "Nancy!" The sound echoed throughout the cavernous hall and brought Mr. Reeves and Mr. Telford rushing from the drawing room.

Suddenly surrounded by Juliana's family, Spencer felt himself impelled toward the center of the group. Questions, accusations, and coarse language bounced from wall to wall until he could take it no longer. "What has happened!" he shouted.

Mr. Telford stepped forward, looking a decade older than he had just the day before. "Juliana received a note asking for a meeting by the cemetery. She thought it was from you—"

"It was not, I can assure you."

Mr. Telford nodded. "That is what I feared."

"Excuse me, sir." A Friday-faced young lady with the cap and apron of a maid addressed them from the bottom stair. "I'm that sorry." She sniffed as if holding back tears. "I checked with Lucy, her that's in the scullery. It were Lucy who gave me the note for Miss Telford. An' . . . an' the gent who passed her the paper . . . well, her said what he looked like. An' . . . an' it sounds like Mr. Pyebald, sir. Mr. Maxwell Pyebald."

The silence in the hall was deafening.

CHAPTER
19

Mr. Maxwell Pyebald did not know what hit him. He didn't see it coming. Juliana had been waiting all day, biding her time.

Her first attempt to extricate herself from his clutches had failed miserably. The moment she entered the post inn, she pulled the keeper aside and asked for assistance. The man laughed. Laughed! Then he patted her on the head and passed her bodily back to Mr. Pyebald. His words made it apparent that the weasel had forewarned the house of her erratic behavior before he had untied her wrists and brought her inside. He had claimed that his sister was touched and likely to regale them with wild stories. And they believed him—they didn't care that her wrists were marked and swollen.

As punishment for the attempt, Juliana was forced to sit through the next two horse changes without alighting. Finally, Juliana's demands for food—which she did not want—and private time—which she needed desperately—were heeded.

This time, however, Juliana did not remain at the inn after using the facilities; she bolted. The scores of passengers coming and going hid her flight. The afternoon light saw her out of the yard and rushing to the nearby village proper. She needed to find a manor or a hall in which to claim sanctuary. The residents of a cottage would not be able to withstand the authority of a gentleman, no matter what Juliana said. But a squire, clergyman, or, even better, a magistrate would be obliged to look into the matter. At least that was the theory.

Naturally the distance was farther than it had seemed. But Juliana led Mr. Pyebald and his coachman on a tense chase for the better part of an hour, nonetheless. A large house on the outskirts of the village had just come into sight when an approaching carriage had sent Juliana into the fields. Mr. Pyebald gave chase, and despite her pleas and calls for aid, no doors opened. No one questioned the commotion.

After running her to the ground, Mr. Pyebald wrapped his arm about Juliana's waist and lifted her roughly, using his hip for leverage. Juliana squirmed and wrenched herself free but fell hard to her knees. Just as Mr. Pyebald grabbed her again, Juliana's hand closed around a rock. It was not large, but it had heft and fit perfectly into the reticule that was dangling from her wrist.

Back in the coach, Juliana stewed with frustration—especially when the demon used her own purse strings to bind her wrists yet again. However, on examination, she decided the attempt had been worth the effort, despite her scraped palms and cruelly slapped cheek. She had delayed the journey to Gretna Green by over an hour, allowing her rescuers to draw closer—she was sure that Spencer, if no other, would be on her trail. But even better than that, she now had a weapon.

Now all she needed was a plan for this formidable rock.

It didn't take long to conceive; her options were rather limited. It was not a complicated plan, nor did it have finesse: Juliana decided to hit Mr. Pyebald on the head with the rock at the next post inn. She would wait until the horses had just turned into the yard and then, while he was insensible, she would rush ahead and secure a room. Juliana would accuse Mr. Pyebald of violence—she was sure her cheek still bore the mark of his ruthless slap—and barricade herself in until either Spencer arrived or a magistrate was brought forward. She would create such a to-do that Mr. Pyebald would be required to explain, or slink off to hide in a deep dark hole, infested with snakes and rats . . . maybe a spider or two . . . knee deep in sheep and pig slop . . . cold and miserable.

With those comforting thoughts, she rested and waited.

Finally, as early evening was upon them, Juliana noted an upcoming post inn. She grimaced with the thought of violence but cast away her horror, took a deep breath, and lifted her bound hands with the rock dangling inside her reticule. She swung the rock back and forth, gaining momentum, and then swung hard, hitting the sleeping Maxwell Pyebald across the temple.

As the coach stopped within the courtyard, Juliana grabbed the handle and jerked it up, almost tumbling to the ground when it opened. Catching herself on the side of the coach, she rushed somewhat awkwardly to The Prancing Unicorn, holding her hands out in front of her as she ran, ignoring the shouts of the abetting coachman.

She stumbled across the threshold, desperately searching for the stairs. She heard Mr. Pyebald's booming shout echo through the common room just as she found the staircase in the back. Barreling past a startled woman who had been descending, Juliana pushed her way into the first room at the head of the stairs. She slammed the door shut and braced her back against the wood. Fortunately, the room was unoccupied. It was small and sparsely furnished, but it did have a large bed and a chair.

Juliana upended the rough-hewn bed and managed to drag it over to the other side of the room, wedging it across the closed door, using the far wall as a brace. For good measure, she dragged the chair over, put it in front of the bed, and sat down.

Her heart pounded, threatening to break her ribs, as she waited, staring at her swelling and bleeding wrists—now cruelly cut by the reticule strings. It didn't matter; she had done it. She was free of that monster. Cocking her head, Juliana listened and waited. Waited for running feet on the stairs. Waited for shouts of outrage. Waited for the weasel to make a move.

Nothing happened. Not for some time.

Juliana's ragged breathing slowed, and then it took on a more natural rhythm. Her heart, which had threatened to burst moments earlier, calmed, and the buzzing in her head and ears cleared. The abject fear subsided.

With her freedom secured, Juliana could now concentrate on breaking her bonds. The edge of the chair was of no use; it bruised her wrists and made no headway on the strings. The windowsill proved to be the same. However, a rusty nail protruding from the ill-fashioned bed was more than up to the job. It made short shrift of her purse strings, leaving them in tatters and her wrists free.

And just as they snapped, Juliana heard the jangle of the doorknob. It was followed by a sickening voice, calling from the other side of the wood. A wheedling sound.

"Juliana, dear. Our little disagreement is causing these good people discomfort. If you open the door, we could discuss it, and I will make arrangements for you to go home. We will not continue if the journey is distressing you, dear."

Juliana couldn't believe his audacity. He was playing to the crowd. How could he possibly think that she would open the door?

Then she heard it.

Footsteps. On the roof. Getting closer.

Juliana looked to the one window in the room. It wasn't large, but a man could still fit through the casement. The weasel wasn't expecting her to open the door; someone was going to come through the window.

Juliana glanced desperately around the room.

She was all out of furniture.

SPENCER WAS WEARY, but his seething anger kept him upright on his horse, and his imagining Juliana's frightened face kept his eyes on the road. He had left Mr. Telford far behind in his landau, as they had planned. Being on horseback meant that Spencer could travel faster and harder. And at last he was gaining.

Locating the stable Pyebald had used to hire a coach had been relatively easy. It was barely outside the fringe of their neighborhood. The man hadn't even tried to be clever, though he wasn't foolish enough to use the highly recognizable family coach. Once the stable was found, it took little persuading and only a few coins to learn the man's intent. Pyebald's lofty attitude and weak purse had piqued the stable master, but he had been downright put out by the driver. The coachman was not one of his own, a rough sort of fellow with dark looks and a mumbling mouth, reported the stable master. The bounder grumbled about every detail of the carriage and even more about heading north at this time of year. Gretna Green was not mentioned but implied.

By the time Spencer had returned to Grays Hill Park, Mr. Telford had the landau ready and waiting. He would follow the most direct road north, stopping at the post inns on the way. If Spencer had doubts and diverted to another road, a message would be waiting.

As much as Miss Reeves wanted to be part of the rescue, it was firmly decided by Mr. Reeves that Juliana would be better served with a warm welcome on her return. Two anxious faces waved them away; Mrs. Reeves was indisposed.

The first post inn eased any fears that he might have had in regard to the direction in which they were headed. A few innocent questions verified that Juliana was, indeed, on the road north. The denizens were still snickering and making snide remarks about the young missy who claimed to have been kidnapped earlier that day. By her brother no less.

Spencer's anger saw him through the next two posts, where she was not sighted at all. He was beginning to fear that he had lost the trail when the next inn brought a smile to his lips.

Juliana had run. His brave, sweet pea-goose had run. She had gotten away. Unfortunately, the innkeeper was sure that the crazy girl had been retaken. The man actually thanked the lucky stars that such a violent girl was not running about murdering people in their beds.

Spencer did not punch him. But it was close.

He rode without regard to the rough condition of the road or his own discomfort. He was possessed; all he could think of was Juliana and what she must be going through. He kept alert by devising one nasty punishment after another. It helped him deal with the terror eating at his gut and the dread that engulfed him.

It was early evening when Spencer sighted The Prancing Unicorn. There was a small crowd of stable hands, postboys, and kitchen wenches with large stained aprons gathered just inside the yard. They stood in the dirt among the chickens and coaches. They were pointing to a small first-floor window of the Tudor black-and-white inn; some smiled, some frowned, and some looked only mildly interested.

Two men hung upside down from the roof; one was forcefully knocking on the casement.

Spencer alit, stretched his legs painfully, and arched his back. As he rubbed at the tense muscles in his neck, he turned to the stable boy who had run over to take his reins.

"Is something amiss?"

"No, sir, not really. Just a lady locked in her room. Don't know how she done it. They'z"— the boy pointed to the antics on the roof —"tryin' to get in, but she won't open da winda. They'z just tryin' ta 'elp, but the daft cow doesn't know it."

Spencer glanced up as the crowd gasped. One of the men had pried the window open a fraction, but the lady had jerked the window from him and slammed it shut. The man was left dangling while his fellow on the roof grabbed at him to prevent a spill.

Intrigued by the high drama, Spencer watched the lady at the window step closer and look down into the yard. She was a slender miss of moderate stature. The sun caught the red highlights in her auburn hair, wavy tendrils had fallen around her pretty oval face, and Spencer knew she had hazel eyes.

It was Juliana. And she had seen him.

The window was immediately flung open—jarring the hanging man's precarious position.

"Spencer!"

There was such joy in her voice that Spencer's feet were in motion before he realized. His heart pumped faster than his legs, and a flood of relief washed over him. He ran into the inn, spied the stairs at the end of the common room, and raced to the back.

But he didn't make it to the stairs. The presence of a man sitting near the bottom brought him to a sudden and resounding halt.

Pyebald was sitting within a crowd of anxious and sympathetic women. He was oblivious to Spencer's entrance, so involved in his own concerns. One woman nodded and patted his shoulder with a large red hand. "There, there," she tutted.

"It is such a trial," the cad moaned, closing his eyes and gingerly fingering the goose egg on his temple. "I try so hard."

Spencer circled the group. "Do you, indeed?"

Pyebald's eyes flew open. "Northam."

"Pyebald." Spencer said calmly just before he slammed his fist into Pyebald's nose. Pyebald flew backward and landed with a thump on the rough wooden floor. He sucked at the air, gasping for breath, but lay still. His eyes were wide and fixed on Spencer's. Blood poured from one nostril.

There was an eerie silence in the room as those nearest slowly backed away.

Pyebald continued to stare up at his attacker. The fool was likely hoping that Spencer was satisfied with one facer. He was destined for disappointment.

Spencer reached over, grabbed Pyebald's neckcloth, and hauled the coward off the floor; then he hit him again. Spencer's fist stung like the devil, but he was too angry to rein in his emotions. Finally roused from his stupor, the blackguard reacted—or he at least tried. Pyebald's defense stood weak and wilted against Spencer's fury.

Dodging a right fist, Spencer planted another facer—though this one was closer to the rat's ear—he followed it with two more punches. A sharp thrust to his gut sent Spencer reeling backward, but only for a moment. Advancing again, Spencer crossed his arms against a body punch, and then he, too, offered a gut jab, with his elbow.

Raising his knee in the most ungentlemanly of assaults, Pyebald aimed for Spencer's nether region. Spencer saw the purpose and, instead, stepped back, grabbing the man's leg. He lifted up—knocking Pyebald's feet out from under him.

The rat crashed hard to the floor, sending chairs flying in all directions, and lay gasping once again. When he rolled over and tried to crawl away, Spencer gave him a swift kick in the rump. Since they were now close to the doorway, he grabbed Pyebald by the collar and trousers and threw him outside into the dirt.

Spencer had just hauled Pyebald up, balled his bleeding fist into another battering ram, and pulled back his arm when a hand touched his elbow. Spencer dropped Pyebald and turned.

Instantly, Juliana was in his arms, her head tucked neatly beneath his chin, and she clung to him as if she would never let go. He could feel her warmth and smell her hair. He kissed the top of her head and said sweet endearments, not one of them making any sense. He rocked her and crooned until she stopped shaking and the world stopped spinning. Spencer thought his heart would burst. She was safe, she was well, and she could still be his.

Slowly, Spencer disentangled Juliana. He could hear Pyebald behind him getting to his feet and spitting, blood, no doubt.

"See, there, all is well." The villain even attempted a laugh—albeit a shaky one. "No harm done. Tempest in a teapot."

Spencer felt Juliana's body stiffen in his arms and looked down into her gentle eyes, surprised to see fiery anger . . . no, an explosion of rage . . . rise up in them. Immediately, his temper flared to boiling, and he turned, ready to plant another fist in Pyebald's face. But he was not fast enough.

Juliana stepped in front of him, and rather than prevent another blow, she swung *her* fist with such speed and force that she knocked Pyebald backward. It was one hit too many. He dropped like a rock into oblivion.

❦

By the time Father stepped over the threshold of The Prancing Unicorn's private parlor, a sense of bustling normalcy had once again settled about the inn. The local surgeon had been called in to tend to bruised, swollen, but, thankfully, unbroken hands, and Juliana's wrists had been bandaged. Father was able to organize and smooth the ruffled feathers of the establishment.

Pyebald received next to no attention. Once it was determined that he had lived, he was scraped from the middle of the yard—where he impeded the comings and goings of the coaches—and dumped unceremoniously onto the hay pile next to the chicken coop.

There was some discussion about notifying the magistrate, but once Pyebald's identity and position in the peerage had been established, the good folk of Hankerly allowed that the kerfuffle might have been a bit of a misunderstanding.

Juliana cared not a whit. She knew that retribution would be meted out by the gullgropers when they came for their money and Pyebald's pockets were still to let. Fear of that alone might force the villain to flee—escape to Spain or the Americas. It really did not matter; the man was out of her life.

Spencer dropped a coin here and there, as it seemed to be the best remedy. Soon, everyone was extolling the entertainment value of the common-room brawl. The cost of the broken chairs had been covered, and it was established that the lady was exactly that, and not a demented soul of whom they need fear.

Juliana was aghast to see the extra lines on her father's face, as well as the gray tinge to his skin. She insisted that he eat and then lie down before they returned to the road. It left Juliana and Spencer with time on their hands, and a quiet stroll on the woodland path behind the inn—well away from the road and prying eyes—seemed like an excellent plan.

Juliana sighed happily; she was both weary and energized at the same time. A strange combination. She lifted her eyes to the sky and closed them briefly. The sun was warm, and the air was flitting about on the wings of a fragrant breeze. She inhaled. Bluebells: the sweet smell was an acknowledgment of spring. Then she heard the call of the wood warbler and the redstart, and she felt all remaining tension drain from her body. She took another deep breath and glanced back at Spencer.

"Miss Telford, do you recall your words . . ." Spencer started to say, then he tensed and his neck flushed.

Juliana tilted her head and frowned. When she realized that she had done so, she made a concerted effort to smooth her brows. She waited for him to continue, but they walked on in silence.

The pathway narrowed slightly as it wended between two large willows. Juliana stepped ahead and down into the greening dale just beyond. It was a pretty little clearing with an ornate wrought-iron bench waiting near a brook; it sat under the umbrella of another drooping willow. Ducks swam in and around the rocks, quacking in great concentration as they searched for food.

Spencer gestured to the bench.

Juliana sat down, but Spencer walked behind the bench and

then turned. He paced behind her for some moments without either one of them making a comment.

As much as Juliana enjoyed the vista, the fresh breeze, and the calmness of the atmosphere, she was very aware that Spencer was oblivious to the day's charms.

"Mr. Northam, is something amiss?" Juliana pulled at the strings of her bonnet. She lifted the hat from her head and wound the ribbons around the arm on the bench, letting it dangle. She couldn't see beyond the wretched brim with it on, certainly not behind her.

"No, not really. I am considering my words. One has to get them right on such occasions, you know."

"Oh dear, one shouldn't have to deal with so many kidnappings that it bears the label of an *occasion*."

Spencer laughed, as had been Juliana's intent. However, his underlying tension was still very much present. "I am not referencing your latest adventure, Miss Telford."

"So you are not going to ring a peal over me for stupidly falling into Pyebald's clutches."

"Of course not, the villain used our . . . our interest in each other to lure you. To know that you thought nothing of meeting someone you supposed to be me on a deserted lane is very telling."

"Is it?"

"Yes. You trust me."

"Of course. You have proved time and time again that you

have my best interests at heart. A lady will always trust her knight in shining armor."

"Is that what I am?"

"Yes. Oh most definitely."

"I quite like that. Knight in shining armor. Yes. Chivalry and all that." Then Spencer took an audible breath. "I am getting sidetracked." He came around to the front of the bench and eased onto the seat beside her. Their knees touched, filling Juliana with a tingling sensation of excitement and warmth.

Taking Juliana's right hand, he turned it and raised it to his lips. Juliana stopped breathing as she watched him press a gentle kiss into her palm. It was warm and soft, and the kiss felt intimate. Blood rushed to her head.

"Miss Telford, when I suggested a false courtship, I did not realize what I was getting into."

"Oh dear. That sounds painful."

"No, no. Just the opposite. The more time I spent with you, the more I got to know you, the more I could revel and wonder and appreciate how truly marvelous you are."

Juliana blinked. If ever there was a time for clever words this was it. "Oh."

"I would like to ask you a question."

"Oh."

"Has your opinion about marriage changed?"

Juliana swallowed, suddenly deaf. The leaves no longer rattled in the trees, the ducks opened their beaks to silence, and her bonnet no longer thumped softly against the wrought-iron leg. Only the loud buzzing of her thoughts penetrated her mist of confusion.

This was not the question she had anticipated. But there was no doubt that it had to be addressed. She had been rather emphatic in her dismissal of the institution of marriage not two months ago. But she had not known Spencer then . . . she had not experienced the strange combination of excitement and peace, yearning and contentment as she basked in his presence. She had not known abject loss, when, for a moment, she had thought him gone—falling onto the rocks at the base of a cliff.

Yes, remembering the tender looks shared between Lord and Lady Strath, the boisterous laughter of the Faredells, and the intimation of closeness at the Maynards' town house had taken her closer to the idea that mutual devotion was possible. Still, it was Spencer, and he alone, who had made her mindful of the joys of love.

"Most definitely."

But it was not Juliana alone who had disparaged marriage.

"But *you* do not believe in the institution, Mr. Northam. You told me so, if you recall, on St. Ives Head."

"I think you were changing my opinion even as it was stated." With those words, he kissed her palm, again and again and, oh-so-gently, again.

She tried to speak, but it came out as a squeak.

"And your father."

"Father?"

"Yes, he was a consideration as well, if I recall correctly. You thought him not amenable to change—thought it might send him into a decline."

Juliana laughed. "Indeed. A classic example of underestimation. I shall have to revise my summation of his character—for I did notice that he quite relies on you already . . . a Telford trait, I'm afraid." Twisting her mouth about as she paused, Juliana frowned. "Where was I?"

"Revising."

"Oh yes. I will now say that interfering with his research—our research—would cause great discontent . . . and leave it at that."

"Though marriage would not necessarily bring about an *end* to your research."

"Not if I marry the right gentleman."

"Such as a gentleman who lived in a bug-infested county in sad need of investigation."

Juliana nodded with a solemn expression, trying to keep her lips from curling into a grin. "Yes, a gentleman such as that. But they are in short supply."

"I know of one."

"Do you? Might I trouble you for an introduction?"

Spencer smiled, but even as she watched—closely—the humor disappeared from his eyes. "Miss Juliana Telford, I would be greatly honored if you would consent to be my wife."

Juliana had never experienced such a flood of relief, joy, and, most important, love. It coursed through her entire body and left her speechless.

Seeing her struggle with words, Spencer leaned closer. "Please consider; even if only for a moment. For if you consider, I may kiss you."

Juliana lifted an eyebrow and smiled. She met his dancing eyes. "You may?"

"Yes, for while you consider, we are both engaged and not engaged at the same time. I would not be upsetting propriety to kiss you under those circumstances, for we might be affianced."

Juliana laughed lightly and opened her mouth to argue, but Spencer was no longer hesitant. He placed his bandaged hand behind her head and drew her close. With his other hand, he gently tilted her chin and then slowly trailed his fingertips down the side of her neck until his hand came to rest on her shoulder. He pulled her closer still, even as their lips touched.

It was a tender kiss at first. Their lips barely met. But the warmth of their shared breath, the press of their bodies, and the heat pulsing between them lengthened the kiss and deepened it. Juliana grabbed tightly at Spencer's lapel.

She heard a soft moan and a hum of pleasure but had no idea which one of them made which sound. It didn't matter. Her eyes were closed, and the only things that existed in the world were Spencer's tender strength and the sense of intoxication rushing through her body, warming her all over. When he let her go, he did so slowly, pausing when their lips were still only inches apart, and then pressing little soft-lipped kisses on her nose and eyes. Then he pulled her back into another embrace that curled her toes and left her with no doubt as to why people would enjoy a love match.

Juliana opened her eyes to see that Spencer had put no distance between them. If she leaned at all, their lips would meet again. A very pleasant thought.

"Juliana, nothing would give me greater pleasure than to spend the rest of my life with you, learning about you, having a family, and growing old together. I love you."

"I love you, too, Spencer, with all my heart. To know that you feel the same way . . . well, it fills me with rapture. There are not enough superlatives in the English language to capture even a tenth of my emotions."

"Say you will marry me."

Juliana looked into the clear blue sky and heard the brook babbling. She smelled the freshness of the fields and knew she would remember this moment forever. She took a deep breath. "Yes."

She was quite pleased with Spencer's nonverbal response.

Glossary

ADDLEPATED: mixed up, confused

BANNS: public announcement in church of a proposed marriage

BEAU MONDE: the world of high society and fashion

BLUESTOCKING: a clever, learned young lady/woman

BLUNT: money

BOUNCER: a large lie

CAT'S PAW: an exploited person

CORKY: bright and lively

CUTTING SHAMS: lying

DANDY: gentleman who pays particular attention to his appearance

DILLYDALLY: waste time, delay, dawdle

DUN TERRITORY: in debt

FRIDAY-FACED: sad-looking

GABSTER: chatty person

GULLGROPERS: moneylenders to gamesters (gamblers)

HAVEY-CAVEY: something of a shady or dishonest nature

HELLS: seamy gambling clubs

LADY BEETLE: ladybug

MEGRIMS: a migraine

PELISSE: woman's coat

POSTHASTE: with all possible speed

QUIZZING GLASS: a monocle

RETICULE: decorated drawstring bag/purse

SARCENET: fine soft fabric, often silk

SPENCER: short-waisted fitted jacket

SPOONY: silly or overly sentimental

TERRA FIRMA: a Latin phrase meaning "solid earth"

THE TON: commonly used term referring to British high society

WALKING STICK: cane

WOOLGATHERING: absorbed in thought

Acknowledgments

Publication has been a dream held close to my heart since I was in grade school—yes, *grade* school. At best, the dream was elusive; at worst, it seemed impossible. And yet, through the years, I have never stopped writing, never stopped dreaming. This dream would not have been realized without many special people whom I would like to acknowledge for support and inspiration.

First, thank you to my husband, my walking encyclopedia and unswerving believer. Thank you to my sister, my steadfast companion on this journey, for her counsel and moral support; she helped me hone my craft. Thank you to my daughter, who keeps my plots honest and dragged me (kicking and screaming) into the world of social media. Better beta readers would be difficult to find. Thank you to my mom for being a devoted fan from day one and to my son, whose enthusiasm is always contagious.

A hearty thanks to my friends—they are always positive and

encouraging. Many thanks to the RWA for great advice, topical information, and the voice of experience.

And last but not least, thank you to the Swoon Reads crew, especially Holly, Christine, and Lauren. You helped me lift *Love, Lies and Spies* out of the cloudy waters of *A Modest Predicament*—all bright and shiny. But more than that, you made a dream come true.

Turn the page for some

Sw♥♥nworthy

Extras...

HISTORICAL NOTES

The Regency

When British King George III was declared unfit to lead in 1811, his eldest son, George, was appointed Prince Regent, ruling as such until his father's death in 1820. These nine years became what is known as the Regency period or era. For the upper crust, it was perceived as a time of frivolity, scandal, and high living.

Napoleonic Wars

Britain fought France in the Napoleonic Wars from 1803 to 1815. At the time this book takes place (1813), Napoleon was a significant threat to England and the rest of the Continent. He was forced to abdicate in 1814, and, after a brief return to power, he was finally defeated in Waterloo, Belgium, in 1815.

War Office and Home Office

The War and Home Offices were two departments of the British government. The War Office was responsible for the British Army from the seventeenth century until 1964, when it was rolled into the Ministry of Defence. The Home Office deals with domestic issues such as smuggling, immigration, and public safety. It is still headquartered in London.

SwoonReads

REFERENCES

For those interested in learning more about the British Regency period, I have compiled a short list of research books (very short, for there are many):

Downing, Sarah Jane. *Fashion in the Time of Jane Austen*. Oxford: Shire Publications, 2010.

Fullerton, Susannah. *A Dance with Jane Austen*. London: Frances Lincoln Ltd., 2012.

Kloester, Jennifer. *Georgette Heyer's Regency World*. London: Random House, 2005.

Pool, Daniel. *What Jane Austen Ate and Charles Dickens Knew*. New York: Simon & Schuster, 1993.

Ross, Josephine. *Jane Austen's Guide to Good Manners*. New York: Bloomsbury, 2006.

SwoonReads

A Tea Date

with author Cindy Anstey
and editors Christine Barcellona and Holly West

"Romance Novels"

Christine Barcellona (CB): What was the first romance novel you ever read?

Cindy Anstey (CA): When I was younger, I read Nancy Drew, and when I started reading romance in my early teens, I went straight into Gothic. I read Victoria Holt, Phyllis A. Whitney, Madeleine Brent—those types of books, a style that doesn't seem to exist anymore. I used to devour those. But as to which particular one, I don't know. It was more a genre that I looked for than one book.

Holly West (HW): Do you have a favorite Regency romance now that you're particularly fond of?

CA: I have favorite Regency romance writers. Jane Austen, of course, Jude Morgan, and some—but not all of—Georgette Heyer. I also enjoy Mary Balogh's traditional regencies. I like the comedy-of-manners style.

HW: In all of media, not just books but movies, TV shows, whatever, do you have a favorite fictional couple?

CA: My favorite couple is Amelia Peabody and Radcliffe Emerson from the Amelia Peabody mysteries, starting with *Crocodile on the Sandbank*. The series is written by Elizabeth Peters, and I absolutely love them.

"Just for Fun"

CB: What's your favorite way to spend a rainy day?

CA: I'd like to say something interesting, like walking down a deserted beach or volunteering at the library, which I have done, but my usual rainy day is spent curled up with a good book or playing *Candy Crush*.

HW: This one is my favorite question: If you were a superhero, what would your power be?
CA: I would love to be very wise—perpetually wise—and I'd like to fly, and I'd like to be a healer. So I would choose to be a wise, flying healer.

CB: Swoon-approved superpower! Next question: If you were stranded on a desert island, who or what would you want for company?
CA: I know it's hokey, but I'd want my husband. He's really smart and he's very handy. He cooks and he makes me laugh. What more do you want on a desert island, right?

HW: I'm sold. So do you have any hobbies?
CA: Yes, I have a plethora of hobbies. Most of them are artsy-fartsy because I'm an artist. Recently I've done mostly graphic design. But when I paint, I use watercolors, and I cross-stitch, which is painting with thread, and I garden, which is painting with flowers.

CB: Did you do the original cover for *Love, Lies and Spies*?
CA: I did. I always thought it would be fun to design a book cover, but I didn't know whether I could do a reasonable job. I tried to do it in a cutout sort of style for a youthful look. It really was fun.

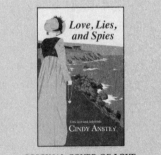

ORIGINAL COVER OF **LOVE, LIES AND SPIES** POSTED ON SWOONREADS.COM

Swoon Reads

"The Swoon Index"

HW: On the site, as you know, we have the Swoon Index, which is meant to measure the amount of heat or laughter or tears or thrills in each book. But for this particular interview, we always like to twist it, and have you tell us what your favorites are. What is something or someone that always turns up the heat for you?
CA: Tenderness and caring.

HW: What always makes you laugh?
CA: Play on words or the absurdity of everyday situations. Like a skit that Ellen [DeGeneres] did when she compared the packaging of batteries and lightbulbs: how batteries are packed so you can't get into them, whereas lightbulbs are barely covered by thin cardboard; it was hilarious. That's the type of thing I find really funny. The absurdities of life.

CB What makes you cry?
CA: Sacrifice. When somebody gives up something for somebody else. That gets to me every time.

HW: What always sets your heart pumping? What's filled with adventure for you?
CA: Travel, I guess. I love traveling, going somewhere new, somewhere different, exotic.

HW: And what always makes you swoon?
CA: Simple moments, simple things. Like a candlelight dinner when we're focusing on each other, sitting on the beach looking at the stars or watching the ocean, or looking up for no reason and finding my husband looking at me, and he smiles or he winks.

HW: Let's talk about Swoon Reads. We always like to talk about us. How did you learn about Swoon Reads?

CA: I read Katie Van Ark's article in the October *Romance Writers Report*. She wrote "An author's perspective on Swoon Reads." We were moving from Europe at the time, and when that issue finally caught up to me, I was super excited. I uploaded *A Modest Predicament* [now retitled as *Love, Lies and Spies*] right away.

HW: What about Swoon Reads drew you to the site? What made you decide "Oh, you've got to do this"?

CA: I really love the idea. Having readers give a critique and seeing if there is any kind of connection. Reaching people right away. You don't have to wait until the book is out. I love that.

CB: What was your experience like on the site before you were chosen?

CA: It was very positive; everyone wrote nice things. It's one thing to have people you know or you love say wonderful things about your work, but to have perfect strangers tell you how much they like your book, it puts you on cloud nine. At first, you make one person happy and then it's two, and so on. It's incremental, but the fact that you've made anybody happy is just amazing. I love that aspect of it.

HW: Once you were chosen, we kind of swore you to secrecy, at least for online and social media. Was it hard for you to keep it a secret?

CA: Oh boy, was it. I wanted to tell everybody. I wanted to stand on the roof and shout it out to the world . . . but I had to wait. It *was* hard.

Swoon Reads

CB: Who was the first person you told?
CA: My husband.

"Writing Life"

HW: Let's talk a little bit about being an author and the writing life. When did you realize that you wanted to be a writer?
CA: Not long after I learned to read. I've always, always wanted to write. I have boxes of stories from high school days . . . and even before. I've always written. I get cranky if I don't write.

HW: Do you have any rituals when you write? Do you have a specific place where you write or anything like that?
CA: As long as my butt's in the chair and nobody's talking to me I can write. And I like it. I don't understand some authors who say they try to avoid writing. I don't get that. I love writing. It's fun; you can live in a different world. When I first started writing seriously, people would call and it would take me a while to refocus. My mind would be in the nineteenth century, and it would take me a few sentences to get my head back in the twenty-first century.

CB: What's your process? Are you an outliner or do you just start writing?
CA: I'm definitely a plotter. I start with a complete outline . . . but characters can and do take over; they change the story. You have to let them, otherwise it's like trying to fit a round peg into a square hole. If you have to redo your plot, you do. That's the way I work, anyway. My characters often dictate where we're going.

HW: For *Love, Lies and Spies*, where did the idea start? Where did it come from?
CA: Most of my ideas come from research followed by "what if?" So,

if I remember correctly, I read about the smuggling during the Napoleonic era, when British smugglers passed French messages. I believe that was the seed, and it grew from there.

CB: What kind of research do you do? I know you're a big researcher.
CA: I love research! I love learning social and cultural history, and I focus on the nineteenth century. I like to read novels that were written in that era as well. I'm more comfortable using books as opposed to the Internet.

CB: Do you remember how extensively you researched for *Love, Lies and Spies*, or are you kind of just always researching a period?
CA: I've always got a nonfiction on the go, as well as a novel, reading back and forth between them all the time. I have more than a few books; my nonfictions are down here. And we have a library upstairs with my fictions.

CB: What was your favorite thing about writing *Love, Lies and Spies*?
CA: Playing with the dialogue. I love writing banter. I can organize a conversation; everybody says what needs to be said. No regrets, no "I wish I had said that."

HW: Do you ever get writer's block?
CA: I never have. Not yet. Knock on wood. If I start rewriting a paragraph or rewriting a page over and over, I'm in the wrong spot. I go back a page or two, and—this is what I love about computers—I put what I have written in another document. If I want to retrieve it, I can. But often the story heads in another direction. So as soon as I start having a problem, I know I'm in the wrong spot and I have to try something else.

HW: That's really great. So what was it like getting the edit letter?
CA: It was a little overwhelming. When I first opened it up, it seemed like a lot of changes. But then you called me and said, "Don't worry about it. It's not very much." And when I started looking at it and figuring out how to address the problems, it really wasn't. I like editing; I know that's weird. I like making things a little stronger, making them better. So once I stopped thinking *Oh my god*, it was fine.

HW: What was the biggest change that you made, and what was the hardest one for you?
CA: The biggest change was flipping the ending. To me that was the hardest and the biggest. I had resolved the romance first on purpose, because I like to know a little about the characters after their declaration of love; I like to see what happens the next day, or the next few months. But I also understood why you preferred it the other way around. It made sense. I did find it hard to do, but I think it turned out well. I was pleased with the way it turned out in the end.

CB: I think you did a great job resolving everything.
CA: Oh, thank you. It was hard to clean up all the broken threads, to make sure that everything was in the right sequence. My sister picked up on the bruises. She said, "Oh, by the way, if it was a week ago, these bruises aren't blue anymore; they've gone yellow."

CB: What's the best writing advice you've ever heard or gotten?
CA: Read—I think that's the standard advice. Somebody once said you have to read, but you have to read what you're really interested in, something that resonates with you. If it doesn't resonate, don't read it. Get something else. I think that is the best advice: read, read, read, read, read.

LOVE, LIES *and* SPIES

Discussion Questions

1. Why was Spencer so surprised by Juliana? What may have made her stand out as different from other women in the Regency period?

2. How did different characters underestimate each other? How did they deceive each other?

3. Early nineteenth century sounds like all parties and matchmaking; what is the reality?

4. Juliana thinks she has a clear understanding of who her father is. Why is she then surprised by his acceptance of Spencer into their lives? Do you think all parent-child relationships have misconceptions?

5. At eighteen years old, Juliana manages an estate and, by the end of the book, she is engaged to be married. Why was an engagement at Juliana's age the norm in the nineteenth century?

6. Do you think Lord Bobbington and Carrie are well suited for each other? Why or why not?

7. At the beginning of the book, Juliana had very firm opinions against marriage. Do you feel they were realistic? What made her opinions change?

8. In Regency England, formal introductions provided entrance into one's social circle. Discuss why this was so important to people who lived during this period.

Swoon Reads

9. Servants made the lives of the gentry possible in Regency England. Discuss the advantages and disadvantages of living so closely with strangers.

10. What are the similar interests of girls in this century with those in the nineteenth? What are the differences?

The only thing more dangerous than
a gentleman with deadly superpowers
is falling in love with one.

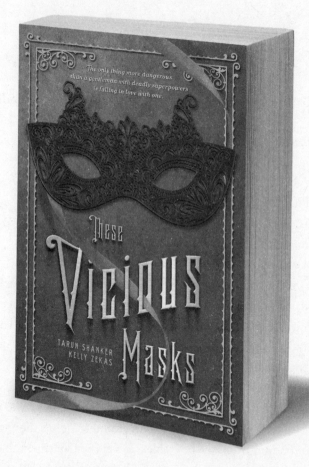

Keep reading for a sneak peek.

One

D EATH. THIS CARRIAGE was taking me straight to my death.

"Rose," I said, turning to my younger sister. "In your esteemed medical opinion, is it possible to die of ennui?"

"I . . . can't recall a documented case."

"What about exhaustion? Monotony?"

"That could lead to madness," Rose offered.

"And drowning in a sea of suitors? After being pushed in by your mother?"

"It would have to be a lot of suitors."

"Evelyn, this is no time to be so morbid," my mother interrupted, simultaneously poking my father awake. "And it is certainly not suitable conversation for dancing. You must enjoy yourself tonight."

"You're ordering me to enjoy myself?"

"Yes, it's a ball, not a funeral."

A funeral might have been preferable. In fact, there was a long list of things I would rather do than attend tonight's monotonous event: thoroughly clean the stables, travel the Continent, have tea with my mother's ten closest friends, travel the Continent, eat my hat, and—oh, yes, of course—travel the Continent. At this moment, my best friend, Catherine Harding, was undoubtedly watching some fabulous new opera in Vienna with an empty seat by her side, meant for me. But when I had modestly, logically suggested to my mother the importance—no, the necessity—of a young woman seeing the world, expanding her mind, and finding her passion, she remained utterly unconvinced.

"Catherine tells me Vienna has grand balls," I put in.

"This isn't the time to discuss that, either," Mother replied.

"But what if tonight, in my sheltered naïveté, I accept a proposal from a pitiless rogue who takes all my money and confines me to an attic?"

"Then better it happens here than on the Continent."

I bit my tongue, for it was quite useless to argue further. Mother would not be swayed and let me leave the country. Instead, she was determined to see me to every ball in England. But what *was* the point of all this? Was anyone truly satisfied with seeing the same people over and over again, mouthing the same false words, feeling nothing, and saying less? Even my London season felt like I was in a prison, trapped in the same routine of balls, dinners, theaters, and concerts that all seemed to blend together, just like the shallow people in attendance. They were so eager to confine themselves to a role and make the correct impression that they'd forget to have any actual thoughts of their own. How would I ever figure out what exactly it was that I wished to do, stuck here in sleepy Bramhurst?

Gazing out the window, I wondered if I should try very hard to have a horrible time tonight to spite my mother, or if we were still close enough to home that I could just throw myself out the door and roll back down the hill. But since we had left, the light pattering of rain had become an angry barrage, while the lightning flashed and the thunder raised its voice in warning. Hopes for an impassable flood took root within me as our carriage swerved and slowed along the slick, muddy road. Suddenly, it jerked to a dead stop, and I believed my prayers answered until the driver shouted down to my father.

"Sir! There's a carriage stopped up ahead! Reckon they're stuck! It'll be just a moment!"

We lurched forward until we saw the outline of a carriage crookedly tilted halfway off the road. Our driver's voice carried: "Hello there! Can we be of assistance?"

Rose and I crowded to her tiny window and found three drenched men—a driver, a passenger, and a near giant—all attempting to push the vehicle back out of a muddy ditch. They paused upon hearing us, and the large man tipped his hat toward our window, the carriage light illuminating his tanned skin and pale lips.

Their driver wiped his brow with a handkerchief as he approached. "Thank you, sir!" he yelled, panting as he waved us along. "It's quite all right! Get your passengers to their destination! We shall manage—" The rest of his words were sucked up by another growl and crackle of thunder.

Whether it was the man's words or the storm that was convincing, our driver decided not to argue and sent the horses forward. As I turned back, watching the three men fade into the blackness, a flash of lightning unveiled them for one last glimpse, their shapes stark against the bright white rip across the sky. But it wasn't any figure that caught my eye. It was their carriage, which seemed to be *lifted* entirely off the ground by the giant man and heaved onto the road before they were swallowed by the darkness again.

"Did you see that?" I asked Rose.

Her raised brow answered the question, but then it furrowed

as she considered the matter. "Is the fair in town? Perhaps he's one of those strong men we always see advertised."

"But . . . still, to lift an entire carriage by himself?"

"Evelyn," Mother interrupted. "I don't wish to hear another story about hallucinations rendering you too ill to attend—"

"Rose saw it, as well!"

"Oh. Excellent. Then we need not risk the health of any of our footmen to fix that driver's foolish mistake," my mother said, in her infinite kindness.

Our conversation died in the din of the storm, but the unnatural image of those four wheels suspended in the air stayed with me as we rolled up the narrow dirt path to the congested entrance of Feydon Hall. Though there was surely a rational explanation, my nerves were now on edge, making Feydon's familiar details seem sinister. At the crest of the hill, the mansion loomed over the rest of the country, and thick clouds roiled menacingly over the magnificent estate. Cracked stone statues of Hades and Charon welcomed visitors in, while gnarled trees reached out to capture all who dared to veer off the path. Towering gargoyles stretched upward as if to attract an ominous flash of lightning. This was ridiculous. Was my mind so tired of Bramhurst that it was conjuring up these gothic images? This must be how girls go mad: It's the only alternative to boredom.

Shaking the absurd thoughts away, I followed Rose and my parents out of the carriage. Umbrella-wielding footmen led us to the front door and into the bright, breathtaking vestibule that set the tone for the rest of the mansion. Though our home was rather large and well kept, Sir Winston's home of Feydon was still awe-inspiring. Vivid paintings glowed in the gaslight against the dark wood paneling. Lush oriental rugs covered the floor, and the ceiling reached toward the sky, providing room for the second-floor balcony—a place where guests wanting for conversation topics had a steady supply of people below to scrutinize.

Still, in spite of the main hall's enormous size, the waves of fashionable men and women rendered it impossible to navigate. This looked to be by far the biggest ball our small town of Bramhurst had seen in years, which unfortunately meant I didn't have to worry about a sea of suitors, but an ocean. We had not gone three steps when my mother fixed her eyes on a boy frozen in perfect imitation of the bronze statue beside him.

She leaned in confidentially. "Evelyn, see there. The eldest from the Ralstons. I hear they have a lovely collection of stained-glass windows." Ah, yes, just my type: a stiff, prideful lord-to-be with impeccable, cold deportment to prove his perfect breeding.

"Set a date," I declared solemnly with a wave of my hand. "I shall marry him immediately."

Christine Anstey

Cindy Anstey spends her time writing and adventuring around the world. She has lived on three continents, had a monkey in her backyard and a scorpion under her sink, dwelled among castles and canals, enjoyed the jazz of Beale Street, and attempted to speak French. Cindy loves history, mystery . . . and a chocolate Labrador called Chester. *Love, Lies and Spies* is her debut novel. She currently resides in Nova Scotia, Canada.